TOM
YOUNG

SEED OF HOPE

THE EMILY SMITH TRILOGY

outskirts press

Seed of Hope
The Emily Smith Trilogy
All Rights Reserved.
Copyright © 2018 Tom Young
v3.0

This is a work of fiction. The events and characters described herein are imaginary and are not intended to refer to specific places or living persons. The opinions expressed in this manuscript are solely the opinions of the author and do not represent the opinions or thoughts of the publisher. The author has represented and warranted full ownership and/or legal right to publish all the materials in this book.

This book may not be reproduced, transmitted, or stored in whole or in part by any means, including graphic, electronic, or mechanical without the express written consent of the publisher except in the case of brief quotations embodied in critical articles and reviews.

Outskirts Press, Inc.
http://www.outskirtspress.com

ISBN: 978-1-4787-3045-3

Library of Congress Control Number: 2017915049

Cover Photo © 2018 thinkstockphotos.com. All rights reserved - used with permission.

Outskirts Press and the "OP" logo are trademarks belonging to Outskirts Press, Inc.

PRINTED IN THE UNITED STATES OF AMERICA

Dedication

This story is dedicated to my son Thomas. May your dreams be my dreams and may I write for you. Love, Dad.

This story is about our, The Human Species, pivotal moment in history. Can we make the right decisions to save ourselves and our good earth? Our decisions in the area of environmental issues to resolve looming destruction are pertinent to our survival. These issues are not fantasy. Sitting around, ignoring the issues, hoping our help will come from the stars, is the fantasy.

To believe we are alone in the Universe is the height of conceit and self-delusion, not to mention great disrespect to our Higher Power. We should remember that a "haughty spirit goes before a fall". We are like the ant looking at an ant hill and saying, "that is all there is to the world", or like others in our past who said the world was flat.

Those that observe will not interfere. Perhaps they intend to inherit the earth. I hope you will enjoy the trilogy of the "Seed of Hope". Emily Smith and her new friends have an exciting future ahead of them.

D.J. Economou; I would like to acknowledge DJ's thoughtful insights and knowledge in regard to publishing.

CONNIE YOUNG; I would be amiss if I did not acknowledge my wife's encouragement in writing this story.

Editors: Linda D. Graham

David K. "Dinty" Moore, Capt. USN Retired

©2012

Contents

1	THE COUNCIL	1
2	ABDUCTION	5
3	CONFIRMATION	10
4	AWAKENING	12
5	EMILY FALLING DOWN	16
6	ROBERT'S INTRODUCTION	26
7	WHERE IS EMILY	31
8	THE REPORT	34
9	THE INVESTIGATION	37
10	SENSITIVE ACTION	43
11	UPMOST DISCRETION	46
12	CONFERENCE	54
13	NO LONGER AFRAID	61
14	STATE HOSPITAL	68
15	ACCIDENT REPORT	73
16	ASSESSMENT	78
17	DECONTAMINATION	82
18	TRAITOR	86
19	CONSPIRITORS	89
20	WHISP OF TRUTH	91
21	THE TRUTH	94
22	ZELEGARK'S SURPRISE	103
23	AWAKENING AND INTERROGATION	105
24	PLAN FORMULATION	113
25	SECOND CHANCE	115

26	THE LANDING	117
27	EMILY SEE'S THE STARS	121
28	FELLOW TRAVELER	126
29	COMPARING NOTES	128
30	TEN CAPTIVES	130
31	EMILY'S ANGER	138
32	REVIEW AND ASSESSMENT	141
33	CAPTAIN SWENSON'S MYSTERY	146
34	PERPLEXED	149
35	KAREN ABBOTT'S ASSESSMENT	151
36	DR. ABBOTT'S OPPORTUNITY	154
37	FAMILIAR FACES	158
38	DR. ABBOTT THE TEACHER	162
39	THEROM'S TRUTH TESTED	164
40	NEW DAWN	168
41	REVELATION	173
42	THE INVITATION	176
43	SELF DELUSION	180
44	MORE ENEMIES	182
45	INTERGALACTIC HOMES	187
46	1SAHARA	193
47	TEDDY BEAR	201
48	RELIEF	204
49	EXCURSIONS	214
50	BRAINSTORM	228
51	REALIZATIONS	230
52	MOONBASE	233
53	OBSERVATIONS	241
54	DEMONSTRATION	243
55	ACKNOWLEDGEMENTS	245

56	NEW ADVENTURE	249
57	THE COUNCIL	252
58	THE SEARCH	255
59	RENDEZVOUS	257
60	NEW ENTITY	261
61	ARRIVALS	266
62	THE REUNION	271
63	NEW GIFT	279
64	AND, JUDGEMENT	287
65	ALLIANCE	290
66	HOME COMMING	296
67	INTERLUDE	302
68	NEW OPPORTUNITIES	305
CHARACTERS IN ORDER OF APPEARANCE		309

CHAPTER 1
THE COUNCIL

"Are you sure they are the legitimate genetic descendants? I do not see how that could be possible. They are limited to almost rudimentary intuitive skills and their neural development appears to be fragmentary. Our "annual children" have greater abilities than their mature adults. And most importantly, they refuse to eliminate the genetically flawed within their species. Something has gone terribly wrong, I fear. I cannot believe they are in any way related to our species. Even though they are our genotype their brains are dulled and asleep. They are sub-human. I believe they should be destroyed from the face of the planet. We can start over. Or better yet, we can take the planet for ourselves before they destroy it with their lack of self-controls."

Klaxo released the neural net as the, "Council of Yield", the governing body of the three interstellar star ships, considered his words. The assessment of the genera inserted by the Twelfth Generation of the Universal Cycle was disturbing. The evaluation of the species was indeed correct. However, nothing like this has ever happened before; so many planets, so many successes. This was unprecedented.

All assembled upon the neural net were solemn. And yet again, Klaxo spoke. "The species should be exterminated from the planet. I do not see any alternative. Should we not do this they would require constant oversight and attention at an enormous expenditure of our meager resources. They have all the resources of this rich planet and they squander them. They refuse to adhere to the greater good! They may even develop advanced space propulsion systems enabling them to travel among the stars and perhaps infect our other colonies with their barbaric thinking and procreation!"

The last statement about procreation was a dangling threat. Star faring species required strict population controls. They could not exist without them. The decision to destroy the specie from the face of the planet was in fact, a very simple and viable option. However the decision to destroy a species from their planet must be unanimous. Quiet ensued on the neural net. The fate of species, Human, hung in the balance.

Shayar, senior member of the, "Council of Yield", then spoke.

"What you have said Klaxo, does appear to be the truth. However, once your option to destroy the species, Human, from the planet is made there will be no going back. The species will be annihilated, not only the planet, but the whole universe."

"As it should be!" Interrupted Klaxo: with strong neural power in an effort to force his opinion.

"Perhaps you may be correct! However, do not ever interrupt me again! You will be removed from the "Council of Yield", and your position given to one more worthy of respect!" Shayar chided and carefully observed

SEED OF HOPE

her colleague.

Klaxo sulked. How he hated that a woman should hold any preeminence over him! His mind was one of the most developed of his specie in all the star systems. Klaxo carefully kept his thoughts shielded. It would not do to have Shayar know what he actually thought of her. Not yet. He would bide his time. Soon! She would have no power over him!

Shayar then spoke again, careful to direct her thoughts to the business at hand. "I suggest an alternative to the immediate destruction of the specie, Human. We should insert a "youngling" into the population and allow the "youngling" to grow and mature. Then we can retrieve the "youngling" at a predetermined point in its maturity cycle and then reevaluate the potential for the species Human to develop, as it should. Thus we can make a more correct assessment for the disposition of this species. It is true we could use the planet to our benefit but we cannot blatantly destroy any species for our personal gain."

Shayar continues, "We do appear to be basically the same. It is just that their neurological functions appear to be asleep, or perhaps, rudimentary in it's' development. Maybe they are not capable of higher cognitive skills. However, there seems to be some sort of strange development near the hypothalamus. We do not know what it is. It is detectable only in trace amounts using our most analytical and advanced instruments and not all Humans possess it. We ourselves do not possess this trace chemical. We need to know more."

The "Council of Yield", agreed with Shayar, not to immediately eliminate species Human at this time. They also agreed to insert not just one "youngling", into the population, but ten.

Shayar watched as Klaxo left the neural net. She could read the fool's carefully guarded thoughts of hate and superiority. Soon, she and the remaining "Council of Yield", members would be required to address his lack of unity of spirit. They could not allow one individual to override and supersede their decisions.

CHAPTER 2
ABDUCTION

"Hello Control. This is Lagrange Point Observer Two. I have a visual of a large object bearing Zebra Quadrant approximately twenty star clicks. It is moving in this direction at a low velocity. It appears to be some sort of space craft."

"Control to Lagrange Point Station Two. That is correct. We have had "Eyes" on it for some time."

"Well Control, thanks a lot! I did not know that, "The Alliance", had spacecraft that large. I guess I have been out here too long. I did not even know that someone else was assigned to this quadrant."

Controls pausing response of, "We don't", sent chills down the Ensigns spine. His eyes glazed over and he had an overwhelming urge to urinate as he rushed to the lavatory where he violently regurgitated his evening meal.

Twenty-Four year old Ensign Robert Aaron had graduated first in his class at the Alliance Space Academy. Thus, he had the privilege of choosing his first duty assignment. He chose Lagrange Point Station Two, because he believed it would probably be the most likely post to be the first observation point to observe any alien space craft approaching the earth; even though the likelihood of that ever happening was truly and emphatically nil. At least up to this moment in time he believed it was nil.

He, as most earth citizens, was kept completely ignorant of the activities going on around them in regard to other worldly beings; this course of action being decided on two generations earlier by well-meaning and self-indulgent powers that be.

Ensign Aaron was in his thirteenth month of a twenty four month rotation of solitary duty on Lagrange Point Station Two which is located about 932,000 miles or 1.5 million kilometers from the earth past the moon, with the earth being between the sun and Lagrange Point Station Two. The distance from the sun to the earth is one astronomical unit or about 92,956,000 miles. The five Lagrange Points of the Earth, Moon, Sun, system, are imaginary points in space where gravity exertion on an object is near zero and thus an object would stay permanently in position with little or no correctional force to maintain position. It was the most advantageous point to place space stations and telescopes for observation of the cosmos.

The modulized station itself was approximately three football fields long mostly consisting of enormous solar arrays, which were used to collect solar energy from the sun to power the numerous research instruments. Ensign Aarons living space was the size of a double wide billet on earth, comfortable, cozy, and sometimes, lonely. Most of his time was spent maintaining experiments where null gravity allowed a more precise measurement in regard to the processes involved. The facility also sported one of earths most advanced space scanning telescopes, which unfortunately for Ensign Aaron, was inoperative

SEED OF HOPE

for three weeks due to a solar storm blast earlier in the month.

Ensign Aaron himself was protected due to an early warning system consisting of two satellites designated as Stereo and Soho, which remained in position due to the suns Lagrange Points. The early warning gave him time to seek refuge by entering a water filled ceramic nano polymer casting that surrounded the safe zone of the habitable part of the station, which would block any debilitating radioactive particles. Therefore, Ensign Aaron only discovered the approaching spacecraft by accident using the light refracting telescope during his leisure time off. By then, the spacecraft was literally at his front door.

Forcing his voice to be calm, Ensign Aaron called Control asking for instructions on what procedure to follow; even though the manual clearly stated: "Contact Space intelligence Control. Avoid contact with aliens." And of course, thought Ensign Aaron, "Why in the hell you did not warn me!"

"Control to Lagrange Point Station Two. Do not engage the aliens. Do not engage the spacecraft. We did not advise you earlier because we did not want you to panic. There is not anything you or we could do to help you. Therefore, collect as much data as possible and relay to Space Intelligence Control."

Ensign Aaron thought, "That is a surety. There is nothing anyone could do to help." Clearing his mind, Ensign Aaron focused all the stations scanners on the approaching spacecraft. Parts of the alien craft had reflective properties and some surfaces did not. As Ensign Aaron began transmitting data to Space Intelligence Control, he observed two luminous objects detach themselves from the larger craft and start his way.

"Oh crap!" Ensign Aaron waited nervously. Suddenly his desire to contact another civilization did not seem like a good idea. The comical, "Take me to your leader", was not funny anymore. Nor did it seem too prudent.

Robert waited. It took sixty-three minutes for the glowing objects to get near the station. As he observed the glowing objects from the small circular view port he was unable to discern any definitive outlines of the crafts, or probes or whatever they were. Robert lowered the sun block visor on his helmet as the nano polymer plexi glass darkened against the ever-increasing glare of the two objects.

The light became so intense within the space station that the instruments began to cease functioning. The light became a kaleidoscope of differentiating light frequencies as the intensity and ethereal power entered thru the very walls of the Lagrange Point Station Two. Ensign Aaron had seen enough. Being already suited up for emergency evacuation he quickly entered into the small escape pod and prepared to abandon station. "They can court martial me if they want to! I am going to get the hell out of here! Obviously the alien craft is much more advanced than ours!"

Robert activated the pods escape sequence and waited for the gravity force as the pre-programmed timer counted down and the escape vehicle was to be blasted away from the station. The timer reached zero. Nothing happened. Instead of blasting away from the station, the vehicle drifted languidly, tumbling away from its ejection point. Robert saw the two alien light craft enter and disappear from view as the tumbling craft floated away from Lagrange Point Station Two. Soon the tumbling stopped. For some reason, movement within the escape pod became impossible. Robert was unable to as much as move his eyes to the left or right. The distant alien spacecraft came within view of the view port in the hole of the escape pod's exit hatch. Then the far distant alien spacecraft grew to impossible dimensions so suddenly that Roberts's mental state went from euphoria as he escaped from the Space platform to sheer terror upon seeing the alien spacecraft immediately before him with a large iris entrance portal opening to swallow him whole!

"It could not have been more than seconds! How could that be?"

Light enveloped the escape pod. The hatch locks turned counter clockwise to the open position. His blood would boil when exposed to the vacuum of space and he would be dead within seconds. In his terror he wanted to die! The hatch opened and what appeared to be a gaseous substance like liquid oxygen poured thru the open hatch whitening out all view. Ensign Robert Aaron's sensation of living…vanished!

CHAPTER 3
CONFIRMATION

Admiral Avery Cleary walked into the Space Intelligence Control Communication Center, immediately upon hearing that two spacecraft had detached themselves from the larger galactic craft and was headed to Lagrange Point Station Two, currently occupied by Ensign Robert Aaron. This was a new development in alien behavior. They had previously steered clear of Earth's space vehicles.

"Bob, "What is happening now? This is really getting out of hand."

Commander Bob Johnson replied, "It appears that Ensign Robert Aaron panicked and egressed from the station. The escape pod was somehow maneuvered into the larger spacecraft. The larger craft then left the quadrant at near the speed of light. It took about two minutes from the time Ensign Aaron exited the station before he was abducted by the two light craft and whisked aboard the larger carrier and the carrier left, presumably with Ensign Aaron aboard the carrier. However, Lagrange Point Station Two does not appear to be harmed and all stations and arrays began functioning properly as soon as the galactic craft left the quadrant".

Commander Bob Johnson was the Commanding Officer of Space Intelligence Command. It was his group's responsibility to keep track of all alien activity within the

SEED OF HOPE

Earths vicinity. The abduction of military personnel from a military installation on the earth or a space facility was indeed a huge breach of normal alien operational procedures and activities. Something was up and it was not good; keying his communicator Commander Johnson said, "Go to Space Con Four until further notice".

CHAPTER 4
AWAKENING

Ensign Aaron could hear muffled sounds. He tried to open his eyes but he could not, they just would not respond. He felt a pinch on the side of his head, a prick in his neck and a hot and cold sensation on his face. The sensations ceased. His mind, for all intents and purposes became clear. Again he heard sounds. They were distinct voices, but he could not understand the language. The voices were definitely human but the words were like a combination of several earth languages combined into impossible combinations. Then he heard his name.

"Robert".

His name was repeated at least five times in rapid-fire succession. It sounded like a microphone check with a reverberator on, the sound diminishing with each successive word. Then he heard, or rather thought he heard, and sensed in his head, "Subject Robert Aaron now in cognitive mode."

"Cognitive mode", what did that mean? The voice sounded feminine. But how could he hear with in his head but not with his ears? Other sensations slowly began to return. He could sense his fingers, toes, legs; fear chilled him as he felt his testicle being touched by someone or something. A sting! Sharp! Painful! Then...blackness.

As Robert regained consciousness the second time,

he became fully awake. All his mental faculties were working and his mind seemed extraordinarily clear. He rubbed his eyes with his hands, which was no longer limp and immobile. Robert blinked his eyes open and looked around. The surroundings appeared to be a laboratory with numerous vats, tubes, and bubbling liquid. He was confused.

"Where am I"?

He could hear the voices again but he could not understand the language. Thinking, Robert tried to make sense of what was happening. "Okay, I know this is not Lagrange Point Station Two. How did I get here?"

His memory appeared to be selective in what he could recall. Again thinking to himself he went over a checklist of things he knew that he knew. "Yes I am an Ensign in the Space Navy. Yes, I am assigned to Lagrange Point Station Two. I did hear a women and I think I talked to her. What was it about? Well I know there are no women on the Lagrange Point Station Two. Therefore, the only logical conclusion is, I must have gone mad. Space Command had to come and get me! What a disgrace! What am I going to tell Mom and Dad? I am obviously in a mental hospital. Oh! What is Dad going to say?"

All these anguished thoughts were going thru his mind when he "heard", the women's voice again. It was the same voice as last time except this time he was fully awake. He knew he "heard" her. Robert looked around expecting to see her. Where was she?

Again the voice, "You cannot see me but am near you. You are doing much better. In fact, we are very pleased;

we did not expect your mental skills to be as pronounced as they are.

Responding, Robert said, "If you are so pleased why do you not show yourself?" Space Command always liked playing their stupid little mind games. Any moron could see right thru them. However, somewhere in his mind's eye Robert remembered a white smoke like liquid nitrogen cloud and seeing his lower body encased in a clear gaseous cylinder. When and where was that? Robert again felt a pinch on his neck and he immediately went to sleep.

Robert felt a gentle touch on his temples, a pleasant massaging sensation. Regaining his consciousness and opening his eyes for the third time, Robert observed he was lying down on a recliner type bed, one end slightly raised. There were not any more of the vats of bubbling liquid he had seen earlier. The light in the room was dark, like twilight, changing colors slowly from deep purple, to blue, to pink, to green, then back to deep purple. The shifting colors of light was not reflected off the walls but moved in waves across the whole room. The effect reminded Robert of a light show he had seen where a smoky, fog filled stadium was laced with dancing laser lights. Those lights moved too but not like this. There was no foggy medium to focus the lasers here.

The soft gentle massaging of his temples stopped. Looking up he saw the silhouette of, a "woman"? Looking down he observed that his waist and legs were no longer encased in a cylinder. He sat up swinging his legs to the floor. He was no longer in uniform either. Instead, he

SEED OF HOPE

was wearing a billowy set of pants, pale blue in color. His shirt was a slipover, open just below the chest area. The shirt was secured around the waist with a narrow purple sash tied to the side with ends hanging down to just above the knees. Actually, they looked just like his karate clothes, except these clothes were super lightweight and super thin.

Robert then looked up and saw the woman standing in the shadows across the room. She was alone, observing him. The light waves washed over her giving her a surreal vestige of regal splendor. She was tall, wearing the same type of clothing, as he except hers was the color of pale sky, morning pink; a darker colored pink sash was hanging from her waist.

Very quietly, in his head he heard her say, "Hello Robert. Welcome to our home."

CHAPTER 5
EMILY FALLING DOWN

Emily, legs crossed, was swinging her leg, watching Dr. Calander as he carefully reread her paper for the third time. He had been attempting to interpret the mathematics now for one hour. He had not spoken a single word. The paper was titled, "Nano Fiber Optic Resolution of Light Frequency Wave Patterns". Emily's platinum blond, shoulder length hair, gently swayed in sync with her swinging leg. She chewed her gum slowly, her eye lids half closed concealing her pale blue eyes.

Emily thought, "This will probably blow his mind."

Emily had always kept a low profile at the Southern University of Physics and Polymer Sciences. She found the math child's play; actually, she had all her life. Her Mom and Dad had always coached her, as long as she could remember, not to reveal her extraordinary gifts and talents for discerning the unknowable. Emily "knew" what Dr. Calander was thinking: just as she seemed to "know" her boyfriend's, Warren, intentions. Emily laughed quietly to herself at that thought. Any female with any brains at all could read a jocks thoughts toward virtually any female. Emily did not find the thoughts unsettling. In fact, in a Neanderthal sort of way, Warren excited her. She knew better than to let him know how she felt.

Dr. Calander looked up bewildered. "Ms. Smith, how

on earth did you leap to these conclusions and put this math together? I mean, I can hardly understand what you are saying. And, even if I did totally understand your precepts, to what purpose and application would the light waves have? And more importantly, where did this come from? You have always been an average student. You never participated in class. And for the most part you seem to be nonchalant and bored."

Emily had hoped Dr. Calander would grasp the significance the light frequency waves and their relationship to space-time travel and nano polymers. He was a brilliant man! Why could he not feel and discern the three-dimensional math exposited in the equations. Linear thinking in mathematics was so lame and limiting!

"Aha!"

Dr. Calander was looking closely at Emily with a down turned mouth and a sneer on his face.

"That Bitch! She is trying to play a game on me! She is trying to make a fool out of me! She is trying to humiliate me!"

"Oh well, I had to try," Thought Emily.

Laughing, Emily reached for the paper on the desk and the laptop with the formulas on the software. Emily looked Dr. Calander in the eye and said, "I knew you would not fall for that gibberish, Dr. Calander. The fraternity jocks put it together and promised me a good running car if I would present it to you. I have been without my own transportation for so long, I thought, what the heck, I had nothing to lose."

Emily knew that Dr. Calander's anger would wipe

away the formulas from his brain. She felt his heat of hate immediately.

"Oh well, I tried, I failed", thought Emily. "Perhaps some other time, some other place, some other person".

Dr. Calander looked at Emily as if she was a detestable specimen he was observing under a microscope, "And yes he would step on her and smash her if he could! She would fail his class, and deservedly so". Emily could almost feel his thoughts imprinted on her brain, his wrath was so great.

Emily, keeping her expressions neutral, was boiling at his blind, arrogant, self-righteous, shallow...whatever else she could heap upon his majesty's stupidity! Keeping her voice calm Emily said, "I am truly sorry for allowing myself to be used by those brutes, surely they have no brains what so ever! I did not think!"

Turning and closing the door behind her, Emily walked down the hall to the exit and out of the building. She did not see any reason to go to her dorm to collect her things. She honestly did not know what to do. She could not just walk away from Warren. Dr. Calander was going to do whatever he could to get her dismissed from the University. She only stayed for Warren anyway. She certainly did not need the money her degree would bring. She had come to respect, no, love Warren. She felt an innate need to protect him. He was so dear. "He wanted so little out of life. He just wanted to get married, have lots of children and love me. That was not such a bad plan. I want that too," thought Emily.

When Emily was with him he could not keep his hands

off of her. It was a constant, gentle fight to control him. And, should the truth be known, she loved every second of it. The other girls in school, including some professors, would have jumped at any attention he would give them. But, he was totally smitten with Emily.

As Emily crossed the street and was walking along the park area she "felt" someone staring at her. She knew someone was staring at her! Stopping and turning around, she observed a young man that appeared to be about twenty-five years of age, certainly not younger, perhaps a few years older. His dress was casual. He was slim build with shoulder length blonde hair that moved perceptively in the light breeze.

"Emily".

She heard her name but did not hear his voice or see his lips move. She was only twenty feet away. "Surely I could see him speaking and hear his voice," thought Emily

She could not see his eyes because he was wearing light blue tinted sunglasses. Again she heard her name, "Emily". Confused, Emily looked around to see if anyone else was nearby. She did not see anyone.

Upon facing the stranger Emily was totally ready to fight or flee because this intrusion into her mind was unprecedented. It had never happened before.

She heard the stranger in her head again. "Emily, you should forgive your Dr. Calander for being unable to grasp your precepts. You are not like him. He is a fine man, a brilliant man, by human standards, but, he is only human", accent on the "is". Then he became silent gauging her reactions.

Emily was confused at first by his statements, "You are not like him. He is only human". A fleeting of human emotions flooded Emily's mind; fear, suspicion, wonder, and then anger. Mostly anger!

"Who are you? What are you doing in my mind?"

Emily was surprised when the stranger smiled at her and replied, "You see. I told you, you are one of us."

Again Emily's anger spiked but was quickly subdued by a twinge of fear. What did he mean by, "I was one of them? How did he know about Dr. Calander?"

"My name is…, well…, Blain. You can call me Blain; my name is unpronounceable by your minds concepts. Come. Let us walk together and I will explain."

Blain turned and walked into the park following a small path expecting Emily to follow. For whatever reason, Emily felt like the invitation to "walk" with him was more of a command, not a casual invitation. Emily, after having the first ever experience of non-verbal communication with another, "human", or, "whatever", was going to find out what was going on. "You're darn right I will follow you and you will darn well tell me what is going on or I will darn well beat the snotty crap out of you!"

Emily hefted her lap top bag farther up on her shoulder and clutched the strap of her purse to her breast and tucked her books under her armpit, and followed "Blain", into the heavily forested park.

After going about twenty yards into the park they entered a clearing. Blain stopped and stepped to the side as he turned around toward Emily, smiling. He said, "Are

SEED OF HOPE

you still going to beat the snotty crap out of me?"

Behind Blain, in the center of the clearing, was a small twenty-foot wide saucer craft hovering silently above the ground by about six feet.

Emily stood dumbstruck, her eyes wide, her mouth agape! She dropped her laptop case, shoulder bag, books and purse on the ground where she stood. Stammering, she verbalized that what she was seeing was impossible. "It was only math, only precepts, child's play, fun, games!"

Emily, for all her composure, self-esteem, self-control, intelligence, or whatever, was afraid. For the first time in her life she was really afraid. She was confronted with the impossible. It began to dawn on her what Blain was implying when he said, "she was one of them." If that was true, what was she? Where was she from? What about Mom and Dad? And, most importantly, why now?

Emily began to back away. She did not know why. It was definitely one of those, "time to flee", things. Stumbling backward thru the brush, Emily's heel caught on a root that caused her to fall backward to the ground. Instinctively Emily swung her arms out in an effort to catch herself. In doing so her arm was lacerated below the elbow by a sharp protrusion extending from a low tree branch. The sleeve of her blouse was torn away as blood flowed freely onto her blouse and surrounding leaves. Because Emily was in shock she felt no pain, just a tremendous dull ache.

Lying on her back with the green trees as a backdrop, Emily saw the young man who identified himself as

Blain, looking down at her with a concerned look on his face. Blain crouched down next to her and took her left arm in his hands and lifted it close so he could examine it. "That is really quite a nasty scratch you have there."

Then, removing a small pouch from inside his jacket, Blain took a small vial from the pouch. Breaking the vial in half over the wound, Emily watched mesmerized and fascinated as green vapor sparkled and flashed as it floated gently into the wound on her arm. The green vapor appeared to be sucked directly inside her arm by some kind of invisible force. The bleeding stopped immediately. Even though there was no pain due to shock, there had been a dull ache. Now the aching was gone.

Blain then removed a small green gauze patch from his pouch and placed it carefully over the wound. The patch too seemed to be sucked into her arm by some invisible force. The patch felt warm, moist and clingy, and more important, soothing.

Blain then looked into Emily's eyes, smiling, and said, "There. That should fix that nasty little scratch. Really, you have no need to fear. I know you have questions. They will all be answered in due time. You have an important role to fulfill. We must go now. Your species fate hangs in the balance!"

Helping Emily to her feet, Blain assisted Emily back to the clearing. Before walking toward the waiting saucer he looked back over his shoulder at the evidence he left behind, the broken vial. Thinking, "Oh well, maybe they can believe we are benevolent." Blain then escorted Emily toward the waiting saucer holding her arm up

SEED OF HOPE

with one hand and his other arm around her shoulder guiding her. As they neared the saucer a small aperture opened in the bottom center of the saucer and a small platform descended being suspended by what appeared to be three cables attached triangularly to a platform. Blain placed Emily to one side of the platform then he stepped beside her still supporting her arm. The cables raised the platform into the saucer. Emily watched as the world she knew and loved slipped out of view.

Looking around the saucer, Emily observed myriads of electronic panels with various colored symbols displayed on what appeared to be liquid screens as the symbols intertwined and wound into wreaths like fine threaded rope coiling around another in a sensuous dance. The center of the saucer was occupied by a large glass looking cylinder that extended from the floor of the saucer into a round circular hole into the ceiling of the compartment. Emily could see between the circular tube and the edge of the "roof". She saw what she believed to be a second deck.

Blain escorted Emily near the center of the craft close to the glass looking tube and carefully placed her within what appeared to be a circle on the deck. The circle began rising from the floor. Upon reaching the second level, Emily had to stay to the center of the craft in order not to bump her head. Again, from the deck to ceiling, the wall was covered with the same type of electronic panels with wreath like symbols attached in chains undulating in a dance with a kaleidoscope of imagery of fantastic colors.

Blain took Emily by the elbow and escorted her

toward two vertical couches. Taking her arms, he pushed her gently back into the couch. The couch was soft and tingly on her bare hands and one wounded arm where her sleeve had ripped away. There was a slight electrical field that raised the hair on her arms and head.

"Don't' move", Blain said. Or, rather did not say, but communicated telepathically. Blain took his position beside her in his respective couch receptacle. Emily felt her arms being raised and crossed against her chest in mummy fashion as two small arm rest rose into position. A clear glass looking cylinder rose up from the deck and encircled her body. She heard an audible click and felt a pressure differentiation as the capsule coupled with the overhead receiving mechanism.

Emily was no longer frightened. She was excited! No. She was beyond excited! She was enthralled with a mystical chemical stimulus flooding the cerebral cortex of her brain. How many hours upon hours had she studied the heavens! Now she, Emily Smith, was going to ride a flying saucer and go…go, who cares! "I would not miss this trip for anything in the world!" Emily thought. Then Emily sobered at that thought; "Perhaps that is exactly what this trip is going to cost me… my world."

Emily felt vibrations as the craft started to rise. Looking thru the container of glass, the craft appeared to begin dissipating. She saw the clearing, the treetops and surrounding buildings. Then suddenly she saw the curvature of the earth, the blackness of space, and a myriad of stars that went on forever!

Emily's tears began to roll down her cheeks as she

SEED OF HOPE

silently wept. "Why am I weeping? The sights I am seeing and beholding are astounding! My God how great Thou art!" The hymn intoned in its entirety in her mind. Again, there was a vibration within the craft and the earth became a tiny sphere as the distance to the earth seemed to fall to immeasurable heights.

Blain, standing beside Emily, could not help but listen to Emily's innermost thoughts. It was wrong, he knew, but he could not help himself. It gave him greater insight into why humans acted and believed the way they did. "Humans are such strange beings. They give all their homage to a mystical, nonexistent god. I wonder what it would be like to have such a wonderful crutch to help solve our every need. If there is one out there I hope he is listening because we are experiencing what may well be the extinguishing of our very existence."

Then, Emily saw a large glowing craft directly in front of her. It was huge! An aperture opened in the side of the craft as the saucer approached. Upon entering the larger craft the saucer glided down a long tunnel where it exited into a large hanger. There was an innumerable number of saucer craft umbilical cord attached to obvious exit ports into the large, what apparently was, "mother" ship.

Emily had to remember to make herself breath as the cylinder around her descended to the floor and the armrest released her arms. Tentatively, Emily stepped forward, her heart rapid, pulse pounding, and her mind again ignited with an excitement that, before this moment, she had never before experienced!

CHAPTER 6
ROBERT'S INTRODUCTION

Robert swung his legs from the recliner to the floor and then noticed they were encased in a form fitting satin material. The material was soft and cool. They matched the dark blue of his sash. After examining his clothes he remembered the woman that was massaging his temples. He half turned to his right on the recliner and he observed her standing about seven feet away next to the paneled wall. She was observing him. She did not move. She was just standing there with her arms to her side. She appeared to be wearing the same type of garment as he.

Her height was about five feet, ten inches tall. Her weight seemed proportionate to her height. Under her billowing slacks and top, it was difficult to be sure. Her breast was...not large. Her face was covered in shadow, not discernible. Then she spoke.

"Robert, you appear to be doing well. How do you feel?"

At least I think she spoke. I know I heard her voice in my head. I could not see her face and I do not think I heard any sounds with my ears. Confused, I replied, "Fine". Who are you and where am I?"

The women took a step forward into the undulating

light. Her hair was long, to the waist. It appeared silver but it was hard to tell with the purple light wave. Her eyes shined in the light, like a trick shot in photography or movies. Turning her hands palms up, she said, "Come. Take my hands"

Again I heard her voice but I did not see her lips move on her angular face. She appeared to be young but then not. She seemed more ageless. I further observed that her eyes were somewhat wide apart but not unattractively so. They still had the silvery gleam. She did not smile.

Still standing with palms up she again said, "Take my hands".

For some reason I believed that, "Take my hands", was a command and not a request. Fear began to creep into my mind and for some inexplicable reason I felt compelled to do as I was told and therefore obeyed.

I scooted off the recliner and stepped forward, my legs firm as my feet touched the floor. I took three steps forward. I could feel the heat from my body as my temperature rose. I could feel sweat on my brow. I reached out my hands almost touching her. Then I saw that she had a thumb but only three fingers. There was a churning in my stomach and instinctively I knew that I did not want to know more. I backed away, legs trembling. My heart felt like it was going to leap from my chest. My brow might have been damp before but now I could feel the sweat running down the side of my face.

Then flashes of memory of what happened on Lagrange Point Station two came to mind; the two pulsating lights exiting the large space ship, my attempt to escape the station, the white fog entering my escape capsule, then…then nothing. I woke up here, where ever or whatever here is. Maybe even whenever! My legs buckled as I fell against the recliner. I felt nauseous and the beads of sweat ran unabated down the side of my face. I was on an alien spacecraft. The woman in front of me was an alien. Mercy! I wanted to go home!

Flata observed the Human specimen with great interest. After all, he was her creation. She could feel all his emotions, follow his thought patterns. She wondered what it would be like to be so ignorant of knowledge and understanding of the cosmos and what it consisted of. How could this specie possibly survive, let alone achieve space travel.

"Peace be unto you Human, Robert Aaron." Flata took a step closer extending her hands once again toward him, palms up.

Robert's terror began to subside, tears came to his eyes blurring his vision as he instinctively and finally realized the hopelessness of his situation. Robert extended his hands palms down and touched the aliens long fingered hands and palms. She enclosed his hands. Her hands were warm, and soft. A gently faint electrical charge danced on the inside of his palms. The charge was like static electricity but less sharp and certainly not painful.

Again he heard the women speak, but he knew now that the communication was telepathic. "How do you feel Robert?"

He started to verbally respond to her question but she

interrupted him and said sharply, "No. Use your mind!"

"Yea right," thought Robert.

Robert looked directly into the mesmerizing silver eyes of his captor and directed his thoughts toward her. "I am twenty three earth years old. I am an Ensign in Earths Space Navy. My job was to maintain the various material and biological experiments on Lagrange Point Station two. And oh," grinning at her he said, "And to report any Aliens in the vicinity! You already knew all these things so why do you ask me?"

Flata, not offended or amused by his reply, said, "I was trying to assess your mental capabilities. They are quiet good for your species. Of course you are part "alien", as you call us, and part human. You seem to be coping better than the others."

All thoughts of possibly being telepathic slipped from Robert's mind as his blood turned ice cold. "What others?"

Flata continued to hold his hand and stared into his eyes. She remained silent, obviously assessing him.

Deep down in some part of his soul he knew what the alien had said was the truth. That would explain his "differentness" he had felt all his life, even since he was a child. Of course he knew his mom was his mom; and his Dad? Without thinking to deeply, Robert fiercely defended his ties to his Father, he had known no other!

He had always noticed his hair was slightly different in texture from his three sisters. His school achievements were like child's play much to the exasperation of his same three sisters. From high school, actually he skipped two years of high school, going into his senior year and from there he went directly to Midwestern Science University. He skipped the first three years after testing out on all the exams for the university curriculum and began working on his Doctorate in theoretical physics. Thus when he joined earth's Space Navy he was able to pick his assignment. He chose the duty as the single, solitary, occupant of Lagrange Point Two, duty station. There, Robert successfully completed experiment after experiment in the material and biological sciences.

Robert remembered well his Father's exasperation and his Mother's confusion in trying to raise a genius son whom they fiercely concealed from special interest groups. His three sisters were just as loyal when the sorority sisters made fun of Robert's apparent lack of social skills when it came to the opposite sex.

"What do you mean by all the others?"

Flata replied, "You will soon see."

As the alien was releasing his grasps, Robert tightened his hands on hers not letting her go.

"Are we on a spaceship? What is your name? Why did you abduct me?" Who are you?"

"Yes we are on a space ship and my name is unpronounceable to you with your current linguistic skills. You can call me Flata. I am the chief geneticist for our group. You will learn soon enough why you have been chosen and taken". With that, the alien named Flata, turned around and left Robert standing alone in the room. He would soon learn that it was his room. For better or for worse, he was home.

CHAPTER 7
WHERE IS EMILY

Warren Abbott looked around Emily's room for the third time searching for clues as to her whereabouts. All her clothing, makeup, toiletries, and lesson manuals were in their usual position. She was supposed to have met him for dinner two hours ago; it was now seven o'clock P.M. She did not answer her calls. She was not anywhere in the dorm nor had any of the other girls living in the area had seen her since Emily went to class earlier in the morning.

He knew Emily could take care of herself. He had seen her take down men three times her size in her karate classes. Although she was only five feet, two inches tall and one hundred and five pounds in weight, her karate skills were phenomenal. She said her father had begun to teach her defensive skills since she learned to walk. He had been an officer in the Special Forces or something.

Warren's heart anguished as he left the dorm to get into his new jaguar convertible. Warren's parents were unbelievable rich. So when Emily expressed her wish to ride in a convertible so she could see the sky, Warren went out immediately and purchased one the very next day. Warren knew the effect he had on women and did not fail to see the looks of envy on men's faces when they were in a crowd. Still, Warren had never been interested in the slightest in any of them from the time his eyes fell upon Emily.

They were in their junior year of high school. The class had been a precursor to advanced mathematical theories. Their eyes had locked onto one another like lasers from opposite sides of the room. How long they had gazed into one another's eyes he did not know. But, in the distance he heard someone calling his name repeatedly. The voice was saying, "Earth calling Abbott. Come in Abbott!" Then he perceived, more than heard, giggles and laughter. Warren realized they were laughing at him. Embarrassed, Warren looked away, the spell dissipating into reality; however, not before he observed Emily's crooked little smile and beet red flushed face.

"Mr. Abbott, thank you for paying attention"...And that was when he learned what love was.

After meeting Emily later in the afternoon, it was as if they both knew there would never be any other significant other persons in their lives. They were mated like swans and were inseparable. Warren had met Emily's parents on one occasion when she invited him home to study with her. They seemed like wonderful people and he liked them very much and they him. They were killed before the end of the year in a car crash. Thus, Emily had become a fixture with his Mom and Dad and two younger brothers. They were all equally smitten with Emily as he was.

Because the Abbotts knew their son, they knew that Emily would always be part of the family. So, when Mr. Abbott answered the phone around six A.M., and heard his sobbing son explain that Emily had been missing since the early evening the night before, he knew that is was serious.

Mr. Abbott had been a software designer for Robotic Space Systems, and had cashed out with several of his many patents. Earl Abbott hung up the phone, collected his wife, Karen; and was enroute on the four-hour drive to The University.

CHAPTER 8
THE REPORT

Warren sat across the desk of the Blaizon Hills, city police detectives, Gary Jessop, and his partner, Carol Reese. The detectives looked at each other knowingly. Their look said, "Poor Chump", with a huge capital "C". They had listened to his story now no less than five times. It never changed. He did not even so much as change a comma in his repeated story. He said they had been going together for five years now and have never had sex. Not even oral! Yeah right!

Det. Reese looked at Mr. Abbott and observed how broken he was. He had already thrown up twice in the last two hours since his arrival. He had come in early in the morning and he was hysterical. He demanded to talk to an investigator about his girlfriend, whose name was Emily Smith. He wanted to report her missing and stated that she had no next of kin but they were to be married when they graduated.

He was now wet with perspiration, snot was running down from his nose to his chin unabated and entirely unnoticed by him. Reese placed a tissue box in front of him that he either did not see or ignored. Det. Reese was at her limits of being objective and distant from young Mr. Abbott. Her career choice demanded that she maintained an emotionless and objective state of mind. However, her "women's intuition", told her that Mr. Abbott was telling the truth.

Det. Reese got up from behind her desk and walked around to Mr. Abbott, placed an arm around his shoulder and reached over pulling a tissue from the Kleenex box. And, like a mother administering to her child, she reached around and started wiping his nose and chin. To her surprise, he leaned into her breast and placed his arms around her waist, and sobbed. She pulled him closer to her bosom as tears slid silently from her eyes.

"Oh yes. She would find this Emily. And, if she was playing young Abbott for a fool, she would beat the living shit out of her. That Bitch!"

Det. Jessop looked on for he too was moved by the young man's sincerity and pain. Being a retired homicide investigator from New York City, he had come to Blaizon Hills PD, for peace and healing, physical and spiritual. He had become bored sitting around his condo in Brooklyn, so he offered his services and expertise to Blaizon Hills, which they accepted immediately.

Det. Rees's story was about the same except she hailed from Los Angeles. Both were divorced and neither had children. Their allegiance was one hundred percent to the job.

Det. Jessop called the University Police Department for the third time. "Yes, they knew of Mr. Abbott's concern about his girlfriend, Emily Smith, and insinuated that he was not related and did not necessarily have a legal right to report her missing, especially after only one night. After all, college girls went off on weekend trips together all the time. No, the Chief was still out to lunch. Yes, they had a list of Ms. Smith's classes including her professor's names and building addresses. They would now fax the information to them".

Hanging up the phone, Det. Jessop walked to the corner of the office to retrieve the fax. Gary whistled when he saw the list of courses Emily was taking. "She certainly was not an under-achiever!" Mused Jessop.

Carol Reese was surprised by the maternal feelings she felt for the young man. Even though he was built like an ox and had the looks of a Greek god, he was truly innocent in each and every way, just as he said he was.

A couple came into the office. Det. Reese looked up and observed the women watching her as Carol held the woman's son to her breast. His sobs had ebbed and as he pulled back he looked up at Det. Reese. Looking down into young Mr. Abbott's eyes, she said, "Warren, we are going to find your Emily. I promise you." Her quiet assured tone sounded comforting and had the ring of truth.

Warren then saw his mother coming toward him. He released Det. Reese's waist and said, "Mother!" rushing into her arms. Mrs. Abbott looked detective Reese in the eye and saw only maternal love there. Saying, "Thank You", she collected her son and they all three of them walked out of the office, Warren in the middle, each parent protectively guiding their son with their arms around his waist and shoulders.

CHAPTER 9
THE INVESTIGATION

Dr. Calander reiterated for the third time carefully the scam that Ms. Smith had attempted to perpetrate upon him. He further explained that he, being a Professor Emeritus of Physics and Mathematics, easily recognized her scribbling's as pure nonsense. Everyone and anyone, anyone with brains that is, know there is no such thing as helix mathematics, light and color frequency deviation relative to space-time travel, and the preposterous notion that gateways to other galaxies thru black holes are possible. He also unabashedly mentioned that no one wrote the textbooks used in all the finer universities other than himself!

Detectives Jessop and Reese listened quietly observing everything, missing nothing. He had been the last person to see Ms. Smith alive. It was obvious that Dr. Calender was trying to laugh off what appeared to him as an attempted scam but it was also obvious that he was still very angry. Motive.

Det. Reese said, "Do you by any chance have any of the notes she showed you? I would like to see them myself."

Dr. Calender looked surprised, then confused, then a half sneer, disdaining look quickly flashed across his face. "Like she could figure her way out of a wet paper bag", thought Dr. Calender. He had not thought of Ms. Smith's notes since she left. The detective's arrival, questioning her disappearance, had come as a surprising shock. "Good, the girl got the message and left school. At least she had enough sense for that". He did not see any of her scribbling's lying around on his desk or in his letters, piled high, and of a course, another indication just how important he was, in his oversized, deep mail receptacle. Then he remembered the formulas he had scratched on a pad and threw away into the wastebasket after Ms. Smith had left. Reaching down into the trash, Dr. Calender rummaged thru the trash and found the copies of his disposed notes. Handing them to Det. Reese he said, "If you are going to keep that please allow me to make a copy". He did not know why he wanted a copy, but why not.

Detectives Jessop and Reese shared space as they looked at the paper. The strange mathematical formulas stringed across the page; some strings intersected diagonally, some vertical and a few intertwined into strange helix coils in an undulating pattern. It was absolutely nothing like anything they had ever seen.

Dr. Calender advised, rather defensively, "She was an average student, nothing special! She had "B's" in all her classes since she has been here at the University. She never participated or seemed particularly interested in course curriculum. Well, with one exception. She always made "A's" in astronomy. Her only known associate was the Abbott boy. They were always together".

Det. Reese walked over to the copy machine and

SEED OF HOPE

made a copy of the strange formulas. She gave the copy to Dr. Calender. She did not know why she made a copy of the formulas; it was just in her innate nature to do so as an investigator. One never knew where the pieces of the puzzle would fit together. Having given the copy to Dr. Calender, she kept the original for herself which she placed in her purse.

Thanking Dr. Calender for his time they left his office. Going out the front door of the building they were standing on a high, large portico overlooking the campus. From their vantage point they could see for blocks and most importantly, into a large heavily wooded meadow across the street. The two detectives did not speak. They did not need too. They both knew where they were going to go next and were fairly certain that perhaps the mystery of the missing girl was soon to be discovered. In their experience, it was usually the all too sad, same outcome.

They walked down the steps and crossed the street to the side that was a heavily forested park area. They had not gone far along the sidewalk when they observed a partially hidden path meandering off into the woods. They both carefully walked the path scrutinizing anything that might be out of place. At about twenty-five yards, Det. Jessop suddenly stopped. Det. Reese, looking away, bumped into his back surprising them both. Smiling to himself, Det. Jessop noticed for the first time that Carol had nice breasts.

They both observed the purse, backpack and computer lying on the ground about ten paces ahead. Then

Det. Reese saw the bloody sleeve, shredded, lying on the ground. Above the sleeve was a protruding, broken branch, about two feet from the ground. It too was covered with blood and thread fibers matching the bloodied sleeve.

Slowly, they backed away trying to preserve as much evidence as possible, retracing their previous foot prints where feasible. There was no doubt this was a crime scene and it needed to be preserved. From long experience they knew the laptop and purse belonged to Ms. Emily Smith. She was last seen wearing a white blouse. The bloody sleeve was white and in all probability, hers.

Det. Jessop called for what constituted a crime scene van, and additional officers to secure the area. They also had officers posted at her room to keep the curious and morbid out, and, perhaps garner more clues as to what happened to Ms. Smith.

After they secured the area, Detectives Jessop and Reese, accompanied by a crime scene officer, re-entered the woods making every effort to stay off of the path. Examining the ground around the tree stub they could see the impression of a body in the lush grass. What appeared to be a knee print and a partial handprint was next to the disturbed earth body print. The tech took several pictures of the area and removed the bloodied cloth with tongs, depositing the cloth in a clean sterilized baggy and noted on the tag, time, date, and location found. It would later be assigned a case number for future reference.

Going forward, they retrieved the purse and carefully extracted the wallet from the purse and confirmed

SEED OF HOPE

the wallet belonged to Ms. Emily Smith. The woman pictured on the driver's license and the school identification card looked young. They were one and the same. Her date of birth indicated that she had just turned twenty years of age. She was very attractive, not beautiful. Her jaw seemed oddly angled but, not uncommonly so. Her hair was platinum blonde.

When Det. Jessop observed her hair he thought, "She certainly is not the proverbial dumb blonde." And, her eyes were a pale artic blue, piercing. Oh, but her smile was genuine, lopsided with natural pink full lips. Det. Jessop could understand young Abbott's attraction to her.

Looking further into Ms. Smith's purse, Det. Jessop saw several wads of one hundred dollar bills. Whatever the reason for missing, the motive certainly was not robbery. Handing the purse to Det. Reese, he went to the computer pack. The computer was still intact and appeared outwardly to be undamaged. This he gave to the crime scene technician.

Walking farther into the woods, followed closely by Det. Reese, they came to the clearing and they could see two sets of prints, side by side, leading to the center of the clearing. The grass in the glen was ankle high and as of yet, had not straightened due to the high humidity and moisture shielded from sun and wind, by the high trees surrounding the glen.

The tracks appeared to stop in the center of the glen. The grass in that area looked like it was depressed in a circular pattern. Detectives Jessop and Reese looked at one another. Det. Reese intoned, "Oh shit". Carefully they circled the glen in opposite directions, making sure there were no exit tracks. They met on the opposite side of the glen. There were none. But in their heart and heads, they knew there would not be any. The area was a fresh crime scene and had not been disturbed.

Agreeing upon a perpendicular approach, they moved toward the circular depression off to the side of the original set of prints. The prints stopped at a smaller depression about four feet in diameter.

Without saying anything, Det. Reese pulled out the earlier discarded paper with the weird math equations, from her purse. Together they looked at the jigsaw puzzle of math equations. Det. Reese said, "I bet you any amount of money that Ms. Smith was trying to set her ole professor along the correct mathematical path and he just failed her test".

"Yep", was all Det. Jessop said, he was a man of few words.

CHAPTER 10
SENSITIVE ACTION

Commander Bob Johnson was sitting at his desk at the Space Defense Intelligence Command Center, when he received an urgent priority alarm on his computer. Staff Sgt. Williams appeared on the screen.
"Yes, Sargent?"
"Sir, it happened again. We believe we just observed an abduction. This time it was a female in upper state Pennsylvania. We were observing a stationary saucer in a wooded area close to the University of Physics and Polymer Sciences. Initially we saw one male occupant exit from the saucer and enter the woods going in the direction of the University. We did not observe him again until about one hour later. He exited the woods escorting a female. He was holding onto her elbow, we assume to help control her. They entered the saucer; it lifted, and then departed rapidly leaving Earth's vicinity meeting up with a larger craft pretty much in the same manner and fashion as the one at Lagrange Point Station two. The larger craft then left the solar system near the speed of light".
"Thank you Sargent. Forward the intelligence to the necessary contacts. We will take it from here."
Commander Johnson was pensive. "What was going on? Both of these abductions are high profile and

unprecedented. The taking of a military officer from a military installation was bad enough. Now, for whatever reason they chose to abduct a civilian student or teacher, from a highly acclaimed University where advanced physics is studied by our brightest and most promising students? No. Something big is going on and we need to know what". The thoughts furrowed Commander Johnson's brow even further.

Picking up the phone Commander Johnson phoned his boss, Admiral Cleary. Admiral Cleary was The Presidents liaison for all matters pertaining to the more frequent visitations to Earth from other worldly visitors.

"Admiral Cleary, Bob Johnson, here. It just happened again sir. This time a female was abducted from the campus of The University of Physics and Polymer Sciences in upper state Pennsylvania. We do not have any further details at this time."

Admiral Cleary responded, "Okay Bob. Get an investigation team up there now and see what kind of evidence you can gather. Money and expense is no object. We need to get to the bottom of this as soon as we can. And Bob, do your best to cover this up. We do not want the locals to start any kind of hysteria. I can see the headlines now, "Aliens kidnapping science students and teachers from prestigious University".

Admiral Cleary rang off. Admiral Cleary leaned back into his chair, thinking. Like Commander Johnson, "He believed that something was going on. They have never been this brazen before. What has changed? Why now? What purpose could the abductees serve to such an enormously advanced being that obviously can travel around the galaxy?"

Admiral Cleary reached for the phone and dialed the number. "Mr. President, we have an unprecedented problem."

CHAPTER 11
UPMOST DISCRETION

After gathering their evidence, both Detectives Jessop and Reese knew that Emily Smith was not on the Earth. They did not know where she was taken but they did not believe that it was out for a weekend vacation. They both sternly counseled the crime scene technician to keep his mouth shut and to help spread the story that she was kidnapped by Gypsies and believed to have been taken to Europe.

"Poor Gypsies", thought Jessop, "they are traditionally blamed and used for all manner of malfeasance". Very convenient though. The crime scene technician was also advised that he would be rewarded for his upmost discretion; he really did not want to know what the implied "or else", involved.

Det. Jessop called his Chief and filled him in on Emily's abduction by Gypsies and that they had discovered they have been travelling thru the area. They were now enroute to New York to follow up on the investigation. They had already decided that any evidence that was retrieved would be conveniently downplayed and misplaced...somewhere.

Det. Jessop and Reese arrived at the Space Intelligence Command Center in New York City, around two P.M., approximately twenty to twenty-four hours after Emily's

SEED OF HOPE

abduction, and six hours after interviewing young Mr. Abbott at the Blaizon Hills Police Department. For the first time in her life, Det. Reese felt like she was not going to be able to solve a case, at least to the resolution of presenting a body and saying, "Here is Emily Smith". She had promised young Abbott that she would find her.

Unknown to them, they had been followed and listened in upon by Space Intelligence Commandoes from the time that Ms. Smith was abducted; they being the senior investigators in the city of Blaizon Hills, were obviously going to be the ones called upon to do the work. Their history files were immediately pulled and forwarded to Commander Bob Johnson. After reading their files, he knew that their next stop, hopefully, would be with Space Intelligence. Lt. Sasha Palangin, in charge of the abduction and cover-up investigation at the University, liked the way the two detectives had handled the investigation and was immensely pleased with their course of action. She could not have done better herself. Her and her team virtually had nothing to do. They did go out and stealthily take soil samples from beneath the location where the saucer had hovered.

Detective Jessop, having spent his career years as an investigator in New York City, had come across all classes of government spooks of one kind or another. He had on one other occasion sent information to them reference a UFO sighting so he believed these were the people they should contact now.

They entered the non-descript building near the wharfs in a seedier part of the city. The building was an old warehouse converted to office space and looked much like all the other dilapidated buildings; the only thing different, if one cared to look, was the huge assortment of antenna tops barely visible along the roofline of the building.

They approached the only desk in the spacious front office area and identified themselves as Detectives from Blaizon Hills Police Department and wanted to talk to someone in charge.

The lady, moderately overweight and voluptuous of breast, laughed and said, "I am in charge here. You can talk to me!" She noted that neither detective smiled at her little innuendo. "Gees guys, lighten up. It is not every day two celebrity detectives walk thru my door."

Jessop and Reese looked at one another. Now what could that mean?

The voluptuous lady reached under her desk and pressed a soundless button that set off a buzzer in some distant part of the building. "Please guys, have a seat over there", indicating to a very uncomfortable looking set of chairs placed away from the desk but not against the wall. Weird!

Detectives Jessop and Reese had no longer sat down than a door on the far wall opened and a man dressed smartly in military uniform approached them extending his hand. "Detective Jessop, Detective Reese, we have been expecting you! Glad you made it in such a timely manner." He then turned to the women at the desk and said, "Thanks Patty, you did a good job. I imagine you got the brains of our two fine detectives churning."

SEED OF HOPE

The lady named Patty laughed and responded, "I did my best boss!" Extending his hand he said, Det. Jessop, Det. Reese, this way please." He tuned on heel and left, obviously expecting them to follow, which they did. Entering thru the first door, which was as all doors, simply a wood frame, they entered into a small foyer. The next door was obviously made of metal and required palm and eye identification to enter. Beyond this door was another world. The warehouse was partitioned with short paneled walls, each cubicle staffed by several uniformed military men and women. They each had earphones, mikes, and were intently staring into computer screens that appeared to display satellite images of the entire earth...and moon?

Their uniformed escort entered an elevator on the far wall and they went up to the third floor of the three-story structure. This area appeared to be staffed in much the same way except at one end of the building there was a huge world map on one side of a large table and a moon map on the other. Small lights seem to move across the various maps. It was then that Jessop figured out it was a three D holographic display on a scale he did not know was possible. One of the blinking lights appeared to be over, The University, in Blaizon Hills.

Turning and indicating for the two detectives to take seats to the side of the display, the uniformed military man then approached a small diminutive woman of about five feet tall who had just entered from a side door. She handed him a thick package. She was wearing jeans and a sweatshirt that was emblazoned with the emblem of, "The University of Physics and Polymer Science". He thanked her and, as she turned to leave, she looked over her shoulder and winked at Det. Jessop. Jessop, being caught unaware that his acute observations of the women was known to her, quickly colored at the collar and looked away.

Reese said, "What's the matter Jessop? Got caught looking did ya!"

The military man, as of still yet unidentified, sat down in a chair across from them. A small coffee table was between them and a full array of small sandwiches and sweets set next to a full pot of coffee and an icy pitcher of milk. He opened the package provided by the "winking women", and started perusing thru the file. Then absently looking up he said, "Please, this is for you. Help yourself. I know neither of you have eaten since this morning. Your morning started rather earlier in the day with the young Mr. Abbott, and got even more interesting from then on." Again he then went back to perusing the file provided by "winking women".

Reese turned to Jessop and said, "Jessop you did not tell me you had such all-knowing friends."

Jessop responded, "Neither did I".

The military man then looked up and said, "Do you have the evidence for me? We need to analyze it as soon as possible. Oh, forgive me; I know so much about you two that I forget not everyone are as privy to information as I. I am Commander Bob Johnson. I am in charge of Space Intelligence Division. We have followed your investigation closely and I am impressed with your work.

Especially your discretion, and, the way you handled the Crime Scene Technician. It did not hurt to put the fear of God into him should he run his mouth. We will see to it that he is amply rewarded. If he does not keep his mouth shut he is a dead man." Commander Johnson looked them both in the eye conveying the unspoken message that it also pertained to them. Was it a hollow threat? Neither Jessop nor Reese believed so.

Without saying anything, Det. Jessop and Det. Reese handed Commander Johnson the packages of evidence they were carrying. He waved to a man standing at parade rest across from the table. The man came forward and received the evidence and left thru a doorway to another part of the building.

Commander Johnson said, "Let's cut to the chase here. We are all professionals. We are up against a unique situation. Normally we, in the military, do not believe that civilian police and military intelligence make a good mix. It involves a different mindscape, a different way of thinking. In effect, we do things that people like you would put people like us in jail for... for, lack of a better word, indiscretions. You would feel your civil liberties were being violated. And that is okay. I can understand your narrow field of view of things. It serves your purpose. But now on the other hand, you also think of the bigger picture. It was interesting the way you made up the Gypsy cover story. It showed a broad understanding of the serious nature of our problem. It is more than just a missing girl and a Hollywood movie money extravaganza opportunity."

Now, I know you both have been in life and death situations. You know what fear is and how to stifle the paralyzing effects. I never have. I have had just a view of violence on the sidelines, from a distance, from an intelligence analyst point of view. So, I am not above telling you that this abduction scares me. In fact, I am terrified." He was not smiling.

Commander Johnson looked serious. He was telling the truth. And, because of his disarming honesty admitting his fear, Jessop and Reese literally loved him all the more. One thing they had learned in their long careers was, when someone was stringing them a line of "untruth", they could discern this. Deceit and lies came natural to the human heart. Honesty was not necessarily so. To them, any man that could admit that he was afraid was a man that they could trust.

"In fact, as I said, I am terrified. We need to know what is going on. And because of the way you two have handled this incident, with supreme professionalism and most importantly, discretion, I would like to extend to you two, full time jobs with Space Intelligence as Special Investigators."

Reese looked at Jessop. He returned her stare. They communicated silently knowing what each was thinking.

Commander Johnson said, "Oh, I assure you it is a legitimate offer. Your time of employment, should you choose to accept, will commence from 0700, yesterday morning."

Detective Jessop looked at his partner and said, "Well

SEED OF HOPE

Carol, what do you think? I have never hunted aliens before."

"Me neither, I'm in," said Detective Reese.

Thus began the careers of Special Investigators Jessop and Reese of the Space Intelligence Agency.

CHAPTER 12
CONFERENCE

Admiral Cleary walked into the conference room at ten A.M., the fourth day after Ms. Emily Smith's abduction and twenty-five days after Ensign Robert Aaron's abduction. "All the, "usual suspects", were already here", mused Admiral Cleary. All the "usual suspects", being Defense Intelligence, appropriate civil defense and scientific groups, military advisors and The President, and his advisors. The President sat at the head of the table. The invited guest of scientist also included a one, Dr. Estevez Calander, Professor Emeritus of physics and mathematics, fame. He looked miserable. "As well as he should be if what he had heard was true in regard to his treatment of Ms. Smith. She had tried to give him the opportunity of a lifetime and he had allowed pride and prejudice to literally take the golden egg from his very hands!" Space intelligence had recorded Detectives Jessup and Reese's interview with him.

Admiral Cleary then approached the two detectives. Their eyes locked onto his, their facial expressions frozen in stone. He knew their reputations and their abilities within hours of their involvement of the Emily Smith abduction. That is why they were "invited" to join the conference meeting and be hired as, Special Investigators, with Space Intelligence. He believed they would make good additions to this work group and staff. "Mercy, they look like husband and wife!" A smile crossed his face at that thought as he introduced himself and welcomed them to the group. They were gracious but they still did not smile. Admiral Cleary returned to the head of the table and took his seat on the dais.

The President stood at the podium. "Ok people! Observe, listen, and above all, think! Commander Johnson, start the holographic video."

Two pictures came up on the screen side by side. On the left was Ms. Emily Smith. Her picture was the same one as the one on her driver's license. On the right was a young, white male, identified as Ensign Robert Aaron. He was in a Space Defense uniform. Detectives Jessop and Reese looked at each other; they both had a look of consternation on their faces. They instinctively knew they did not like where this scenario was going to go.

Commander Johnson stepped to the podium beneath the holographic photographs, and introduced himself. "For those of you who do not know me, I am Commander Bob Johnson, Commander of Space Intelligence Center. I serve at the pleasure of Admiral Cleary.

Starting his analysis he pointed to the picture of the white male identified as Ensign Robert Aaron. "Ensign Robert Aaron was assigned to Lagrange Point Two observation station" Commander Johnson indicated on a space map Lagrange Point Two's location on the Earth-Moon solar map. "The duty assignment on this station is considered by many, including Ensign Aaron, to be the plum assignment in Space Intelligence. All be it, it is a solitary duty assignment of twenty-four months."

"Ensign Aaron consistently scored at the very top in his intelligence categories. Indeed, we were not really able to score him well because we were at a loss as to what to compare him too. He was one of a kind. He was one of the most prolific producers of science experiments aboard Lagrange Point Two station. No one has ever come close to the amount of scientific data he accomplished in the short thirteen months he served aboard the station. His science data in the areas of chemistry, physics, and biology are simply astounding."

Pointing his laser to the picture on the left, he said, "This is Ms. Emily Smith. She was a senior at, Southern University of Physics and Polymer Sciences, in Blaizon Hills, Pennsylvania. The only thing they seem to have in common is their above average intelligence."

"Now, Ms. Smith is another interesting matter. All of her grades indicated she was an average "B" student; with the exception of astronomy. In astronomy she always got "A's". Now…, in regard to her "B's", Ms. Smith was always exactly average. She was never a point higher or a point lower, ever, all her life! She skated under the radar, invisible! Indeed, her only higher intelligence indicator is this one piece of paper with mathematical equations copied by Dr. Calander, her physics and math professor."

Pausing for effect, he continued, "And, her laptop recovered by Detectives Jessop and Reese. Oh, and by the way, they discovered all the evidence within one hour of reaching point zero!"

SEED OF HOPE

The president stepped up to the podium leaning forward into the mike saying, "Thanks to the both of you for a job well done. We are all grateful and fortunate to have you two on board, Thank you again". He returned to his seat.

Commander Johnson watched the two veteran detectives as the accolades from, The President, was being presented. He could not help but smiling. Both detectives were caught totally by surprise! He was sure that being caught by surprise was something that rarely, if ever, happened in regard to them. At first they looked like deer caught by the high beam of the headlights. They had frozen completely still, eyes gone wide, mouths slightly agape! Then they began to perceptibly slink down into their seats. These two hard, seasoned crime fighters were never appreciated in their work. More often than not, petty politicians used them as political scapegoats.

Commander Johnson was surer than ever that he had made the right decision to bring the two detectives on board as members of his new elite task force. Of course he had to have the approval of Admiral Cleary. It was highly unusual to incorporate civilian law enforcement into military operations. Admiral Cleary had at first been hesitant but acquiesced saying he trusted his judgment.

He thought his judgment was sound. They both have impressive service records. Their records indicated time and again that, "they were loners, they did not "play well with others", and more often than not, "they went over the heads of their local supervisors", under mitigating circumstances. But, each and every time their judgment was sound, just like at Blaizon Hills.

Together they had a multitude of accommodations for valor above and beyond! And, they had both been shot, stabbed, beat upon, on several occasions. Jessop had been in twelve firefights and been hospitalized for up to nine months. None of the people he had a gunfight with survived.

Reese had been in a total of nine firefights and had been hospitalized for up to three months. Only one person survived a gunfight with her and that was because he was a fellow cop. She had allowed him to live.

There were wagers with real money within their respective department that bet that they would not survive to retirement. Those that bet against them lost their money. After reviewing their service records in detail, Commander Johnson was very hesitant indeed about bringing them on board. But viewing the satellite imagery of how they carefully reconnoitered the crime scene, and hidden surveillance cameras within the PD, showing how Reese's maternal instinct surfaced when comforting young Mr. Abbott, provided insight into their professional and personal character. Det. Reese's maternal instincts were a completely hidden character trait on her part and did not appear in any assessment by any previous supervisor. The tears he observed on her cheeks were real. Commander Johnson figured it probably surprised her even more than it would have any previous supervisor.

The investigative reports were well written, concise, accurate, and, where facts were not necessarily clear, accurate judgmental truth was presented and noted as their judgment. Commander Johnson was also impressed with the knee print and three-fingered thumbprint carefully preserved in a casting. They knew instinctively it was odd and important, but they did not really know why at the time.

But most important to Commander Johnson, was their utmost discretion in reporting the crime. They bypassed the University Police, and Blaizon Hills Police, and all normal chains of command and reported directly to Space Intelligence. They did not know that an intelligence team was already on the ground in the area ready to take over the investigation, but was not necessary due to their discretion. Abduction at a highly prestigious university of sciences, by aliens, of one of their students, would have caused panic. To assure the silence of the crime scene investigator, he was promised a good crime scene investigative position within the government. Fortunately, he was a good investigator and worthy of the opportunity.

The meeting going over the evidence and the final analysis of the abduction took most of the day. Other items discussed were the latest sightings of saucer craft in the area of jurisdiction of the Space Intelligence Command. The sphere of observation extended way beyond the earth and the moon. It was apparent that some new dynamic was in the works. They just did not know what it was or how much time they had. At the end of the meeting at nine P.M., Detectives Jessop and Reese stood off by themselves facing one another. They both held out their hands palms up. They both had visibly shaking hands. Detective Jessop, looking down into Detective Reese's eyes said, "The ax is falling".

Detective Reese responded with a heartfelt, "May God help us all!"

CHAPTER 13
NO LONGER AFRAID

Ensign Aaron was sitting in a viewing room where he could look out at the cosmos. He never tired of the view. It was so humbling on one hand and it could create despair on the other. One just had to restructure the order of how you fit into the milieu of your surroundings. It had become obvious to Robert, that, whatever purposes his existence was now serving; it no longer could be compared to his former life. He had been aboard the intergalactic cruiser now for at least, what? The twenty-four hour day was not the standard of measurement. But, to the best of his recollection, it should be around twenty-five earth days. Surely, sooner or later there must be a more direct contact and dialogue with his alien captors so he could find out what is going on.

Since Aaron had accepted his fate, he was no longer frightened. His "indoctrination", if that is what it was, had been fascinating. He was usually placed in a lecture setting similar to the many university courses that he had attended. Then various groups of aliens would be allowed to interview him; primarily giving him a sort of intelligence test.

What amazed him most was their intelligence. Their intellectual abilities were staggering when it came to math and physics. Most of the concepts and precepts were currently beyond his abilities. However, he was becoming more aware, and his own intellectual abilities seemed to be becoming more enhanced. Now he could communicate telepathically where before he could only "hear", their thoughts and commands. A telepathic conversation was no longer an ordeal and had become the natural order of things. It was difficult for him to be the least knowledgeable individual in a group. Here the role was reversed. He felt like he was the really dumb one. And, in actuality, he was. This was very humbling.

When in the class setting the questions would start simple, at least for him. Other humans would not find them so simple. With the interviewers, the most uncomfortable group was the pre-adolescents. Their emotions were not as controlled and refined as the adults. Sometime he could sense disdain, a lot of superiority and now and then, tinges of outright hostility. But for the most part, he was nothing more than a human specimen.

Robert had access to much of the public areas of the ship. As of yet he was not allowed on the bridge, engine rooms, or any other technical areas that enabled the ship to function. He really wanted to see the hydroponic section and learn how they so easily manufactured air. Perhaps later.

From time to time he would see a group in the distance that he believed was human, but he was not sure. They were kept separate and he was not allowed to communicate with anyone including his guides. The guides were always present but at a certain distance and always silent.

SEED OF HOPE

After one of the sessions with a group of young aliens, a female alien approached him. She appeared to be about the same age as he. She was holding her three-fingered hand across her breast in a fashion Robert had come to recognize as a greeting, generally from a superior to an inferior. This greeting startled Robert, even if it was one of condescension. He, without realizing it, bowed his head and placed his right hand flat across his midsection fingers spread wide apart, thumb straight up, like holding in his stomach.

In his mind Robert heard, "Robert Aaron, I have been given the privilege by, the "Council of Yield", to further assess the Human-Andrian bonding experiment. Andrian is our species and it is about as close as you can ever come to pronunciation. We come from a galaxy accessed by what you would call a wormhole, but what we call terminal gates. We have visited your galaxy on many occasions and have colonies throughout this star system. My name is Breveka. My specialty is inter-dimensional specie dynamics. Again, that is the closest approximation of what I do to which you may possibly grasp the concepts."

Robert was astounded. It was the first time he had ever been addressed by name and had been provided any information about whom his abductors were or where they were from, or even why he was here. He was some kind of experiment.

Robert observed the Alien, Breveka. She was slender as they all were. Her hair was cut short at the front, swept back over the ears in a style he would consider sort of "dikey". The hair color was blonde. Her face was not unattractive, the slightly cantilevered or almond shaped eyes, looked exotic. The color of her irises was pale yellow-green. Her lips were full and light pink. And, like all the other Andrian females, her breast, though not ample, was nicely formed and shaped, as evidenced by the sheer garment. Her flowing garment hid her hips and waist. Only her slippered feet peeked from beneath the light green, ankle length, and colored garment.

Breveka said, "Do I meet your human standard of attractiveness?"

The question caught Robert off guard. He felt heat on his face as his face colored. The opposite sex had never been his forte, so to speak. He just had difficulty relating to women. Robert replied, "I am ssssorry! I did not mean to stare!"

"Human Robert Aaron, you are strange even by human standards. You show much promise intellectually; not withstanding your inability to interact socially. You seem incapable of establishing relationships not only with females, but with males also. You do not fit into the milieu of your life form. In our society you would not be allowed to use the precious resources and you would have been eliminated. The elimination of the feeble, body or mind, the lame, or the criminal, is necessary for any society to function in a cohesive fashion. Your failure, as specie, to eliminate the refuse, makes you weak. You do not realize it but your very survival is at stake!"

The statement by Breveka that the Human Species was in crises and in danger was by itself a shattering

SEED OF HOPE

revelation. It was a very sobering thought. However, her statement that he would be eliminated if he was a member of their society, shook his very soul. He was unaware of the tears that ran down his cheeks. He quickly came to realize that all his life he had romanticized what aliens would be like. He knew they would obviously have to be super intelligent. They were certainly that. He had assumed they would have "human" compassion, love, and respect for others that were "lesser" than they. If they could so coldly and calculating destroy members of their own species, then humans must be extremely abhorrent to them. This revelation shook him to the core and caused a twinge of fear and anxiety within Robert!

Robert tried to reason out if they were the way they were because they were a star faring specie? Were the same standards, attitudes, and mores, practiced on their planets as on their star ships? Did they even try to populate planets? Robert had not thought much about what a society would be like that spent their entire lives, maybe generations, traveling among the stars, in a tightly controlled environment. It was now obvious to him it was necessary to control the population. Exactly how would one go about controlling a population? What methods of policing would be required? Then Robert thought about Flata, the Andrians chief geneticist. She had to be absolutely the most important and powerful women on the ship. Robert thought, "I will definitely go see her. I need answers to my questions!"

Breveka interrupted his train of thought. He had been so engrossed thinking thru the processes of population control he had completely forgot that Breveka was there or that she could read his mind, hear every thought, and feel every emotion. To Robert that was mental rape!

"Robert, would you like to know my assessment of you? Are you perhaps curious as to how I, an Andrian female, find you as a Human male? I have met several. Most of them put on a brave front. Outwardly they were not afraid. But we, as a species, have higher cognitive functions. We can know what you think as we can know what others of our specie think. Your cognitive function is higher than any one of them, but to us, still very primitive. Yet, you are improving which indicates you may serve our purposes sufficiently well. That purpose will be explained to you later. You were not chosen at random."

Robert listened dumfounded. He was, "chosen"? Chosen for what?

Breveka continued, "Robert, comparing you to an Andrian male, you are equal physically in your height, weight, and musculature. You were physically stronger when you were first brought aboard our ship. However, after several months in space, you are in a weakened condition and are thus on par with Andrian males who have spent years in space."

Robert was taken aback. "What do you mean I have been here several months? I think I have been here maybe twenty-three days or so, just a few days more or less?"

"Yes Robert, you have been awake for the time you mentioned. However, you were unconscious and in detoxification for a period of three of your earth months. It was necessary for you to be detoxed down to the molecular level before allowing you among our people. Had we not done so you would have contaminated the entire contingent of our ship, which is our home."

"Now, your face…, should we ever have a mixed neural exchange of mind and body, a process we call, "ambrosias", I would not want to look at you. You are not necessarily undesirable by human standards, but to us you are deformed. Your round eyes look deformed, your chin is too pronounced, and I imagine that should we ever share "ambrosias", your energy level would be to intense and painful for me. Our physical contact is minimal and Andrian females would not be able to encompass your body and your bestial mind."

Robert smiled for the first time since being abducted and brought aboard the space ship. "Ambrosias", huh? Too intense you say? Well I could not possibly be a good judge there because I am a virgin and have never been with a woman."

Breveka was taken aback by his declaration of never being with a woman. Perhaps it means something else to humans? Breveka turned preparing to leave the room. 'We will commune more later, Human, Robert Aaron. You are a superb specimen for our needs." Breveka left the room with the door sliding silently shut behind her.

Robert was smiling and greeting each and every Andrian female courteously, bowing expansively for the rest of the day. He did not know or understand why he was so happy but he was. However, his heart was still heavy and the new knowledge that his sexual prowess would in all probability be too much for the Andrian females would not release the heavy tension wrapped around about his chest.

CHAPTER 14
STATE HOSPITAL

Detective Jessop and Reese were going thru the accident report that had been generated when Emily Smith's parents were killed in the vehicle accident. At the time of the accident no foul play was suspected therefore the report, though thorough, did not look for any other mitigating circumstances. It appeared their car crashed thru a barrier and descended into a ravine. The vehicle caught on fire and both Mr. and Mrs. Smith, died. The report indicated that the road was dry. There were no skid marks. It was unknown why Mr. Smith drove off the roadway. However, there was one redeeming note in the report. An individual was listed as a witness. His address was listed at a state hospital. His name was Mr. James Carroll, no other information.

Detectives Jessop and Reese found the address of "The Peace Time State Hospital". It was right outside of Philadelphia. Upon arriving at the facility they found a large landscaped, tree-covered campus with a wrought iron fence surrounding about ten acres of pristine property. The building was at the end of a tree-lined drive that curved to the front door portico. The building itself, was a two-story structure with white walls and pale green shutters and tile roof. It was a very beautiful facility and no doubt pricey. However, neither detective had ever

SEED OF HOPE

seen such a state facility. It looked more like a private resort.

After parking in visitor parking, which was empty except for three other cars, the detectives went up the steps to the entrance. The glass door access was locked and they had to be electronically admitted. However not until after stating who they were and what their business was in regard too. The foyer was sterile with four straight back chairs against the wall. There was no table with magazines, thus, it did not have a homey inviting feeling to make visitors feel comfortable and welcomed.

Behind a glassed in receptionist desk sat a replica of the proverbial "Nurse Ratchett", of Coo Coo Nest fame. And, she was not smiling. After introducing themselves again and producing, gold federal shields embossed with the identification of the "Space Defense Command Intelligence Service", they again stated their business and that their intention was to speak to Mr. James Carroll.

Without a word, "Nurse Ratchet Replica", got up from her desk and went out a side door. Det. Reese perused the foyer area and receptionist area and observed three surveillance cameras, and pointed them out to Det. Jessop.

"Exactly what kind of facility is this Jessop? It does not look like the run of the mill state hospital?"

"Nope", was the only response Jessop gave but he agreed with Reese that it did seem kind of over kill for housing run of the mill mentally deficient patients.

When checking background on Mr. Carroll, they did not find any evidence of his existence. He did not have a criminal history. There was a birth record for a James Carroll but he was a juvenile. He was certainly too young to be in a state institution. Other than being listed as a witness on the accident report, he did not exist.

After waiting about fifteen minutes, "Nurse Ratchet Replica", returned with a male attendant. You could easily label him as, "Mr. Nurse Ratchet". As of yet neither employee offered any type of identification. And instead of responding to Det. Jessop's questions, they started rapid-fire interrogation questions themselves.

Reese had had enough. Slamming her ID down on the window counter she said, "Cut the bull shit! This is a federal investigation. Present Mr. Carroll immediately or you will be arrested and your facility quarantined. Now!"

Both "Ratchets" physically paled when they realized that Det. Reese was indeed, sincere. They could see it in her eyes. They had stared at many eyes like that but they had all been under lock and key. And, they certainly did not have guns. Both detectives had moved their jackets back and exposed their weapons, casually of course. Casual or not, the "Ratchets" got the message. Nurse "Ratchet" pressed the intercom button and ordered an unknown individual to escort Mr. Carroll to the front office immediately.

Within two minutes the door to the foyer opened and the third attendant escorted a young blonde man with slightly angular face and slim build into the room. He released Mr. Carroll's arm and re-entered the inner sanctum without as much as a word.

Both detectives looked at each other. Mr. Carroll

SEED OF HOPE

looked so much like Emily Smith they could have been siblings. They then observed both "Ratchets pick up telephones. Det. Jessop boomed out a command for them to desist. They looked at each other for guidance until Jessop removed his service revolver and pointed it at the two "Ratchets".

"Have all your employees come to the office! Now!"

Reese looked out the front door and observed the third attendant sprinting to his vehicle. Running out the door, service weapon in hand, Reese commanded him to stop. He did not even slow down. He reached for the door handle of the late model vehicle. Reese aimed the weapon and fired one shot thru the front window of the vehicle punching a hole thru the glass and headrest, which exploded in a mass of stuffing. The attendant stopped, putting his hands in the air. Det. Reese removed a communicator and pushed a button. The Space Defense Intelligence Center was immediately notified that back up assistance was needed immediately.

The "Space Defense Intelligence Center" directed one of its satellite assets to focus on the area provided by the communicator. They also launched a ready response team who would fly to their location in an Osprey style aircraft. They would arrive with in fifteen minutes.

Reese cuffed the attendant and marched him into the foyer. Det. Jessop had the two "Nurse Ratchets", cuffed and seated in the foyer. They both looked around apprehensively, eyes wide, and obviously very much afraid.

Det. Jessop said, "What kind of drug did you give Mr. Carroll? And is it fatal?"

"Nurse Ratchet", replied, "No sir, not fatal. It is just a heavy sedative. It makes him sleepy and non-responsive.

Det. Jessop took Mr. Carroll by the arm and led him to a chair and placed him opposite of the two handcuffed attendants. Mr. Carroll who was sitting in one of the chairs, looked at Nurse Ratchet, grinning from ear to ear, spit out a pill that landed on the floor in front of her. Then he slowly stuck his tongue out at them.

Det. Jessop retrieved the pill for evidence and assessed that Mr. Carroll appeared to be alright.

About twenty minutes after receiving the assistance call from Det. Rees's communicator, an Osprey landed in the parking lot kicking up dust and gravel. The back opened up and twenty heavily armed men in tactical uniforms emerged. Two of the commandoes were in the new heavily armored robotic assist suits that could literally tear a steel door from its hinges.

CHAPTER 15
ACCIDENT REPORT

Commander Bob Johnson was beside himself with satisfaction. Again his two detectives had worked miracles, this time from an innocuous accident report. Following up on the accident report they had found an alleged state hospital, which was in fact a prison housing ten individuals and had been doing so for years.

The ten individuals were now ensconced in a "safe house" on a military base. In effect, he admitted they went from one prison in which they were kept in total isolation, to a more "adequate", accommodation, that was more like a resort. However, since they were not free to leave it was still a form of incarceration, thus a prison.

The total number of attendants taken into custody from the prison hospital was twelve. They too were imprisoned on the base. Their accommodations were slightly harsher than those they themselves had incarcerated at the hospital. They were subject to sodium pentothal and several other new drugs used by intelligence services to extract information. And, Commander Johnson was not proud of himself, but he also allowed the use of mild shock therapy, with the threat and promise of more severe infliction of pain if they seemed stubborn and refused to talk. He did not justify his actions.

What the Space Intelligence Services did learn is that

the original "Nurse Ratchet", was the only one of the twelve who had ever had any contact with the individual who had set up the financing of the facility. She alone was responsible for hiring necessary personnel, payroll, supplies and medications. She further advised that the individual identified himself as Mr. Jones. They also learned the twelve employees received very handsome salaries for keeping the ten prisoners sedated on the drugs. The facility had not been open for more than four years. All of the young people that were incarcerated came in their early teens.

It was further learned that only one employee was terminated. He was the one who absently left the front door unlocked and allowed Mr. Carroll to walk out of the front door of the facility. That employee was found hanging in the employee dining room with a note attached to his chest saying he was terminated for dereliction of duty. The note further stated that he was to be buried behind the building, as a reminder to anyone else who thought of leaving the employment services of the hospital or who made similar mistakes. No one knew how or when he was murdered even though there were surveillance cameras in the dining area. They did not show anything. He seemed to have just appeared.

Because of the death of the employee at the hospital, all the prisoners were kept under twenty-four-hour surveillance. The military members involved in the detention of the twelve prisoners and the ten former prisoners were made aware of what had happened to the other employee and of the abduction of two citizens by aliens that

SEED OF HOPE

were somehow connected to the aforementioned groups. Thus, the service members involved were very diligent in their duties.

On that day, four years earlier, when Mr. James Carroll walked from the facility, he did so with the intention of warning Mr. and Mrs. Smith of their impending danger. How he knew of their danger he did not know. He was also aware of their daughter Emily and knew that she too was in mortal danger. He and Emily were the same age. He had caught a cab and had him drop him off near where the accident was supposed to take place. His mental powers included the ability to make the cab driver believe he had already been paid. He was only able to do this because the same attendant that left the door un-locked, forgot to inject him with the stupor inducing drugs that morning. And, the same attendant left the door unlocked because Mr. Carroll had weaved a neural pattern into his brain causing him to forget.

Mr. Carroll knew the Smiths' would be driving along the winding road within the next hour thus he was waiting for them when they came around the curve. He stepped into their path waving his arms. When Mr. Smith pulled over and stopped, Mr. Carroll approached the driver's window. He told Mr. Smith that he and his wife were going to be killed if they continued on their journey along the winding road. He also told them he did not know how he knew these things. But when he mentioned that their daughter Emily was also in danger, they became afraid and drove away. It did not help when Mr. Smith observed the logo and name, "Peace Time State

Hospital", on Mr. Carroll's shirt.

On the next outside curve, both front tires blew and Mr. Smith, unable to control the vehicle, drove thru the wooden barrier and over the edge into the steep ravine. Mr. Carroll also told Detectives Jessop and Reese that he saw a man near the front of the car after it had come to rest. The Smiths survived the decent into the ravine even though it was rough and rocky. They were incapacitated and unable to move and exit the vehicle but they were alive. The unidentified man pointed a pistol like device, which emitted a white beam of light that ignited the vehicle into a ball of flames. Mr. and Mrs. Smith died instantly. The first vehicle responding to the car fire was a police officer. Mr. Carroll told the police officer the same story as he had told detectives Jessop and Reese. When he told the officer that he lived at the "Peace Time State Hospital", and then the same officer, observing the hospital shirt on Mr. Carroll, contacted the hospital notifying them of his whereabouts, the officer dismissed Mr. Carroll's claim of seeing a man using some kind of light weapon to set the car on fire.

Attendants from the hospital speedily came and retrieved Mr. Carroll, immediately sedating him so he could speak no further. However, the officer did write his name and address on the accident report but chose not to include his story. Upon follow-up of Mr. Carroll's story, detectives Jessop and Reese interviewed the investigating officer that filed the accident report. The officer confirmed word for word the incident as reported by Mr. Carroll. He did not think that it was important because, after all, he was mental patient who had escaped the hospital. With the hospital picking up Mr. Carroll, it saved him a lot of complications in conducting his routine, though be it fatal, accident investigation.

CHAPTER 16
ASSESSMENT

Det. Jessop and Reese carefully interviewed each of the young people that had been incarcerated in the facility that masqueraded as a hospital. They were all in the same age group within two years of one another. That age pattern was consistent with that of Ms. Emily Smith and Ensign Robert Aaron, with them being at the top end of the age scale. Ms. Smith was twenty and Ensign Aaron was twenty-one. The other young people ranged from seventeen to nineteen years of age. Because they had been sedated for several years a lot of things were totally new to them. For most people, the obstacles to achieving "normalcy", after such a long absence would have been a very long and intensive process. However, because of their above average intelligence and their ability to make fast friends with one another, the process of socialization took a matter of weeks. They exhibited a unity of spirit that appeared to be instrumental in aiding in healing.

The military takes great pride in assessment of individual skill and achievement levels as that is an integral part of creating an effective fighting force. Thus, in the assessment of the young people they were scrambling to find and generate new parameters of comparison to effectively evaluate their abilities and skills. Their intelligence skills were off the charts and there really was no

SEED OF HOPE

current adequate measure for comparison. Therefore, they had to stand alone within their own assessment categories. Fortunately for the men and women who were appointed to liaison with them, the young people were solid, loving and kind, no doubt the fruits of loving parents. Each adult that was assigned to the group felt a personal responsibility to help heal them of their pains and sorrows.

In regard to demographics, four of the young people were from the U.S., three from Germany, one respectively from France, Russia and Nigeria. All of them had been subdued in the same manner. Two men walked up to them, smiled, and then sprayed them in the face with some kind of sedative mist. When they awoke, they were in captivity and kept in heavy sedation. The abductions took place in isolated areas like parking lots, parks, or movie houses.

It was not until later in the interviews that it became apparent that each of their parents had died in accidents of one kind of another. Det. Jessop and Reese investigated each death and on the surface they all appeared to be accidents. However, due to the circumstances surrounding the children's incarceration, it became apparent that the parents had been murdered even though they were unable to find identifiable evidence that would have specifically indicated as such.

The staff had decided that at the present moment they should not reveal to them that they were human-alien hybrids. The young people knew they were "special", because they had developed cognitive and telepathic skills on their own. They had all had physicals and blood was routinely drawn. The blood analysis occurred at the molecular level. It was discovered that all the young people had two extra chromosomes, and as of yet, another unidentifiable chemical matrix of nano particles. It was basically these two markers that set the children apart from other individuals of the human species. However, blood test were not routinely conducted on the molecular level, and therefore, it was unknown how much of an aberration from the general population the indicators were. Admiral Cleary had immediately instituted a requirement for all personnel assigned to the" Space Intelligence Command", to be routinely tested on the molecular level.

There were five young men and five young women, adding Emily Smith, and, Robert Aaron, that made a total of twelve human-alien hybrids that they knew of. The questions surrounding them, was as perplexing as were the young people themselves. All of them were friendly, open, outgoing, and affectionate and, not one of them exhibited the least bit of guile. What was their purpose?

One afternoon after interviewing the ten children about their parents, Det. Reese said, "You know, if we had kids, I would want them to be just like them, they are really good kids." Det. Jessop looked straight ahead and said, "Yep, if we had them kids as our own, they would do us proud." That was about as close to either of them could come to verbally committing themselves to one another...at least for now.

The abduction of the ten young people and placement in the bogus hospital was different from Ms. Smith's abduction. Ms. Smith appeared to go willingly, being helped by her escort. It appeared that somehow she had eluded her would be captors who would have certainly placed her in the hospital like the other ten captives.

Det. Reese said, "It looks like we have two different groups of captors at work."

Det. Jessop replied, "Yep".

CHAPTER 17
DECONTAMINATION

Emily was escorted by Blain into a medium sized room that looked like a laboratory. It was the same room Ensign Robert Aaron awoke in after being taken from Lagrange Point Station Two. Blain pointed out a couch and indicated for Emily to have a seat. He then excused himself saying he had other duties to fulfill and that he would see her later. Looking around Emily was fascinated with the vials and vats of bubbling chemicals. There was no odor of chemicals. It seemed strange to her that there was no odor in the room.

Emily sat with one leg crossed over the other, slightly swinging her leg, much as she had done when she was in Dr. Calander's office. She held her arms crossed at her breast and her eyes were slightly hooded. Again, the exact same pose and demeanor she had exhibited for Dr. Calander. Even though she looked relaxed, her mental alertness was running at one hundred and ten percent.

A female entered the room and sat in a chair across from Emily. She crossed her arms and legs in a similar fashion as Emily. They sat quietly studying one another for about five minutes. Both women made silent appraisals of the other.

Emily thought, "Guess this is a version of an alien standoff".

SEED OF HOPE

Emily heard telepathically the women's greeting. She did not see her lips move.

Emily thought, "Uh oh, another telepath".

The women smiled slightly. "My name is Flata. I am the chief geneticist for our group. I am pleased to see you are doing well and have already achieved telepathic abilities. Blain told me you were superb and spoke highly of your cognizant and intellectual abilities."

Emily remained silent, trying to process what the women identified as Flata had meant. Why would she be pleased with her, Emily's, telepathic abilities?

Emily responded verbally, "What do you want and why am I here?"

Flata smiled fully and replied, "First things first. Please, respond telepathically. You may not proceed any further into our ship, our home if you will, without being decontaminated. Therefore, remove all your clothes and place them in that container." Flata indicated a tube container next to the couch Emily was seated upon. "They will be destroyed. Remove all your jewelry and place them in the box on the table next to the couch. They will go thru a separate decontamination process. I am sure you will be pleased with the outcome. After you remove your clothing you are to stand in the circle." Flata indicated a circle on the floor next to a large bubbling vat. Once within the circle, a clear cylinder will descend and seal you in. Do not move. And do not be afraid. A fog like gas will fill the container up to your neck. The gas will turn gelatinous forming a seal around you locking you gently in place. Because this is a cellular level decontamination it will be necessary for you to be put to sleep. A tube will extend from over your head and insert itself into your mouth. Do not fight it. It is not uncomfortable. As soon as the tube is inserted, you will go to sleep. Then the remaining portion of the cylinder will fill with gas, turn gelatinous and seal your head and hair. This is necessary because when the diseases and toxins are expelled from your body they will be trapped within the gel and neutralized by nano plasma. When the process is complete you will awaken healthier than you have been in your entire life. You will be refreshed and most importantly, you will not be a contagion threat to our people nor us to you."

Emily looked at Flata, then the circle, then back to Flata. "How long will I be out?"

Flata was pleased with Emily's question. The young woman was apprehensive but she showed no fear. Then Flata looked Emily in the eyes and replied, "You will be asleep for three of your earth months. You will dream. The dreams you dream will be stored for your later viewing. You will lose nothing. You will be the same person coming out as going in. Even though we are telepaths, we do not delve into the secret recesses of your mind.

Without saying a word, Emily stripped off her shirt with the torn and bloody sleeve; she removed her bra, her shoes, socks, jeans and panties. She threw the clothes into the container as directed and watched fascinated as they disappeared in a bright flash of light. She then removed her earrings, finger rings, and a necklace that had been given to her by Warren, and deposited them in the indicated box. A lid slid shut over the opening.

Emily, thus being naked, walked over and stood within the circle eying Flata as the clear tube lowered itself over her from head to toe. She glanced at the cloudy mist as it rose from her feet to her neck. She then felt a tingling sensation as the mist turned gelatinous locking her in place. A tube descended from over her head and inserted itself into her mouth, clamping a rubber like device over her lips and nose. She breathed once and fell instantly into a deep sleep.

Flata watched Emily as she went thru the above processes and fell asleep. She was pleased with the Human-Alien hybrid, Emily Smith. After all, she was her creation. And, she seemed by far a more superb specimen than Robert Aaron.

Flata thought, "I wish I knew where the others were." Within the last five years the remaining eight hybrids had disappeared. "Several of our own must be working against us," thought Flata. With that thought in mind and Human-Andrian Emily safely in hibernation decontamination, Flata, sought out the Council of Yield.

CHAPTER 18
TRAITOR

"**Flata, report your** current findings in regard to the species Human," Shayar, Council of Yield commanded.

Flata replied, "As you know we have a traitor among us. I name the traitor Klaxo. He has made every effort to thwart our efforts to make our assessment of species-Human. All of the returnees by klaxo and his companions were not hybrids but regular humans. None of them exhibit any higher cognitive skills or telepathic abilities. We believe two may be retarded in their mental development. Even though these two exhibit pockets of brilliance they are incapable of functioning in our society much less their own. One of them is blind and the other is lame. Both have been afflicted since birth. I recommended that they be eliminated. The strange trait that afflicts the specie-Human upon the earth is exhibited in each and every single returnee. They coddle and care for the two mental and physically impaired. They place them ahead of themselves, even when we reduce their rations to starvation level. We do not understand their concept of compassion in these instances. When we indicated that we would eliminate the deficient, they became aggressively war like and we believe they would inflict mortal wounds upon us should we continue with our efforts. Three of the more robust and healthy ones even offered

SEED OF HOPE

themselves up unto termination."

"However, the last two returnees are true Human-Andrian hybrids. They exhibit intelligence way above their standard specie-Human, peers. The female, earth name Emily Smith, has highly developed cognitive telepathic skills. The human male we retrieved from the human's space lab is also beginning to develop his cognitive telepathic skills. He is also able to grasp multi-dimensional math. His skill level is elementary but he is increasingly becoming more advanced."

"The female specie-Human, earth name Emily, already possessed both cognitive telepathic skill and multi-dimensional math skills. She tried to reveal multi-dimensional math to her earthling physics professor but he was unable to grasp even the most elementary prospective. In fact, he even threatened to destroy her university career for trying to fool him. She will be presented to the quorums within one cycle of ships time, they will more adequately assess her cognitive skills."

"As of yet we have been unable to locate the eight remaining hybrids. Traitor Klaxo has killed their parental pairs. Immediately afterwards, the children disappeared. No doubt Klaxo has either had them killed or is hiding them somewhere, most probably on the planet. Klaxo has successfully thwarted our efforts to find them. In addition to the other murders, Klaxo murdered the human parental pair of specie Human-Adrian, Emily Smith. How she managed to escape we do not yet know. Klaxo entirely missed parental pair unit of Robert Aaron. We do not know how or why."

Shayar listened to the assessment by Flata. The rebellious Klaxo troubled her. She had underestimated his hostility toward the "Council of Yield's" conceptual plan to save the specie-Human, from extinction. His greed for power and his disregard for life forms upon the planet have allowed his hidden character to manifest itself. When he is found he will be eliminated, the sooner the better.

CHAPTER 19
CONSPIRITORS

Klaxo and his one hundred and fifty co-conspirators sat ensconced in a chamber within Jupiter's moon, Europa. They were discussing how they should terminate the earths Human-Andrian hybrids and make it appear that humans themselves destroyed them. Then surely "The Council of Yield", would have no alternative but to destroy humanity from the earth. Then they, the Andrians, could colonize the earth with their own children. The intergalactic space ship home was reaching critical mass and would soon begin to convolute it's regeneration processes and many if not all would die.

Zelegark advised, "The Human-Andrian hybrids Emily Smith and Ensign Robert Aaron have successfully evaded our capture efforts. The magnetic cognito pulse analyzer has never been able to locate their neuro frequency spatial parameters. Both have somehow successfully slipped thru our neural net.

The Smith's parental units were easily destroyed despite the interference of the Human-Andrian hybrid James Carroll. He was successfully returned to the capture facility but not before he spoke to earth authorities. Our agent in place was able to focus neural disturbances causing the earth authority subject to forget the accident information given to him by James Carroll. We eliminated the human that allowed the escape of prisoner Carroll."

Klaxo was not pleased that the two Human-Andrian hybrids escaped capture. And, the James Carroll escape could have caused the planets authorities to become suspicious and thus interfere with their plans. They have already spent too much time and effort to allow simple errors to thwart their activities.

"Zelegark, you are to return to earth and destroy the hybrids and human caretakers. Make it look like and accident. Take two other spec units with you. Do not raise the suspicion of the Earth authorities!"

Zelegark hissed his response, "It is about time! We should make our move now! The "Council of Yield", will not be pleased with our actions but after all the Humans are destroyed from the earth, they will have to accept our actions."

Zelegark carefully selected a total of eight men, three men for each of the three ships. This would be an easy assignment. He had killed so many humans without raising the suspicions of the earth authority that it was like child's play. Humans were so naive. They were so stupid. They were so everything that begged for destruction! They never ever realized they were in mortal danger until it was too late. Then most of them never new then, by that time they were dead.

CHAPTER 20
WHISP OF TRUTH

Marla Raines, age eighteen, was sitting under a tree with her new friend and confident Allen Paisley, nineteen. They were both just coming to grips with the fact that someone had kidnapped them, kept them mostly unconscious for nearly four years. For what purpose, to what end?

Marla said, "Allen, How could anyone do the things that were done to us. We basically lost three to four years of our lives? We never harmed anyone. Gosh, my parents have been dead now almost four years. It is like they died yesterday or even last month! They died in a terrible house fire."

Allen looked at Marla in surprise, "Yes, now this is strange. My parents died in a private plane crash. They never could find anything wrong with the plane. I wonder how many of us here have had similar experiences. Perhaps it has something to do with our being taken prisoner and drugged all of these years. Man that would be a real bummer!"

"Mercy, Allen! I was just wondering the same thing. It is almost like I could read your mind!" Marla laughed at the thought. Together, hand in hand, they started walking back to the community center. "It felt so good just to have someone to talk to much less touch and hold hands with after being drugged all those years. Something really bad must be going on, "thought Marla.

"I think it is about time we get together with the others and see how many pieces of the puzzle we can put together. I, for one, am getting tired of just sitting around here and not accomplishing a thing," advised Marla.

The two young people walked across the manicured lawn and returned to the community room where the other six young people were gathered. They wanted to have a serious discussion about exactly what was going on.

Commander Johnson and now, Special Investigators, Jessop and Reese, were in an intense conversation with Admiral Cleary, and wanted to go ahead and advise the children of all the information they knew. They had learned quite a lot in their investigations. However, they still did not have a motive for the imprisonment of the young people.

"Ok Commander, we have been watching and listening for two months. Not any of them have an inkling of what is going on. As soon as they start talking to one another they will soon realize that all of their parents have been murdered. Sooner or later those responsible are going to return and finish the job. We owe it to them to tell them the truth, or at least as much of the truth as we know. If they put all the pieces together before we tell them, they will not ever trust us again." That was a very long speech for the former, "Detective Jessop", now known as "Special Investigator Jessop", of the Space Defense Intelligence Service.

SEED OF HOPE

"He is right, Commander. That is the very least that we owe them. They are all very good kids. Someone very cruelly has taken four years of their lives away from them. Who knows, perhaps they were placed here for very benevolent purposes and there is disagreement among the powers that be", said Special Investigator Reese.

Both men looked at Agent Reese in surprise. Neither of them had ever ventured a guess as to what the gifted children's purpose was. Commander Johnson thought about what Agent Reese had said. It was becoming obvious that something needed to be done in regards to telling the children what was going on. The intelligence service only had bits and pieces of the puzzle. Perhaps the young people could be a good resource in resolving the security issues. And, while we are at it, why not make Emily Smith's notebook and computer available to them? The Department of Defense Scientist could not make heads or tails out of the mathematical formulas.

CHAPTER 21
THE TRUTH

Commander Bob Johnson, accompanied by several other members of the intelligence community seated themselves along the wall. Agents Jessop and Reese were to initiate the process of enlightenment. The young people looked on expectantly. They had just had their first group session with all of them present noting the similarities in their abductions and the deaths of their parents. All of them had been saddened, several of them had been angry. They wanted to know what was going on.

Agent Jessop was up first with Agent Reese at his side. Seen from the perspective, and eyes of the young people assembled in the room, he appeared to be about fifty-five years of age. He was well built and in excellent condition...for his age, the eternal youthful clincher in describing individuals senior to them, those individuals mostly being over thirty. His face was ruggedly handsome. His nose was slightly a kilter; it appeared to have at one time or another to have been broken. There was what appeared to be a fine scar that ran from his forehead, diagonally across his lips to his chin. His brown eyes were clear, friendly and warming. And his hair! It would make a marine drill sergeant look like a hippie.

"Wow, he must have been in a bad accident," whispered Marla.

SEED OF HOPE

Marla thought the lady standing next to him, obviously his wife, was about the same age. She was well built...for a woman her age. Her coal black hair was cut short and swept back over her ears almost covering them.

Allen was a careful observer too and it looked to Allen that half of her left ear was gone which he pointed out to Marla. She too exhibited light scars on her face. And, when she looked you in the eye, you could sense...sadness, pain, and yes, a fierce determination to protect. To protect who from what was a mystery, but it was there. "Wow, I would hate to make her angry", intoned Allen to Marla.

Agent Jessop began. "I hope you are all comfortable. The couches look comfy! Do not go to sleep." A nervous laugh came from the lady next to the man who was speaking. The "psychologist", who name was Jessop, continued, "You have been here going on two months and one week. You each have been healing from your wounds, physical and mental. You all have been heavily drugged and sedated for several years. The detox program to remove the drugs from your system has been complex and extensive. We believe you are now completely free of contaminants.

"I suppose we should get this show on the road. We all know that a picture is worth a thousand words so we are going to show you some video and listen to some audio of some recent events." The room darkened and the screen lit up showing a video of a man floating in one-half gravity. They listened as he informed Space Intelligence Command, of a large craft approaching the

Lagrange Point Station Two. You could hear a pin drop after the film ended with the large spacecraft leaving the system at an incredible speed taking the man with it.

"The man you saw abducted in the film was Ensign Robert Aaron, of the Space Intelligence Service. That was three months ago this month. No, we have no further information regarding his fate."

Agent Reese then said, "Now watch this second film obtained by a Space Intelligence Satellite."

Again the film lit the screen, this time showing a clear overhead view of a saucer in a wooded clearing. A man emerged from under the saucer and entered the woods. The same man returned escorting a blonde female holding her hand and elbow. You could see she had been injured but otherwise not being coerced or forced to the saucer. A few minutes later the saucer lifted and flew away. Once the saucer was airborne the intelligence satellite had trouble keeping it in focus. They did observe the saucer enter a large mother ship. The ship disappeared leaving a black void pinpointed by the stars.

Jessop and Reese looked at the group of young people. Reese voiced their concern, "What does this have to do with me, with us?"

Reese advised, "These two events have nothing to do with you." Immediately she saw and sensed relief. "However, we believe you are the key to solving these two events." "We believe the best defense is a strong offense".

Agent Reese stopped and Agent Jessop began, "And, in order to present a strong offense, we must be honest

SEED OF HOPE

with you and withhold nothing from you. The bare boned truth is, we need you, and you need us."

"The young women you observed boarding and leaving in the saucer, her name is Emily Smith. She too has been gone for three months. They were taken, abducted, the same week five days apart."

"Now, you know me as Gary and this lady here as Carol. And, you suppose you are in a hospital recovering from the effects of being drugged for years. You are right about the hospital part. Everything within the government's power has been laid at your disposal to assist you in your recovery. No expense has been spared. You each have your own personal nurse and doctor. And of course there is us old "psychologist", which brought a few chuckles.

Jessop's face changed as did Reese's. "I am a retired homicide detective from New York City. I took early retirement to heal physically and mentally. Then I took a cushy job as chief investigator at Blaizon Hills Police Department".

Reese then intoned, "I am a retired homicide investigator from Las Angeles PD. Together, we have sixty years' experience as police investigators. I too took a cushy retirement job at Blaizon Hills PD. I took the job to heal from my wounds, psychic and otherwise."

"It was at Blaizon Hills where Jessop and I paired up. It was fun. We drank coffee, ate donuts, and did cross word puzzle". Chuckles came from the young people. "All that changed when an emotionally distraught young man demanded to see police investigators reference his missing girlfriend. The girlfriend was Emily Smith, the young lady you observed being escorted to the saucer."

"We found the saucer location within fifteen minutes of leaving Emily's Physics teacher's office at the university. She was a senior. We also found her laptop, notes, and purse. We were able to determine Ms. Smith injured her arm when she tripped over backwards, striking a broken stub of a limb. No doubt she saw the saucer, she became afraid, backed up tripping over the root and fell to the ground. We believe the unknown man administered first aid to her injured arm as we found a broken vial with an unknown substance that has, as of yet not been identified. We submitted our reports to contacts in New York City, bypassing the usual police channels. The contact was the Space Defense Intelligence Service."

"Subsequently, we contacted Commander Bob Johnson, Commander of the Space Defense Intelligence Center." Agent Jessop indicated Commander Johnson who was sitting on the stage. Commander Johnson gave a brief nod in acknowledgement.

All the young people were spell bound, eyes wide, mouths agape. This was so much more information than they expected. After all, they were in a "hospital".

"Agent Jessop continued, "Because we were involved in the initial investigation we were asked if we would be willing to continue our investigation under the auspices of the Space Defense Intelligence Command. Thus we gave up being detectives and are now "Special Investigators", with the Space Defense Intelligence Command." He laughed trying to ease the tension that

SEED OF HOPE

had risen palatably within the room.

Agent Reese began, "We did not know who Emily Smith was. We knew she was intelligent. At least she seemed to be. We recovered a piece of paper with what our scientist say they believe is, "multi-dimensional math". At least that is what we were later advised that is what it was."

"During our investigation we discovered that Emily's parents had died in a car wreck two years earlier." Looking each of them in the eye, Reese waited a minute. "Does that sound familiar to you or ring a bell with anyone of you in this room?"

"Fortunately while Jessop and I were investigating the fatal accident of the Smiths, there was one witness listed on the report. It stated that he lived at the "Peace Time State Hospital". This is the same hospital in which you all had been imprisoned. His name was Mr. James Carroll."

Everyone turned and looked at Mr. Carroll in awe. Mr. Carroll just grinned and shrugged his shoulders.

"We were able to free you and nurse you back to health. Physically you are basically well. We know there is so much to grasp. You are still healing mentally, sort of like us when we took that cushy job at Blaizon Hills PD." Everyone did laugh at that one!

"But, here is the real kicker. We believe you are still in grave danger. You are in a hospital alright, but it is also a "safe house", owned and operated by the Space Intelligence Service. You are being guarded twenty-four hours a day by dedicated men and women who know your plight. However, I guess from your point of view you have traded one prison for another, regardless of how benevolent we may be. You are still imprisoned."

Reese continued, "Thus comes the crux of the situation. We are willing to share with you what we know. We hope that, instead of being victims, and part of the problem, you will join us and help us by providing a solution to the problem. The decision is yours. I do not personally believe you will live very long should you choose to leave our protection. On the other hand we cannot promise to keep you alive even in our facility."

"We know we are up against beings with far greater intelligence than what we possess. They have space travel technologies we cannot duplicate. There medicine is a mystery. Their mental capabilities cannot be matched by humans. But yet, someone of their group believed it was necessary to murder your parents, kidnap you, drug you and keep you incarcerated. Someone else in their group felt it necessary to single out Ensign Robert Aaron and Emily Smith and whisk them away from the earth. Why? Was it to protect them? Are they still looking for you? Would they harm you? We do not believe that those that took Robert and Emily have evil intentions to ward you. However, what your purpose is and how you and they fit into the equation is not clear to us."

Reese and Jessop looked around and carefully observed each person. There was one hundred percent rapt attention. Reese could feel a kind of drawing or pulling sensation in her mind. They wanted to know everything and they wanted to know it now!

SEED OF HOPE

Reese sighed, taking a deep breath, braced for what, she did not know. Just before she began, the lights dimmed enough to give privacy. "In fact, you are a lot like them. We do not know how they did it. There is no record of unaccounted time in your parent's lives. The only ones that might possibly have the answer are your counterparts, Miss. Emily Smith, and Mr. Robert Aaron. You are part human and part...part..., we think..., another type of humanoid species that look like us but their intelligence skills are way above what we currently possess." Quietly Reese said, "And, we all love you dearly."

There was silence in the room. Each individual had to deal with the revelation as best as they could. It was deemed necessary by all involved that if the young people were to live, they must be told the truth.

Tears rolled down Reese's cheeks. "Damn, this is the second time I cried in the last three months. I must be going thru the change of life or something."

Reese and Jessop both left their positions on the raised stage and walked among the ten young people touching each of their shoulders giving them a squeeze of reassurance.

Jessop said, "Look, me and Carol here, we never had any children of our own. We have both been married and were both divorced. Our job stresses did not allow any time for anyone else in either of our lives. We were extraordinarily busy trying to make those that committed heinous acts of violence and took innocent lives, to pay for the things, which they had done. And yes, saving our own. I know that I speak for Carol as well as for me. We consider you family. Families we never had. We too have been orphaned at an early age, younger than most of you. And like you, we do share some pain and thus we can understand somewhat of what you are feeling.

My father was killed in Washington, D.C., in the nuclear blast, as was so many others. He was in the marines. I was twelve years of age. Carol's father, a patrolman in Seattle, was gunned down by bank robbers. She was nine. We know… We know what it is like to be alone, to lose, and more importantly, to survive; and, for the first time in our adult lives, to love."

"Yes, we seemed to have succumbed to the forces of stress and have fallen in love with one another. We would be proud if all of you could consider us as part of your family. For better or for worse, we will see this strange thing thru. Let us all work together and learn what your purpose here on the earth is for. Help us find those who murdered your parents. I promise you, not only Carol and I will make them pay, but every man and women in this room and the surrounding area are of one mind and one heart. We all love you." Jessop took Carols hand and they returned to their seats at the front of the stage. The room was very quiet indeed.

CHAPTER 22
ZELEGARK'S SURPRISE

Zelegark landed his craft in a clearing behind the hospital facility in broad daylight. After all, he was not expected so why so why should he be over cautious. This would only take a few minutes. He and two of his fellow assassins moved silently approaching the building knowing exactly what they were going to find. They had each been here before on several occasions and have come to believe all humans were weak, undisciplined, and incapable of withstanding superior technology. Plus, humans were just plain stupid.

Approaching the rear entrance, Zelegark pointed his shaeller tool at the electronic lock. The tool easily decoded the locking mechanism, unlocking the door. They entered the room in single file coming in from the bright outdoor sunlight into the gloom of the darkened room. As the door shut behind them, the room darkened even more. Before their eyes were able to become accustomed to the darkness there was a series of blinding flashes and deafening explosions. Almost immediately all three aliens were tasered and they fell to the ground quivering and groaning until they passed out.

Captain Swenson radioed command center, and using code, advised that the three aliens had been subdued and had been injected with Demerol, a mild sedative used in operations to put patients in a twilight sleep. A rotary hovercraft landed outside the door. The three aliens, firmly secured, were placed on stretchers and attached to the receiving mechanisms in the craft. Each alien also had a head covered with a metal Mylar hood with a magnetic field pulsating in various strengths to minimize their telepathic abilities. That additional touch was at the suggestion of the ten young people that had chosen to work with the Intelligence Command. After they were placed in the craft, they were whisked away to a secret location, the same secret location where the children were staying.

CHAPTER 23
AWAKENING AND INTERROGATION

Zelegark awoke slowly. He could hear mumbled voices but he could not sense anything. He felt like he was blind. He was unable to contact his fellow assassins. Then, he became aware that he was bound, unable to move his legs, arms or head. He had some kind of hood over his head. Then he almost panicked when he felt a slight cool breeze blowing across his body. He was naked! How could that be? Then he remembered entering the hospital prison on a mission to kill everyone there. What had happened then? Bright flashes of light, deafening noises, and the excruciating pain of electricity as it flowed thru his body. Then... nothing. He had been rendered unconscious. Now he, Zelegark, the master assassin, was himself taken prisoner, by Humans! Even though that was impossible it evidently was the truth.

Zelegark felt the table he was laying on move from a lateral position to a vertical upright position. He felt the hood he was wearing being lifted from his head. The room was very bright with spotlights shining on him. All he could see was a wall. There was several of their primitive observation units pointed at him. Even though the cloth cover had been removed from his head he could still feel a bowl like object covering his head at the hairline. Only his face and ears was exposed. And, there was a needle inserted into his arm with a line running out of view behind him.

On the other side of the wall in the observation room, there was standing room only. The ten hybrid young people were sitting on the second row of the amphitheater. Admiral Cleary, Commander Johnson, and The President, along with Agents Jessop and Reese were sitting on the front row. The large screens showed the alien's front and side view. The alien was male as evidenced by his penis. At present time it was pretty flaccid. He was slender by earth standards. His eyes were blue and he had pale blonde shoulder length hair. He was looking about defiantly. The skullcap was kept in place as his telepathic skills and abilities were unknown and every effort was made to shield the audience from whatever powers he may have had. That too was the young people's suggestion.

In front of Zelegark there was a view screen that showed two people, Agents Jessop and Reese. They both looked at his hands and magnified the pictured, which showed the alien had three fingers and an opposing thumb. The hands were busy forming a fist then relaxing. There was no worry about him escaping. Gas nozzles were located near his head suspended from the ceiling. Should he try anything he would receive a knock out gas. Should he break free he would be eliminated with high voltage electricity from wiring that was embedded in the floor and the walls.

SEED OF HOPE

When the alien was sedated and unconscious a whole slew of biological test were performed. They had found the same chromosome number as evidenced in humans, 2N, two extra chemicals believed to be amino acids, a chemical matrix believed to be macrophage particles, and other unknown markers which were not evident in the Hybrid young people.

A note was passed to Agent Jessop, which said that the alien was known to the hospital captors as Mr. Jones. The former hospital workers were in the very last row in the top tier of seats

Agent Jessop began the interview.

"Good evening Mr. Jones".

The alien looked at the com link. He was clearly startled that they knew his earth name. He remained silent, trying to determine what they knew.

"I am Detective Jessop, my partner is Detective Reese." He had unconsciously fallen into the habitual mode of homicide investigator investigating a serial killer suspect.

"At this point I would ordinarily advise you of your rights as provided by the Constitution. However, I do not think they apply to you."

Detective Reese cut in. Her eyes were blue and she had a steady gaze; her voice soft and purring. "We know you understand our language and are somewhat familiar with our system of government so we will skip the preliminaries and get to the immediate subject at hand. Why have you come to our planet and kidnapped our citizens, murdered the parents of a group of young people who we know now are a human-alien hybrid? And why did you murder an employee of your prison hospital?"

Everyone watched the alien closely. The computer scanners constantly scanned the alien's facial expressions and eyes for clues to his demeanor. He was clearly surprised when Reese had mentioned the abductees and the murder of their parents.

Zelegark experienced and alien equivalent of "thunderstruck", at the mention of the abductees and murders. "How could they possibly know? It just was not possible," thought Zelegark.

The two trained homicide detectives watched the train of emotion and surprise imprint the aliens face. "Ha! Count one for the humans!" thought Detective Jessop.

Much to their surprise the alien responded. "My name is ZZZelegark! With your limited capacity to think, those of your world find it unpronounceable in my language. As for the murders and kidnappings you speak of, I know nothing of those." He then unconsciously slipped into the plural. "We have done no such thing".

On cue, Detective Jessop said, "Well now, that is not what your partners said. How else would we know about the abductions and murders?"

That was exactly what Zelegark was furiously thinking and his face showed his turmoil on the screen.

"I have nothing to say," replied Zelegark, looking out at them with a haughty, superior gaze.

Detective Jessop looked at Detective Reese. She nodded to him. It was obvious they were not going to get anything further from the alien Zelegark. Detective

SEED OF HOPE

Jessop pushed a button on the desk. The button activated the electric circuit that started the flow of truth serum, sodium pentothal, into the alien Zelegark's arm. Sodium Pentothal was used by intelligence agencies worldwide to secure information from otherwise unwilling participants.

Zelegark could feel a warm feeling going into his arm.

"What is this!" bellowed Zelegark. He was thinking, "Is that it? Am I going to die now?"

Zelegark was not knowledgeable about sodium pentothal. His race of beings had no need for such a crude chemical. Since they were telepaths, they could enter your mind at will.

Zelegark became dreamy, happy, and secure; he laughed to himself thinking, "This cannot be too bad if this is all they have!"

Thru the fog in his mind he heard the female human say, "Tell me about the abductees."

Thinking the answer was of no consequence he replied, "Ha! I was told to return the Human-Andrian crosses for evaluation." Bitterly he then said, "What a waste of time on obviously inferior specie. You should be wiped from the face of the planet. We have a desperate need for the space for our own people. You turned out to be a weird, non-thinking, polluting species. But, the "Council of Yield", wanted to give you earth worms another chance. Thus they tried to help lift you up by cross transferring your DNA with ours. Our children are more intelligent than you. And, you further degrade your species by actually saving your invalid, blind, lame, and mentally impotent. What possibly could a species such as you offer to those of us so enlightened?"

He finished his tirade with a sneer. "You will be exterminated from the face of the earth! I and my followers will see to that!"

Everyone in the room was frozen in place. Even for the veteran detectives who had already heard and seen "everything", was suddenly confronted with something new. Both detectives kept their faces as stone, not so much as a twitch was emitted from their souls. They both knew that any information they could get from the Andrian alien, Zelegark, helped increase their chances for survival, not only them, but evidently the entire human species.

Detective Reese purred, "Tell me about the abductees. Why are they so important to you?"

Zelegark rose from his stupor and replied, "Ha! I was responsible for returning the Human-Andrian cross specie to the "Council of Yield", for evaluation. I believed it was time to act. I found others who thought as I and together we thwarted, the "Council of Yield's", plan to save your precious selves! Our leader is even a member of the "Council of Yield". We all left the star cruiser and constructed a hidden base on Jupiter's moon, Europa."

Zelegark had the self-satisfied sneer and smile of all serial killers Detectives Jessop and Reese had hunted down, arrested, and saw to the execution chamber. They were still smiling their smug, superior smile as the chemicals flowed into their veins, often leaving the hideous smile stamped on their faces. Both detectives recognized

SEED OF HOPE

the exhibited feelings of superiority and a "god" complex. This race might be more intelligent but it appeared that diseased mental processes worked the same in both species.

Detective Jessop said, "Tell me again about the abductees." He was confused as to why Smith and Aaron were allowed to go to the "mother ship" and the rest were imprisoned on earth.

Zelegark laughed, still feeling the euphoria and self-satisfaction and superiority due to the constant flow of sodium pentothal. "We fooled the "Council of Yield". Instead of providing them the hybrids we gave them your everyday human!" Zelegark laughed even more heartily. "One was even blind! But the lame one was the absolute best!" Laughing loudly till tears ran down his face, he was barely able to continue. "He actually got out of his wheelchair and ran about ten feet before we caught him!"

Both detectives were stunned. They only knew of Smith and Aaron, and of course the ten young people that was previously imprisoned in the "State Hospital". Jessop looked at Commander Johnson inquiringly. He shrugged his shoulders and held up his hands. It appeared that no one had any clue what the Andrian Alien was talking about.

Casually Reese said, "And how many humans did you deliver to the "Council of Yield?"

Answering because he thought he wanted to he replied, "Ten. They were even stupid by your standards. They were actually going to terminate anyone that hurt the lame and the blind. Not only that, there were several that offered themselves for termination instead of allowing the dregs to be terminated. How stupid is that? It is certainly a weakness in any specie to want to die for the dregs!" The video and audio link was turned off to the howling laughter of the Andrian alien. Detectives Jessop and Reese both stood facing, The President. Everyone in the room had tears in their eyes. They did not know who the other ten captives were but they knew they were the absolute best that humanity had to offer.

Together they said, "We got to get them back Mr. President. We are going after them!" The ten young people that previously was held hostage said in chorus, "We are going too!" The President just nodded his head. He was still too moved to speak.

CHAPTER 24
PLAN FORMULATION

As **Admiral Cleary** and Commander Johnson were leaving the meeting, Cleary asked Johnson, "What of the other two saucers? Do we still have them under surveillance? And most importantly, is our saucer secured?"

"Yes Admiral, our saucer is secured and we are tracking the other two saucers. They are staying in the vicinity of Blaizon Hills. Obviously they are confused as to what happened to the other saucer and Zelegark. It has been forty-eight hours since they last had contact with him."

"We have set a trap around the hospital and have people coming and going with deliveries to make everything look as normal as possible. We were lucky with the first capture in that the other saucers were not around. We have been trying to intercept their communications but it appears that they are using pinpoint lasers. It is impossible to intercept their communication with the technologies we have."

"The room where Zelegark and his team initially entered the hospital is now wired with a mesh neural net. That way, if one of the other teams comes inside, they cannot call out for outside help. At least we hope they can't. We are also busy creating other very ingenious surprises. I think our engineers are truly inspired."

"That sounds good Commander. Keep me informed

when they drop in."

"Yes Sir, Admiral, I will. We could sure use those other two saucers."

Admiral Cleary left with his entourage to go back to the command center. The President left with his aides and advisors to return to the" New Capitol", in Greenland. The Washington D.C. complex was abandoned after a successful nuclear attack by terrorist forty-two years earlier. The United States responded with a devastating nuclear response on three countries harboring, sympathizing and supporting terrorist groups. At the time, sympathizing and harboring was loosely interpreted. It was the terrorist act and the United States response to that act that enabled the creation of the New Earth Alliance Government. It was also the attack that killed Detective Jessop's father. The feelings and attitudes of most everyone in the world was that it was deemed necessary to provide a worldwide front against political groups that would find great joy in destroying the world. No one faulted the magnitude of the United States response. The establishment of the new form of government provided the vehicle to respond quickly across national boundaries to prevent another terrorist nuclear attack. The president of one country was hanged, and, presidents of two other countries were incarcerated for life. Organized terrorism as seen in the early twentieth century no longer raised its ugly head.

CHAPTER 25
SECOND CHANCE

Commander Johnson's communicator lit up with a coded string of letters and numbers interspaced with a few words. Target points were referred to as tree varieties. Beechnut was the hospital. They had agreed that no voice communication was to be used in regard to the trap being set for the aliens. The aliens, being telepaths, and earthlings being verbal communicators, seemed to offer an easy way to deceive aliens as they expected humans to talk. Thus chatter was increased on military frequencies, which constantly reported bogus UFO sightings to misdirect the aliens in their search for Zelegark. The novel idea was again a product of the young people who had been abducted and incarcerated, and it worked beautifully.

In an effort to devise a trap to neutralize the aliens, test were conducted on two of the captives that had been with Zelegark. It was determined that the aliens had a tremendously low tolerance for VLF, very low frequency, and sound waves. It was known that VLF waves using high-energy decibels, or power, could physically move dense matter, like ones intestines. The higher the decibels the more intense the sound, thus, the more incapacitated with pain they became. It was certainly uncomfortable to have ones intestines and stomach rearranged. Therefore, a huge speaker system had been installed in the entrance room. The walls had been heavily padded and baffled so all the sound waves would stay within the twenty by twenty foot hospital entrance room.

Commander Johnson thought, "Our only hope for success was to lure them into this one room, and, a lot of prayer!"

The message on the communicator indicated that two saucers had landed on the back lot of the hospital. Now was the time of truth.

Chapter 26
THE LANDING

Captain Swenson and his team waited quietly while the saucer landed, again in broad daylight. His twenty-man team was clothed in the new nano polymer suits with the chameleon background changing technology. The suits were invisible in infrared and visible light. The reflective pixels changed with the background. They all blended in with the surrounding shrubbery and landscape.

Captain Swenson divided his twenty-man squad into two groups. Ten men were inside and ten men were outside. The outside team was responsible for securing the saucers and the building exit door. If they were unable to physically take the saucers they were to destroy them before they left the ground. Fortunately they had the other saucer so they had a training model and knew what to expect as far as the interior layout.

Captain Swenson watched as the two saucers landed side by side. Three men from each saucer exited the bottom as the saucer hovered overhead about six feet from the ground. The men were clothed in light blue form fitting coveralls. Three men carried what was obviously the spaceman's version of assault rifles. Two of the men carried a kind of handgun and the third carried a rod like instrument that was later used to open the door.

As the aliens reached the rear door, the one in the

lead pointed the rod like instrument at the locking mechanism on the door and it slowly unlocked the door. The leader swung the door open and entered the building followed by the rest of the spacemen. The last man in turned around, looked about once and then closed the door.

Just as quickly as the door closed, two commandoes raised themselves from the ground carrying a large metal bar six feet in length. They silently placed the rubber encased steel bar across the door into two braces on each side of the door that was camouflaged as lamp holders. They then returned to their predetermined defensive positions in case the aliens in the room blasted their way free, which in all probability, they would.

As the aliens entered the room, the extra bright lights went out making it totally dark. The extra bright lights were an effort to compromise their vision. That was not a problem for the aliens because they had viewing goggles on which adjusted to the light with a range greater than anything upon the earth. Then the flash bangs lit up the room with bright light and loud pulsating explosions. That too was not a problem for the aliens because they had enhanced ear protection with completely sealed communication capabilities, therefore, it took about a second or too for the aliens to realize they were under attack. Once they did, they opened fire with their plasma rifles. The inside assault team was immediately and desperately loosing. Five members of the assault team were quickly vaporized along with two of the four walls. Fortunately for the team, the Taser guns were automatic and remotely controlled by computer for just this sort of

SEED OF HOPE

scenario. All ten Tasers fired automatically as soon as the first shot was fired but not in time to save the five commandoes. The Tasers struck all six aliens. Again, the coveralls served as light weight body armor and the aliens were slow going down as the body armor almost nullified the effects of the Tasers, but not quite. However all the aliens did drop their weapons and they fell to the floor twitching. The remaining five commandoes rushed into the room and tasered them at close range until they were unconscious. One alien was struck in the neck and the high power setting burned thru his neck and his head dropped to the floor before the body.

The aliens had known something had happened to Zelegark and his team but they believed his saucer had crashed or perhaps they had already murdered the inhabitants of the hospital and had returned to the base on Jupiter's moon, Europa. They were just checking the hospital to make sure that everyone was dead then they too were going to return to Jupiter.

It never entered their mind that humans could have taken Zelegark prisoner. Fortunately for their error in judgment the aliens only half prepared for the reconnaissance of the hospital. Had they used combat armor instead of planetary landing suits, all the commandoes would have been killed and a large, deep, smoking hole would be where the hospital once stood. Once again, surprise and underestimating their enemy was the alien's downfall. But with their mindset, after all, the enemy was only, "stupid humans". They would all be dead soon enough.

Captain Swenson contacted Commander Johnson again using coded numbers and letters. The message indicated that the aliens, which had been designated as "dung beetle", had been captured and or killed. Two dung beetle nests, i.e., the saucers, had been secured. And five members of the Space Defense Commando unit had been killed. Commander Johnson was elated at the news that once again, they had been able to take the aliens by surprise and obtain two saucers. He was also deeply saddened by the loss of five commandoes.

Commander Johnson thought they had planned so meticulously and still they almost failed. Sooner or later they will not be able to surprise the aliens. Then, he was sure; it would all be but over for Earth's defense forces, and all mankind upon the face of the planet Earth.

Shaking off the morose thoughts, Commander Johnson signaled back acknowledgement of the receipt of the message and noted that it was a job well done. He knew that Captain Swenson would be grieving for his men, but not yet, there was still much to do. He then sent Admiral Cleary a communiqué informing him of the outcome of the mission.

CHAPTER 27
EMILY SEE'S THE STARS

Emily awakened languidly from the most restful sleep that she could ever remember. Yawning, she stretched her arms above her head for a satisfying stretch. Opening her eyes the first thing she noticed was the lavender billowing sleeves, which had slid down to her elbows. At first she was confused as she knew that she did not own such a blouse. She sat up swinging her legs off the bed and observed the same color and style of billowing slacks that went to her ankle. Examining the garment closer she found it was a one piece suit, tight around her waist which was secured with a darker lavender sash, and, a deep cut open blouse which exposed her cleavage.

Looking up, Emily then saw a woman seated about ten feet away silently observing her. She was dressed in the same style of clothing, same color. She also looked familiar. Emily then remembered where she had seen the women and who she was. She was the geneticist, Flata.

Glancing around the room, Emily observed several large clear containers of bubbling liquids. None of the liquids were the same color. It looked like a college chemistry lab except on a much, much, grander scale. Then there were the light waves, which moved thru the room like waves upon the water, in strait lines, in sync with one another; they were multiple colors and somehow the color lines were definitive, not bleeding in one to another.

The women said, "Welcome back Emily. Remember me? I am Flata, the chief geneticist. You have recovered well for being under such a long time. Sometime the detox can be very difficult."

Emily then remembered how she came to be where she was and considered what being on a large intergalactic craft was going to be like. She found it exciting and exhilarating.

"May I see out? I want to see the heavens."

Flata stood up and extended her hand, which Emily took. She could feel a slight tingling like electricity as they touched. Flata then placed her arm into the crook of Emily's arm at the elbow and they walked from the room. Emily felt comfortable walking with the alien named Flata, in this manner, it seemed normal and satisfying. It was sort of like walking to lunch with one of her dorm sisters. That seemed like a hundred years ago.

The main passageways were wide enough to accommodate four abreast. The smaller passageways off to the sides were large enough for only two crewmen. The lighting was muted and soft on the eyes; the walls glowed with wave lighting like what was in the room in which she woke up. They walked down several corridors until they came to a lift. The lift was in a tube shaft and one could see the decks as they flashed by at an incredible speed.

Once they exited the elevator, Emily saw other aliens along the passageway who stared at her but otherwise they showed little interest. They passed her in silence,

SEED OF HOPE

verbal and otherwise. However, she did get a mental impression that they knew who she was and was somewhat known to them.

Flata stopped in front of an exit door and pointed for Emily to go first. As Emily approached the door, it slid laterally into the wall allowing unobstructed entrance into a large room. Emily looked around in awe and approached the edge of the room. The entire wall was transparent. The black void was sprinkled with diamonds, which disappeared into the black void of the cosmos. Out the left side of the view port Emily could see a small galaxy with billions of stars in a classic spiral swirl, which appeared to be suspended by invisible appendages. A large colorful nebula appeared to be flowing outward in suspended animation, was visible out the right side of the view port. Other small galaxies seem to float in different positions as their distance increased from her relative point of view soon becoming pinpoints of light, which were in reality more galaxies.

Emily's heart beat so hard that she thought that it was going to leap from her chest. Without thinking she put her hand over her heart and placed her other hand on the back of a chair for support. It was so beautiful. As often as she had studied the sky thru telescopes on the earth her mind had never imagined how stunningly beautiful the cosmos would be. She looked hard and long as she wanted to remember this first view of the cosmos forever.

Tears streaked down her cheeks onto her blouse as she intoned, "My God, how great thou art!"

Flata stood by silently observing but otherwise not

intruding into what was obviously a sacred moment for Human-Andrian Emily. To her it was strange that when every single human was brought into this room to view the cosmos, each had invoked their Deity in humility and awe. Perhaps this was the wellspring of the human's inner strength, their preoccupation with their deity.

Slightly smiling to herself, Flata thought, "I guess that makes me their god."

"Where is Earth?" Emily asked in a subdued monotone voice trying to see a planet. Silently, Flata pointed to the small galaxy suspended in the void on the left side of the window.

Emily sucked in her breath and fell to her knees. Tears running unabated down her cheeks in streaming rivulets. Emily cried out, " My God where are you now because I really need you!"

Flata waited until Emily had totally cried herself out, and then said, "Emily, you will have the opportunity to go home again. Although it is up to the "Council of Yield", you and nine other subjects are to be evaluated to determine whether your species is worthy of life. However, we have been able to recover only one other subject who was part of our experiment; his name is Ensign Robert Aaron. I will take you to meet him after you rest.

We also have ten other humans on board which were returned by a traitor named, Klaxo. Klaxo is trying to thwart the "Council of Yield's" assessment of the new Human-Andrian Hybrids ability to preserve the planet thus saving the specie. We believe he may be holding the other eight Human-Andrian Hybrids in prison or he may have already killed them. We do not know. That is why

SEED OF HOPE

we left your galaxy. We do not know for certain how many traitors there are among us and we must insure your safety.

Our group consists of three intergalactic carriers with nine thousand Andrians on each carrier. We do know there are a total of one-hundred and fifty Andrians unaccounted for and we believe they are in consort with Klaxo to destroy our "Council's Plan". They also took twenty saucers. Any single saucer can defeat all of your earth military forces combined without getting close to the planet.

Emily was in shock. Her planet was in dire danger. Warren was in danger! However, her superior intellect allowed her to place those serious items into a mental compartment until she could do something about it. So instead, she asked, "What about the other ten human earthlings? When will I get to meet them?"

Flata replied, "Yes, you will get to meet the other ten human subjects in due time. However, we deem it necessary that you meet the other captive Human, Robert Aaron, first."

Emily was now in shock and was totally exhausted. It was more of a revelation than even her land locked mind could take in.

"You will meet the Human, Robert, after you sleep. Rest now on the recliner. Allow the "Spirit of the Eternal Stars", enter into your being. Be at peace Emily Smith."

Emily was totally exhausted, emotionally and physically. "Yes, I need peace". Emily lay down on the recliner and stared out at the diamond-studded cosmos. Yes, she needed peace. Soon she was fast asleep in a deep slumber.

CHAPTER 28
FELLOW TRAVELER

Breveka entered the room where Human-Andrian, Robert Aaron, was intently studying; he was beginning to master the polymer concepts for Three Dimensional Mathematics. The constructs were mind blowing and Robert reveled in the rotating, diagonal numerical concepts, especially the ones that were formed in a double helix. So deep and intent was his concentration that he never heard Breveka enter into the room, thus when he looked up and saw her standing there he was caught completely by surprise. He verbally stammered a greeting. It took him a moment to clear his mind of the swirling math symbols that seemed to flash thru his mind before he noticed another women standing behind and to the side of Breveka. She was furiously filling in the mathematical equations in the rotating maze of numbers and symbols as quickly as she could write on the three dimensional holographic construct. Somehow, this women "seemed" different but he could not fathom what it was, he was not all that versed with the opposite sex.

Breveka said, "Human-Andrian, Robert Aaron, I would like you to meet, Human-Andrian, Emily Smith".

Robert stood quickly, excited to be this close to another Human. They both faced each other, hands out palms up, greeting each other as equals in Andrian fashion. The greeting came so natural. Their eyes were lasered together, each taking appraisal of the other.

Emily believed Robert to be about twenty-three earth year's old, "earth years", becoming a new concept for time. She probed his mind. He looked surprised and responded in like manner. He was finally getting a handle on mental telepathy. They both stepped toward one another flinging their arms around one another in a fierce hug, both verbally talking at once.

Breveka observed their interaction "tasting" and "feeling" their emotions. They were definitely far superior to the un-enhanced Humans. However, they all exhibited the same cohesiveness and unity of spirit. This in and of itself was the same required trait of Andrians. There was no room for selfishness. This was another positive indicator making Humans worth saving from extinction.

Breveka left the room as the two Human-Andrians verbalized loudly, both talking at once, and throwing their arms one way then another. Breveka thought, "The arm throwing is obviously some primitive form of non-verbal communication, I will report to the "Council of Yield", what I have learned. I now believe it imperative that the other eight Human-Andrian subjects be located, retrieved, and evaluated."

CHAPTER 29
COMPARING NOTES

Robert sat across from Emily at their dinner table and listened raptly as Emily told him what she knew about their circumstances. Up to this very moment Robert did not know he was literally a Human-Andrian Hybrid. When Emily revealed his hybrid status to him, his life with so many incomprehensible pieces of jumbled puzzle, fell into place. The most obvious physical characteristic was his fine hair, his mental abilities, which always exasperated his family, was another.

Robert said, "Well Emily, why did they not tell me? They told you."

Emily responded, "I do not know Robert, but did you know about the other ten humans that was also abducted and are here on the carrier?"

"No! Let's go to them right now and find out who they are and why they are here!"

"Robert they were abducted to confuse and thwart the plans of the "Council of Yield", to evaluate the Human species. Their evaluation was to determine whether or not our species was worthy of life. An Andrian named Klaxo is the leader of other Andrians who want to destroy us from the face of the earth.

Robert became more agitated and excited. "I want to

SEED OF HOPE

go to them now! We must see if we can help them in any way!"

Emily, noting his defiance and the lack of regard for common sense, telepathically said, "Oh, be at peace Robert!"; She said that naturally because that is what Flata had told her when she was scared or agitated. "We must prepare and plan on what to say and not to say."

Immediately Robert began to calm down. "Yes, you are correct Emily. I am sorry I went off half-cocked. Of course we need to devise a plan of introduction. It will be very important to say only the correct things to them."

Emily, on the other hand, was quiet surprised to see that her telepathic command to, "be at peace", actually worked. They had been verbalizing instead of silent communication because that was their lifetime habit. She grinned her lopsided, crooked little smile that Warren found so endearing.

"Warren"! Thought Emily suddenly becoming aware that she had not thought of him since her abduction by Blain! "Poor Warren, how long has it been? Certainly at least four months. I wonder if ships time is the same as Earth time. We are not even in the Milky Way Galaxy! Maybe he is an old man already! I certainly hope not!" They both decided that the next time they saw Breveka they would request that they be allowed to see the other captives.

CHAPTER 30
TEN CAPTIVES

Early the next morning Breveka escorted Robert and Emily to a different section of the ship. Upon entering a secured door they entered a veritable paradise of lush plant growth. They were both amazed with the variety of flora that was growing from the floor, walls, and ceiling, and the mist that floated above their heads. This was the first time that Robert or Emily had seen this type of area on the carrier. Robert had always wanted to visit the hydroponic section but was never allowed to do so. There was real dirt on the floor. The grass was cropped short and evenly cut. The ceiling was at least a hundred feet high and plants grew across the entire area. The distance was indiscernible because of a mist, which shrouded the trees and other flora.

Breveka advised, "This is one of twenty hydroponic sections on the carrier. All of our oxygen is generated from the plants and they also filter the air and water. The plants have been genetically enhanced to generate the maximum amount of oxygen possible."

A small path wound thru the foliage and as they followed the path they quickly examined the plants and flowers in passing. All the plants appeared to be the same varieties as ones found on the earth. In all probability, they were earth plants. The path ended in a clearing.

SEED OF HOPE

The clearing was occupied by ten scraggily, malnourished, men and women. They were all similarly clothed in bright red jump suits. Obviously the color was meant to easily locate the subjects visually when one of them was in the room. Each "subject" was also tagged with a nano chip that controlled where they could and could not go.

The group of ten captives was sitting around a table talking when Robert and Emily stepped into the clearing. They became very quiet and stared at the newcomers. They studied one another trying to figure out how each other fit within the parameters of their new reality. It was obvious to the captives that the newcomers were well fed, dressed in the same fashion as the alien captors and thus obviously, the enemy. Then they noticed their hands and observed they had all their fingers. They were human. What was that all about?

Emily and Robert were stunned because of the dire condition their fellow humans were in. They could taste and feel the anger toward them. Then, Breveka stepped into view from behind the foliage. The feeling of anger toward them changed instantly to open and intense hate, collectively, for her. They, as one, turned their backs toward them and totally ignored them conversing quietly among themselves. Another human would not have guessed at the depth of hate and vitriol that possessed the group because all their faces turned to stony indifference and their backs were nonchalantly turned toward them.

Breveka retreated to a bench that was shielded from

the view of the captive's line of sight and quietly sat down. She wanted to observe the behavior of the interaction of the Human-Andrian and Humans first hand. Moving the foliage aside with her three fingered hand she listened with her mind and ears and observed with her eyes. She knew that she could review the interactions later on a holographic vid at her leisure, but for some reason she found excitement to see firsthand human interaction with group dynamics.

Emily looked over the group of the ten human captives. She noted that one was blind and one had two twisted legs, obviously deformed from birth. He was unable to walk and had difficulty sitting in a normal chair. The group, using materials at hand, had fashioned him a chair that would more easily accommodate his disability. All the group members were malnourished and their expressions were grim.

A tall man got up from the table and walked toward Emily and Robert. It was obvious that he used to be formidable in built but he was now a shell of his former self. He had a menacing countenance. He stopped in front of them crossing his arms across his chest and stood with his legs apart. Malnourished or not he still sported large muscular arms. He pretty much looked like the "Mr. Clean" caricature except, he was not smiling.

With a heavy New York accent he said, "Who are you and whudda ya want?"

Emily very calmly walked up to him. The top of her head came up to his armpits. When she got closer to him she could see multiple burn marks and small dark

SEED OF HOPE

punctures on his bare arms and head. "Control marks," thought Emily.

Looking up at him into his eyes, Emily said, "My name is Emily Smith. His name," pointing toward Robert, "is Robert Aaron. We are human like you."

Emily did not extend both hands palms up in the alien greeting fashion but caught herself just in time. She extended her right hand for a traditional human handshake.

Breveka, observing from the concealment of the foliage smiled thinking, "Yes, our Emily Smith is really very smart." However, being alien, she did not really understand the significance and bonding of a simple human handshake.

The large man uncrossed his arms, taken by surprise by the small women's open sincerity. Extending his hand he shook Emily's hand. Emily's small hand was lost in his.

"My name is David Longoria. I am from Queens."

Robert came forward and extended his hand. I am Ensign Robert Aaron of the Space Defense Command. I was assigned to Lagrange Point Two Observation Post when I was abducted. I am very pleased to meet you, wish it was under more normal circumstances."

That drew laughter from everyone around the table and they all got up and crowded around Robert and Emily. The man with the twisted and deformed legs hobbled over on modified crutches. Everyone in the group made room for him when he approached.

"Well as I said, my name is Emily Smith. I was a senior

at Southern University. I was studying physics and mathematics before I was abducted. I think it was about four or five months ago. I do not know for sure because I was in detox for at least three months. I do not really know for sure." Everyone had gone thru the detox experience and was well aware of how confusing time became.

A young red headed women with dark circles around her eyes about twenty years of age and thirty pounds under weight, asked, "How come you and Robert are dressed like one of them?"

It was a direct question with a challenge and one, which she and Robert had discussed at some length. They had both decided that if they really wanted to help their fellow captives, they must keep their hybrid status secret.

Robert replied first. "We have all been pretty much herded thru the same processes and test. We have been interviewed by children that make even the brightest of us look utterly stupid. I am sure you all agree that we have all been treated pretty much like circus animals and mice in a maze." There was loud agreement to that.

Then Emily said, "It appears that these humanoid aliens have a different scale and standard by which they judge ones worth, than we do on earth. They are a star faring species and travel among the stars. They even travel to different galaxies."

Everyone saw the somber, haunted, and vacant look, in Emily's eyes before she could redirect her thoughts. They knew that particular look of despair could not be manufactured up at will. It was genuine.

"They are much like our early seafaring forefathers

SEED OF HOPE

when they travelled across the oceans of earth. I am sure you all can agree our seafaring forefathers were a pretty hard lot. Sometimes life was cheap and expendable. Ones worth was determined by what he or she could contribute to the greater good. If there is absolutely nothing one could contribute then it made little sense to expend precious resources such as food and water to maintain that particular individual; especially when every one's life was at stake. Now, multiply scarce resources by one hundred thousand and then maybe you can begin to understand our predicament."

Emily waited for that thought to sink in. They all began to talk at once protesting that they never asked to be here and asked myriads of questions, most of which, they knew that it was in the captives best interest not to answer.

Finally a middle aged man, who, by the alien's standard of knowledge, was a generic human being, spoke quietly, without raising his voice, but one which they all listened to, said, "What do you and Robert contribute? You are obviously human, you are well fed, well dressed, and yet, you are accompanied by that she devil alien?" It was not really a question. It was a demand for an answer, a clarification of status.

At the mention of the "she devil alien", they all turned and stared toward the bushes where Breveka was seated in concealment. Breveka could sense the open hatred that poured forth from the human captives like a flood of lava from a ruptured volcano. Normally, Breveka would not have entered the compound where the humans were living, without being escorted by a defense guide. But she believed that Human-Andrians, Emily and Robert, could control them. "How could they not. After all, they are far superior to the captives", thought Breveka.

Finally Emily raised her hands and told them to quiet down.

"Do any of you possess any science or mathematical skills?"

There was a muted quiet murmuring among the group.

"We did not asked to be here", exclaimed a man loudly from back of the group.

All the captives began talking at the same time agreeing with the man in the back of the group.

Emily again took command. "Ok, ok! None of us asked to be here. It has not been a picnic for any of us; even less so for you, than Robert and I! We are fortunate that we both excel in science and mathematics. It seems that is the only redeeming skill that we possess and it happens to be the only scale of measure that these aliens," gesturing in the air pointing in the direction of Breveka's location, "use to determine ones worth and value."

Robert then added, "When I first met Breveka, that is her name, she told me that even though I was extremely intelligent, by earth standards, and being a mathematical genius, again by earth standards, that I would still be eliminated because I was awkward and unable to assimilate into the milieu of the group. I was always a loner and never developed interpersonal skills. I had three sisters to fend for me. So yes, I am intelligent and possess highly developed mathematical skills. But I would have been eliminated from their group because of my inability to work well with others. They have not yet revealed to us our purpose for being here."...a partial lie, but one they believed served better under the current circumstances than the truth.

Emily would never reveal to them or any other human, of their Human-Andrian hybrid status, or of their telepathic abilities. Their skills had increased tenfold under the tutoring of skilled Andrian facilitators. Emily and Robert both have been experiencing a veritable renaissance in the evolution of human understanding and cognitive mental skills. Sometime it scared her when she realized what mental powers she possessed.

Both she and Robert knew that these ten individuals represented a microcosm of all humans upon the earth. If they could not convince them here then they would not be able to convince those that dwelled upon the earth. Then the image of the small galaxy floating far away came to mind, and she thought, "I may never get the chance!"

Again the haunted look came to her eyes. It seemed to be the one window into her soul that she could not control. The group, having experienced a much greater degree of adversity for a much longer period of time, instantly recognized the clouded, lost look, in Emily's eyes, and came to believe that she, like them all, was just putting on a brave front. They all crowded around Emily and Robert and embraced them in an outpouring of tears of compassion. Emily and Robert wept too. It was no act. It was anguish of soul and spirit. They alone, in the entire group, knew and understood the dire extent of their circumstances.

CHAPTER 31
EMILY'S ANGER

After **receiving consolation** from the group, they each individually met each captive and assessed their needs. That was relatively easy. The most pressing need was adequate food. Their accommodations were relatively adequate; they shared two large sleeping areas with beds for each individual. They advised they were no longer paraded before groups of aliens. They believed the aliens no longer found them amusing and the cheap entertainment came with a cost. Almost on every outing the prisoners became belligerent and if possible, they attacked their guards. Of course the consequences were extreme and painful, but it just seemed to be the thing to do. If one is treated like an animal, one became an animal. That seemed to be part of the innate human nature. Especially when there did not appear to be any hope of reprieve.

The young blind man grasps Emily arm as she interviewed him. He said, "Please help us if you can. They seem to show you favor."

Emily responded quietly, "I promise."

After Emily had visited and talked to each and every captive and listened to their abduction stories, she was fuming. She separated herself from the group several feet. They were standing around watching her expectantly. Surely she could help them in some way.

SEED OF HOPE

Emily said, "Breveka, show yourself." Her voice was quiet and purring and showed no outward sign of her inner rage.

Breveka walked from behind the trees and came closer to Emily; her facial expression neutral, arms at her sides. Breveka could feel the intensity and heat of Emily's anger. She had never experienced her anger as Emily had always been congenial and resigned to her fate, and enjoyed learning. She had a voracious appetite for knowledge and did not seem to be satisfied with shallow answers.

"Yes Emily?"

Emily's anger began to boil. She was angry at being abducted, she was angry at being taken away from the love of her life, she was angry for the ten abductees being treated like animals. But mostly she was angry at being... being...only God knew where!

Breveka watched Emily with rapt attention. She received Emily's telepathic command, yes command!... Her command was, "attend to the needs of the hostages and to have Flata the chief geneticist, to attend to the blind and the lame." And, most importantly, "she demanded to have a "face to face" conference with the "Council of Yield." And, "Do it now!" Emily's body language seemed strange to her and yet in some mystifying way, it seemed to accent her every command.

The abductees observed Emily take a few steps away from them. They followed forming a semi-circle on either side of her. Emily verbally called to the alien whose name they now knew as Breveka. Then in a very quiet and soft voice she told her to attend to their needs. That was the verbal language. Body language showed her standing with her right hip thrust to the side, her hand was on her hip, and her eyes were partially hooded. She moved her head in such of a way her hair swung around her face onto the back of her shoulder. And, she was lightly tapping her left foot.

The men in the group instantly recognized one pissed off earth women. They had all met someone like her somewhere in their life! All the women too took the same stance, consciously or unconsciously. It was definitely a defiant, synchronized action.

Breveka verbalized, "Yes Emily". She then turned around and left.

CHAPTER 32
REVIEW AND ASSESSMENT

Admiral Cleary was standing at the laser board pointing to a mechanical schematic of the alien saucer. He was presenting engineering and intelligence data to a large group of military officers and science advisors regarding the information they had gleaned from their latest captives. Everyone was listening with rapt attention and all were dedicated to the projects they were assigned.

"Each saucer craft can carry up to twenty commandoes. We are starting our assault training exercises as we speak. We do not know where we are going yet but we want to be prepared. Now, we have not been able to duplicate the power source. It is some kind of hydrogen plasma drive that is maintained in a high-energy magnetic force field and driven by fusion generators. Any questions?"

Everyone in the room laughed. No one had any idea of how the saucer really worked.

There are laser systems on board and we have learned to operate them to a certain degree. We think they may be strong enough to blow a hole thru our moon. However, we have been practicing on expendable rockets. If we can get far enough distance from earth we may be able to practice on an asteroid or two. Now, Commander Johnson will present what we have learned from the captured aliens."

Commander Johnson then began his presentation and placed pictures of the five most recently captured aliens on the holograph. They all had the same haughty and superior look pasted to their faces. All of them believed this was just a temporary setback and they would soon be freed by Klaxo.

"We were very successful in our interrogation of the captives. It seems our truth serum, sodium pentothal, along with a couple of other drugs whipped up by our science research and development lab, renders the aliens into a most pleasant, pliable and talkative mood. We played on their sense of superiority of their specie over our specie and that really gets them going. They just will not stop talking! Lucky us."

Everyone in the room laughed. It was difficult to find things to laugh at, especially after the death of the five commandoes that was killed during the aliens capture.

Continuing, Commander Johnson said, "They are a dangerous and powerful foe. Should they have a mind too, they could easily destroy us from the face of the earth, totally and completely. In fact, there is just such a plan being formulated, right now! Fortunately for us these malcontents are in the minority, at least for now."

"There is a governing body among them that is long on patience, it encompasses human generations. The governing body is called the "Council of Yield". But we must make no mistake, should they deem us unworthy of this

SEED OF HOPE

planet, they will wipe us from the face of the earth and we will never see it coming. For now we have received a reprieve. The reprieve has something to do with the ten young people we rescued from captivity."

"The malcontent I spoke of earlier is named Klaxo. He was a member of their governing body until he rebelled against them. He has one hundred and fifty followers and twenty saucers at his disposal. We have currently relieved him of three saucers so that leaves them with seventeen saucers. At this time we have a total of eight aliens in captivity and one alien was killed during our attempted capture."

"It appears that the "Council of Yield", was the initiators to save the Human species from extinction on the earth. Their efforts consisted of genetic experimentation with our genome. At some point in time they abducted ten adult females and ten adult males and took them aboard the intergalactic carrier. There, the semen of the man and the eggs of the women were bonded with Andrian, oh, by the way, they call themselves Andrians, DNA markers and other genetic materials they call matrix rhesus. This procedure is supposed to enhance our intelligence and reduce our compassion and tolerance."

"It seems our compassion is considered a fatal flaw. They specifically mentioned our caring for the blind and the lame. Remember, two of the captives that were returned by Klaxo were blind and lame. And, they reiterated to no end, how stupid we were, in that we were destroying our own lives by destroying the environment; and we do that with no place to go! I guess we all could certainly agree with that one! It does not seem too bright. I truly believe considering the source of that particular assessment we should take serious heed".

"I guess the crux of the problem, from the malefactor's point of view is that if we do not care enough about our planet to take care of it then there are those on their ships that will take the opportunity to do so. There is no difference of opinion between the malefactor's point of view and the "Council of Yield's", point of view in that we are destroying the planet. The difference comes when one decides on what do to about the problem."

"We have also learned that they are not the only star faring specie that sail the cosmos. We are far enough away from the center of traffic that we are not considered a pleasant tourist attraction. The Andrians are another matter entirely. They are not only star faring specie but intergalactic travelling specie as well. Try to process our odds with something like that. "

"Planets of the quality of Earth are evidently few and far between. Should we manage to come out of this intact then we had better heed the warning, clean up our act, and take giant steps to preserving what we have. All of our reports are being forwarded to, "The President", and his advisors. I imagine there are going to be some changes around here.

"And, I think we should consider the ten young people with extraordinary intelligence, and whom by the way, are above average in compassion, as a gift from the stars! We could not find more loving children anywhere on Earth, no pun intended. All records of them being Human-Andrian hybrids are being expunged as we speak, by order of The President. Now I turn the floor over to Captain Swenson for his analysis and assessment of what we have accomplished and what we must do. Captain Swenson, if you please."

CHAPTER 33

CAPTAIN SWENSON'S MYSTERY

Captain Swenson stood at the front of the room. This was one of the few presentations for which Agents Jessop and Reese were not present. They were out interviewing Robert Aaron's family. There was a large presence of scientist and military personnel.

After clearing his throat in an effort to gain every one attention, Captain Swenson began his presentation. "We may have their saucers but as of yet we do not know how to fly them to the moon. We are barely able to go past the space station. We have been unable to operate the weapon systems except for a small laser. We found other lasers and a pen mike communication device and we are studying them now."

"And by the way, the three young people that are working with us are astronautically endowed geniuses. We would not be able to fly the saucers at all without their assistance. In fact we have offered all ten of them positions with in our service until the immediate crises is over at which time they can choose other fields; which brings up a very interesting question. If we have ten young people and they have two young people and all of them are Human-Andrian Hybrids, where did the extra two people come from?"

"All of the eight alien captives say there are only ten Human-Andrian Hybrids. They had all been incarcerated in the prison hospital that Agents Jessop and Reese found. If that is true, where did the other two captives, Emily Smith and Ensign Robert Aaron, come from? It is obvious that the "Council of Yield" believed them to be Human-Andrians, as they were willing to risk a lot of exposure to retrieve them. And, all medical records indicate that the twelve young people have the same genome markers. This is a true mystery."

"Ok, We will solve that mystery when we able to retrieve Emily and Robert. Now, I believe the best chance of success is to wait for the intergalactic carriers to return. We know they stopped beyond Lagrange Point Station Two last time. I believe they will stay in the asteroid belt between Mars and Jupiter or the Kuiper belt beyond Neptune. We need to be able to fly the saucers at least as far as Mars. I am sure that would get their attention."

"And then when we contact them we can we can board them and "demand" our citizens back. Yea, Right! Maybe we can get a conference before the "Council of Yield". They seem more reasonable than Klaxo and his group. If that does not work we can blow ourselves and them up. We have nothing to lose."

Everyone in the room was quiet. That was a very bleak assessment. It sounded crazy. But really, how did one deal with a specie that was far more advanced than yourself in each and every way; and that some members of that specie wanted to annihilate you."

"And of course, how do we reach the group on Jupiter's moon, Europa. They are currently beyond our reach. It is imperative we learn how to fly the saucers and take the war to them" Captain Swenson paused with a surprised look on his face. It was the first time anyone had used the term "war", in regard to the aliens. It was truly so.

CHAPTER 34
PERPLEXED

Klaxo was seated up on the Calais looking over the assembled group assessing their capabilities. They were a magnificent group. Most importantly, they were loyal to him. As of yet the three ships sent to retrieve or destroy the Human-Adrian Hybrids, at the hospital prison had not yet returned. Obviously nothing could have gone wrong but he was perplexed that they had not at least communicated indicating position and status.

Klaxo stood to address the assembled group. He believed he had manipulated them superbly by including them all in the decision making process and calling them, "The Council". Of course they did his bidding. They just thought it was a new kind of democratic process. It was something he had learned while on Earth.

"Members of "The Council", Zelegark has not returned. We have not heard from him or the two groups that accompanied him to Earth. It may be that a solar storm near the inner planets is keeping the laser ion beam from formulating a proper carrier. However, he should have completed his task and returned by now. It is not possible they could have failed and fallen into the hands of the imbecilic, stupid, Humans. Therefore, if not a solar storm, the saucer craft must have been affected by an ion-neutrino blast from a black hole. Because of this, they have been unable to navigate."

"I propose, with your approval, of course, that we send three more saucer craft to look for Zelegark, and go to the prison hospital Zelegark established for detaining the ten Human-Andrian hybrids, and observe what is going on. The two other craft should search the area for the other saucers. If you are unable to locate the craft you should enter the hospital, kill all the Humans and Hybrids. Make it look like they were killed by the Human staff. Then burn the hospital to the ground. If you encounter any problems, which I cannot perceive how that would be possible, blast the hospital and anyone else that gets in your way. Find Zelegark and the others and return here to base. We will be waiting for you. After your return we will release a toxin that will destroy all life on the planet."

Klaxo did not lack for volunteers for the mission; it was a simple extermination and extraction. Nine more men and three additional saucers left the base after a leisurely lunch.

CHAPTER 35
KAREN ABBOTT'S ASSESSMENT

Karen Abbott was reading over the missing persons report generated by Blaizon Hills Police department. She could not count the number of times she had read the report. Ten? Twenty? Karen had the report memorized and could quote it verbatim should she be required to do so.

"You know Earl," who was lying beside her trying to go to sleep, "there is something strange about this whole Emily thing. I mean, you just cannot just disappear like that. She has been missing for four months or more, and not a word from her. And what about those two cops, Jessop and Reese? It is like they fell down the same rabbit hole as Emily. When I finally got to talk to the Chief of Police, he was working hard to avoid me; he said that they left the very next day. They did not even clear out their desk. He said he has not heard hide nor hair from them. And, you know what else? Earl! Earl! Are you listening to me?"

"Yes dear", replied Earl, turning over to face his wife. He knew he was not going to get any sleep as long as she was on a tear.

"Earl, did you know that nice young man that was the crime tech? Well he is missing too. Just gone! Just like that! I also checked at the University and his professors said that he quit coming to class about four months ago. That is about the same time as those two detectives disappeared."

"There is something strange going on here. Earl, you have contacts in Space Intelligence. Why don't you put out some feelers or something? I mean look at the detective's police report. A gnat's ass could not go unnoticed by them. Then at the end, which ends rather abruptly, they say that Emily was allegedly kidnapped by a band of Gypsies that was reportedly moving thru the area. For goodness sakes, everyone knows the only thing they do is allegedly break into vending machines. Kidnapping is way over the top! I mean, how preposterous is that? They might put and evil spell on you or something like that but that is all."

"You know we are the only family Emily has. We are her only ties to earth, for heaven's sake! She is like our daughter. I mean poor Warren is totally devastated. And you know, Earl, they love each other just like we love one another. And Billy and Skip love her just as much as Warren. Sometimes I think they love her more than me! And you know what else Earl, because of her tutoring they are almost as smart as you in mathematics and science. I mean those boys are literally genesis."

Earl was resigned that there would be no sleep until he satisfied Karen's concern so he said, "You know Karen, I have actually been thinking the same thing for quite some time. And, I did make a few inquiries. The response was disquieting."

SEED OF HOPE

"I was told the two detectives now work for Space Intelligence as Special Investigators. Furthermore, this is the largest, most secret, most far reaching...most anything and everything investigation in the history of Space Intelligence, with the most consequences for human kind ever conducted! It really sounds serious! And Emily is right in the middle of it! And what does that mean? I do not have the foggiest idea."

Karen ran her index finger in a small circle in the center of his bare chest where Earl had the most hair and said, "Well dear, you have more patents purchased by Space Intelligence than any other single inventor. Why do you not call up that nice Admiral Cleavage, or something like that, and see if you can help and maybe find out what is going on with our daughter, Emily?"

"It is Clealand dear...or something like that."

"Well whatever; I am sure there is some kind of major crises brewing and you may even be of assistance."

Earl responded with an eager, "You know, I think you may be right. I will fly up there in the morning and contact Admiral Clealand, or something like that, of the Space Intelligence Command. Do you want to come with me?"

"I would not miss it for the world dear. I do not trust those pretty, young, female intelligence types. I have seen them eyeing your beautiful body!"

"They lust after my brain dear, not my body!" Earl then gathered Karen in his arms and they promptly went to sleep, having put aside a worrying, nagging problem.

CHAPTER 36
DR. ABBOTT'S OPPORTUNITY

Admiral Cleary stood when Mr. and Mrs. Earl and Karen Abbott, entered his office. Admiral Cleary being run ragged day and night trying to resolve the alien issues, had made a ten-minute slot for Dr. Abbott's visit. He did not have the slightest idea what was wanted of him but they had been very demanding in meeting with him and no one else. But then, Dr. Abbott was an exceptional scientist and inventor and a little courtesy on his part was the least he could do. Admiral Cleary mused, "Just imagine what he could accomplish with a support staff." Admiral Cleary pointed to the two seats indicating for Dr. Abbott and his wife, Karen, to have a seat, which they did after shaking hands.

Before Admiral Cleary could say a word, Dr. Abbot said, "I know your time is precious and therefore I will get right to the point Admiral."

"Thank you Earl that is one of the things I love about you most. You do not bull...corn around;" changing his verbal response in midsentence as he glanced at Mrs. Abbott.

"This is the short and sweet of it Admiral, What has happened to Emily Smith? She is my son's fiancée."

SEED OF HOPE

Admiral Cleary's face visibly paled from tanned to white at the curve that just hit him in the chest. To gather his wits about him he reached for the pitcher of water on his desk and poured himself and the Abbotts a glass of water. Thinking to himself he mused that, "If anyone could ferret out a secret at Space Intelligence, it would be the shy and unassuming Earl Abbott. How much should I divulge?"

Swinging his chair back and forth looking Earl in the eyes, Admiral Cleary blurted something out that surprised himself and Earl Abbott. "Dr. Abbott, how would you like to come to work for Space Intelligence, say, for a three year contract, and one which you could terminate at any time no questions asked? We could certainly use your expertise about now".

Earl and Karen both were taken aback by the sudden shift in focus with a job offer.

Karen spoke first. "Will it help Emily if Earl works for Space Intelligence?"

"There it was," mused Earl. "Clean and simple, Karen did have a way of getting to the crux of a problem."

Admiral Cleary gazed out the window, again swinging his chair from side to side. Then sitting straight up and clasping his hands together on the desk, he said, "Yes".

Karen answered for Earl before he could respond, "Earl would love to come and work at Space Intelligence, Admiral Cleary"

Earl looked down at his wife then shrugging his shoulders said, "Sure, when can I start? Earl then mused,

"Now there is a real twist for you. I never even thought of getting on the "inside". That Karen, she is so sharp!"

Admiral Cleary pushed a button on the side of his desk. A very attractive, very young, uniformed woman promptly entered the office from a side door.

"Yes Admiral?"

"Take Dr. Abbott here and process him for a three year contract. And Lieutenant, he gets the highest clearance. He will be working on project "Andrian", and he is to be assigned to the propulsion systems."

The young Lieutenant looked surprised. She gave Earl Abbott a discerning "look over", and then said, "Yes Admiral".

Addressing Earl, she said, "Right this way Dr. Abbott."

Earl leaned over and kissed Karen on the cheek. She said, "Do not worry dear. I will be at home with the boys. We will be waiting to hear from you…and Emily." At which point Earl followed the attractive young, curvy, Lieutenant from the room.

As the door was closing behind Earl, Karen called out, "Remember what I warned you about Earl" The door closed quietly behind him. She was smiling when she turned her attention back to the Admiral.

Admiral Cleary looked Karen up and down. He observed her and believed her to be fit, trim and in apparently good condition. She was certainly tanned.

Karen, used to male scrutiny and noticing the Admiral obvious and intent assessment, said, "Do I meet with your approval Admiral?"

SEED OF HOPE

Admiral Cleary looked Karen in the eyes. Her eyes had a glint and she had a pretty, petulant, smile on her full lips. "No wonder Earl married her, she was absolutely beautiful!"

"Yes, Mrs. Abbott. Do you think you are up to a free ride home, courtesy of the Space Intelligence Command? Perhaps you would enjoy a short tour in one of our newest stealth fighter jets? We will have your vehicle delivered to your home at the earliest moment. And by the way, the stealth fighter jet was made possible by several of Earl's research patents."

Karen gave Admiral Cleary one of her most endearing and charming smiles and said, "Why Admiral, I thought you would never ask!"

CHAPTER 37
FAMILIAR FACES

Three days after the meeting with Admiral Cleary, Earl found himself in a large room with at least one hundred people in attendance. There were chairs around a large table placed in the middle of the room and chairs two deep against the walls. He had been seated against the wall no more than several minutes when a man and women came and sat down on either side of him. They looked somewhat familiar but of course he could not possibly know them. I mean, "I am on a top secret base in the middle of nowhere", thought Earl.

"Hello Mr. Abbott", the lady on his left said. She extended her hand, which he shook. He looked her in the face. Yes, she did look familiar but where on earth could he know her from? Social settings were not Earl's strong suit. He was much more at home with Mathematics and Physics. Karen was the social butterfly of the family.

Then the man on his right extended his hand and greeted him by name also. "This is really odd and disconcerting," thought Earl. "I do not know these people."

Reese and Jessop could easily see the man was confused as to who they were and where he had seen them. To his credit, he had only seen them briefly when he and his wife had collected their son Warren.

"I am detective Reese and this is detective Jessop. We

SEED OF HOPE

were at Blaizon Hills Police Department."

"Ohm", said Earl. "You were working on Emily's disappearance. Well I am certainly surprised to see you two here".

Both detectives looked at one another. Reese shrugged her shoulders, and replied, "As we are to see you here. And by the way, how is Warren? He was totally broken up by Emily's disappearance?"

"Well thank you for asking Detective but truthfully, Warren is not doing well. He dropped out of The University. He is pretty down."

"Sorry to hear that," said Detective Jessop. He is really a good young man."

At that time the lights dimmed and the screen lit up. Earl saw three saucer craft in a hanger resting on support pylons. Admiral Cleary stood at the podium and began his bi-weekly assessment. Earl listened with rapt attention, spell bound as the scenario was laid out before the audience. Nothing was withheld. It was imperative that they all be on the same page without misunderstandings.

Earl was surprised to hear of Emily's math and science skills. He knew she was smart. She really helped the boys increase their understanding of math and science. When Earl saw the examples of Three Dimensional Mathematics, he was beyond excitement! He could hardly sit still. When Admiral Cleary advised that as of yet, they have not been able to decipher the math matrixes, he just had to say something.

Earl was beside himself as he knew some of the answers. He jumped up and said, "Let me try Admiral! I have been dreaming of something like this for several years!"

"Come on up Earl," said Admiral Cleary. "Ladies and gentleman, I would like to introduce you to Dr. Earl Abbott. He is one of the Space Intelligence Commands, most prolific inventors. We would not be on Lagrange Point Two, if Dr. Abbott did not share his inventions. And oh, by the way, Emily Smith is his son Warren's, fiancé.

Agents Jessop and Reese looked at one another. "Wonders never cease," thought Reese. Leaning over to Jessop she said in his ear, "Maybe Emily was the source of his dreams he said he had," whispered Reese to Jessop. "Yep", said Jessop.

The intelligence briefing lasted most of the day. After the meeting Jessop and Reese stepped outside in the cool of the evening and gazed at the stars. Touching hands on the railing, Jessop said, "What does all this mean Carol? I mean we know what they did and basically why they did it but what does it really mean for us and all mankind? I am being forced to look up and think about things I have never even considered before. It looks like solving men's little murder mysteries are actually simple compared to trying to assess this dilemma."

Carol squeezed his hand. Jessop had echoed her exact sentiments. They really were like a coin with two sides, they complimented one another. "It is a good thing we believe in a higher power, Gary. And I do not mean alien power and intelligence. The same God that made us made them. I really believe we can solve this thing,

SEED OF HOPE

whatever it is."

Arm in arm they strolled to their temporary quarters overlooking a lake with the moon's pale light reflected from the surface. They knew that if they were going to solve this mystery they were going to have to have clear minds.

CHAPTER 38
DR. ABBOTT THE TEACHER

Two days later, in a classroom setting, Earl was walking back and forth expounding on a mathematical concept. He was furiously thinking more to himself and was almost breathless as his words flowed from his lips. The ten young people in the class were in awe and listened raptly, hanging on to every precept he carefully and methodically extracted from the spherical mathematical equation. The mathematical formulas were woven in a helix and at times crossed over to the other strand in a diagonal supposition that resulted in amazing clarity postulating warping of time to achieve unimaginable distances. In effect, it was concepts that enabled one to travel near the speed of light. It was also probably safe to say that he was unaware of their presence. He made the concepts somewhat understandable. Of the ten students in his class, two of them were able to somewhat comprehend what he was expositing, the rest were barely able to see the thread that he wove thru the helix. But, they were getting brighter as Earl continued to expound.

Suddenly, he stopped his pacing and he turned to his class. He had made an intuitive leap in understanding. He said, "Those numerous symbols on the walls of the

SEED OF HOPE

saucer craft, they represent three dimensional mathematical formulas. We need to interpret those symbols then we should be able to zip out to Jupiter or Neptune in no time at all, so to speak!"

He was smiling. His hair was scattered every which way. There were dark circles under his eyes. His lab coat was buttoned lopsided and was askew. Even so, all the students literally loved him. Somehow he could make connections with them like no one else ever had. It was like he could almost read their minds.

Jake and Ashley got up from their respective seats. Jake took a cold bottle of water from the cooler, removed the cap and placed the bottle in Earl's hand. Earl took the water, took a sip and walked away never stopping the lecture. When he returned, Ashley placed two fig newtons in his other hand, his favorite snack. Earl took a bite of his fig newton, another sip of water and walked away. Both students returned to their respective seats.

This instruction scenario continued for ten more days and would have continued for another ten had not Admiral Cleary ordered Earl to be sedated. Then, after Dr. Abbott was sedated, all the students fell into an exhausted and dreamless sleep. They were so weary from the mental exercises in spherical math they did not need any prodding to take to their beds.

CHAPTER 39
THEROM'S TRUTH TESTED

True to Dr. Abbott's words, the symbols on the panels in the saucer craft represented three-dimensional mathematical formulas. It had been slow going, but working together the ten students translated about sixty percent of the symbols into cognizant, understandable, mathematical formulas. They believed they had the operational controls of the craft figured out and were sure they could travel anywhere in the solar system.

Seated in front of Admiral Cleary, Earl appeared every bit of the caricature of the mad scientist as he had ever seen. Earl said, "Admiral, we have worked out the navigation and propulsion systems and we are ready to take the saucer out for a test run. We need to test our hypothesis and the students are the ones to do it! We have worked nonstop for at least three months, except of course, the times you had me forcibly sedated." Earl was quiet peeved about that.

Admiral Cleary responded, "Sorry Earl, it was necessary. Everyone needed a break. You and the students were going nonstop for weeks at a time." Admiral Cleary could never accuse Dr. Abbott of being a slacker.

Swinging his chair back and forth in contemplation,

SEED OF HOPE

Admiral Cleary was wary to turn loose one of the saucers for a test run. But, this is why he had brought Earl on board. If anyone could solve the mystery of the saucer's intricate operational systems, it was Earl Abbott. Now he wanted to fly one of the saucers. It was time. Questioning his own judgment he said, "Ok Earl. It has to be a short flight. You can take five students and five commandoes to test the operational systems. However, take only you're brightest and best."

So far earth scientist and military had been able to operate the saucer craft on short hops up to the edge of the atmosphere; they were never able to engage the time warp drive. Now the five students who were well versed with the three dimensional math and the symbols in the craft believed they were ready for the test run.

Earl had chosen his five student pilots carefully. He made sure that they knew that they could possibly be obliterated should they get the formulas wrong. All five students said they were ready and able to fly the saucer and were eager to go.

The five students, Earl, and five commando pilots entered the craft and took up their respective positions. Soon they were all encased in their respective clear tubes and the white chemical cloud filled the tube to their neck. The young student identified as Tommy, engaged the controls and the walls of the saucer became transparent and they lifted quickly into the air. Soon the moon slid into the view of the occupants.

Earl said, "Ok Tommy, see if you can use your mind and manipulate the symbols and try to get us to Jupiter.

And please, do not break Admiral Cleary's toy! "

"Yes Sir! A piece of cake" replied Tommy.

Tommy began to concentrate on the symbols flashing across the three-D imagers. The mathematical formulas began undulating and turning upon one another. They could feel the craft vibrate and shake for several minutes. The wall visual had become opaque with bright flashes intermittently streaking across their field of view. The streaks of light appeared like the floor indicator lights on a rapidly ascending elevator, which at times traveled in a lateral direction. And then the vibration stopped. The opaque walls turned black. Stars like diamonds steadily lit the distant black velvet canopy. As the craft hung suspended in the black void rotating slowly, Jupiter and its angry red spot floated into view. It slowly moved across their field of view. No one said anything. Indeed, not so much as the intake of breath could be heard. The silence was sustained until Jupiter slowly slid from view as the craft hovered in vacuum, rotating.

One of the commando pilots said, "Well professor, it looks like you and your young people were successful. I suppose that until we can develop this telepathic mind control asset that you and your students possess, we will have to use you as pilots and astrogators. Can you take us home now, at least as far as Earth's atmosphere? We can take it from there."

"Sure", replied Earl. "Tommy, take us home son!"

Tommy worked what appeared to be magic to the uninitiated. Again there was a slight vibration. The streaks of light flashed across the wall and soon the earth floated

SEED OF HOPE

in silhouette blocking the suns bright light, the moon off to the side, gray and dead. All sighed audible sighs of relief when the lead commando advised they would take control of the craft at the edge of earth's atmosphere. The mission was successful.

CHAPTER 40
NEW DAWN

Breveka stood before the "Council of Yield". She was not used to feeling uncertain and has always been positive about every assessment she gave pertaining to any and every specie they have ever encountered. This Emily and Robert, the true Human-Andrian hybrids, forced Breveka to think in ways and dimensions she had never considered before.

Bowing her head, Breveka began..."My most enlightened and eminent Presence. I must say I am mystified and unsure exactly what my assessment should be regarding the Human-Andrian hybrids. Flata and I believe they could possibly be a new species of humanoid form, different from Human and different from Andrian. Although they have both of our DNA and genome properties, they have exhibited exceptional neurological growth patterns into areas of the cerebral cortex that we do not possess, nor was it anticipated."

"For instance, they seem to have pre-cognitive senses in that they know what I am going to ask before I myself know what I am going to ask; for example, I am starting to think of a certain task for them to accomplish in number compilation. They just look at me then turn around and begin writing the answer before I can formulate the entire thought in my mind. I may begin to think of a chemical rhesus evaluation and again they will have exactly what I want before I finish my thoughts. I wanted to review a section of nebula with the ion telescope using a light frequency that enhanced spectral imaging. They handed me the results when I arrived at the lab. We were not even the same room!"

"It is not just an enhanced sense of telepathy. They have both become highly skilled in all learning processes and the cerebral cortex region of the brain controlling telepathy exhibits a highly excited neural process. But very importantly, the difference we noted earlier in most all humans, in regard to the area next to the hypo-thalamus, the small unidentifiable nodule which we do not possess, is rapidly changing in density, color, texture, and size, in Human-Andrian, Emily and Robert. Even though the changes are minute, they are there nonetheless. In addition to these changes there is now a presence of a trace chemical that as of yet we cannot identify. It is barely within our scientific skill to measure it. This is in and of itself indicative of an evolutionary process in the early forming stages. They, the new genetic species, may even become more biologically and neurologically advanced than we ourselves."

"Flata believes that perhaps we have controlled our own evolution for so long by manipulating our own genetic processes, that even though we are currently far superior mentally to humans, we may have thwarted our opportunity to evolve to the next higher level. We do not, as a species, even have a trace of this new, unknown chemical. This new variant of Human-Andrian genome is superior to not only regular humans, but even to us. And, if this turns out to be true, then the question of whether or not we allow humans to continue to live upon their planet is irrelevant. Since we have discovered this trace chemical molecule in the Human-Adrian hybrids, we have researched our records and have discovered this same trace chemical molecule in several of our previous human captives. The diminutive amount of trace chemical consisted of only a molecule or two thus, was easily missed."

"So now, my Eminent Presence, the question is therefore, for the sake of our posterity, should we not advance our posterities neurological processes by combining human DNA and Andrian DNA until all of our genome throughout the galaxies are enhanced? Or, should we do nothing and allow humans to advance beyond our capabilities?"

Breveka continues, "We should think upon these things. We believe their aggressive and warlike trait is unworthy of allowing the specie to exist. I have researched our own history back to the time before we became an intergalactic star faring species. Most information is lost in the mist of the cosmos and is not didactic information. The sources are fragmentary and mystical legends. It seems that in that far distant earlier time period our species too warred constantly with one another. We almost destroyed ourselves and our planet. But, there was an intervention of some kind by an unknown entity. Shortly after the intervention we achieved space-traveling capabilities, and also solved many other significant

SEED OF HOPE

problems with our own home world environment. In effect, there seems to be a parallel with our ancient past and the Human's present situation. We are perhaps, in effect, "their unknown entity", as we are now at this very moment in time trying to improve the human genome."

"Therefore, perhaps this new Human-Andrian, combination, is not an advanced Human, but is instead, a whole new species. Humans had the "sleeper", DNA all along. Our genetic inclusion of our genome acted as a catalyst and thus helped create a life form similar in genotype but neurologically superior. We only had to introduce the Hybrids, Emily and Robert, to our knowledge base and now, strange as it seems, they are superior to us in some areas of problem solving".

"Furthermore, and more disconcerting, Human-Andrian Emily Smith, commanded me, not requested, that I tell Flata to use our sciences to relieve the diseased ones of their afflictions. I was also commanded to provide the ten detainees with more sustenance, and, to tell you that she demands, mind you, demands, an audience with you! And do you know what is so depressing? I was compelled to do everything she demanded whither I wanted to or not! Now, their blind can see and the lame can walk, and they have plenty to eat even though our resources are precious. And most galling, instead of acknowledging the source of their good fortune, they are praising their invisible, unknown, "God", for the "miracles", our science supplied!"

The "Council of Yield", upon hearing this assessment became troubled and communicating among themselves decided to grant the Human-Andrian, Emily Smith, her request for an audience. This in and of itself was unprecedented as only the most elective was allowed to view them in person and never had that included a Human.

Therefore, council member Shayar advised, "It was my idea to insert our genome into their DNA to create a more advanced Human. Evidently the process appears to have succeeded beyond all our expectations. I would deem it imperative that we must grant Human-Andrian, Emily Smith, her request, and also Robert Aaron. We should listen to their thoughts. Furthermore, we should return to the vicinity of their planet, Earth, and make every effort to locate, retrieve and evaluate the other eight Human-Andrian Hybrids. And, most importantly, we must locate and destroy Klaxo and his followers before they destroy all Human life upon the planet.

All the "Council of Yield" agreed upon the two proposed courses of action. They then sent for the two Human-Andrians for their evaluation.

CHAPTER 41
REVELATION

Emily and Robert escorted the ten other earthlings into the same viewing room that Flata had taken her and Robert earlier. The scene was…humbling. The Milky Way Galaxy was directly in front of the viewing room window. It was positioned in the elliptic, thus allowing one to see the complete circular pattern. Other galaxies floated farther away in an ever-unending scroll of black velvet.

No one spoke. Each had their own thoughts. If any of the group was not necessarily religious before, they certainly were now; religious as in being aware of the omnipresence of an omnipotent God, not man's subscription of one sectarian theological doctrine over another. The view of the heavens on earth's starry night just provided an inkling of the omnipotence of God. The view from here blasted away any and all pretenses of self-importance and literally shouted the glory and omnipotence of God. Emily recalled the scripture in Psalm 8, that her Father had said should be her anchor, "When I consider thy heavens, the work of thy fingers, the moon and the stars, which thou hast ordained; what is man that thou art mindful of him? And the son of man, that thou has visitest him." With Emily being far more intelligent than those around her, her Father and Mother wanted to instill within her a sense of humility. They succeeded. Tears rolled down her cheeks as they did on each and every captive's cheeks.

The soft-spoken man who was usually quiet, but when he spoke, every one listened, said, "God help us now." There was a unanimous chorus of, "Amen".

The "Council of Yield", along with Flata, Breveka, and Blain, observed the humans on the laser video system. They could observe a single individual or the entire group, read their minds, and, feel their emotions. For the Andrians, it was a stunning moment. Each and every human believed in a Supreme Being. The Andrians had been an intergalactic traveling specie for so long, had gathered so much knowledge, skill, and finding out that as of yet, they were the most intelligent specie yet encountered, had long since forgotten the sense of awe, respect and adoration for their supreme being. Their requirement of being self-sufficient or die in the voids of space, had over time, leached away that dependence on their supreme being. Their ancient books were rarely, if ever, consulted.

The group of twelve human's kneeled before the view of the galactic panorama, humbled and subdued by God's majestic power. All fear left them, "the peace that passeth all understanding", imbued their very souls. Their Spirit was at last at peace.

The Council of Twelve decided in that very moment that the humans, as flawed and weak as they were, were well worth saving. Their faith in their God, humility of spirit and their evidentially providential metamorphous into exceedingly advanced specie, assured them that their initial decision to return to the solar system to hunt down Klaxo and his minions was the correct one. It was indeed perhaps providential that they, the Andrians, must save the specie, Human.

The Human-Andrian Hybrids exhibited the same sense of awe. They felt no sense of superiority over their fellow, less endowed, humans. They really were no different. Or, perhaps as the Council of Yield had been told, and Flata believed, the Human-Andrians were new specie all together. And it appeared, if that was true, it was for the better of both the Human and Andrian species that the Humans survive.

The eleven members of The Council unanimously agreed to return to earth's solar system. They must find the traitor Klaxo and his followers before he destroyed all life on the planet earth. The order was given to prepare for intergalactic travel.

CHAPTER 42
THE INVITATION

Emily was in the group area listening to the various captives retell their abduction stories. Each individual never varied so much as a period or coma as they rehashed their experiences. For each of them it was sheer terror. Klaxo and his minions had enjoyed causing as much fear and pain as possible. Emily thought, "I suppose that is the way we humans pretty much treat lab animals."

Blain entered the area very quietly, listening to the Humans retell their abduction stories. He was very much aware of the sheer terror that Klaxo and Zelegark had caused. He was not proud of their methods which were driven by hate. He thought back to how he had retrieved Emily. It had been so easy, so natural. Was Emily truly that much different from the other humans? She was certainly afraid initially. She even tried to run but tripped on a root and fell backwards injuring her arm. He did not really force her to come with him. He had reasoned with her. Of course she had telepathic skills the other humans totally lacked.

And, unlike Emily, the Human Aaron was totally panicked. His retrieval of Aaron was orchestrated with patience and finesse. Of course he could not get away. Where could he possibly have gone? The little escape pod would have provided enough air for a nice slow death before becoming a coffin. Yes he was scared. Who would not be scared when one is being abducted by and unknown entity in the middle of space? Even though Aaron did not have active telepathic skills at the time, he would not have been able to communicate. But since Aaron had been on the intergalactic spacecraft, his telepathic skills have developed tenfold.

Emily "felt" Blain looking at her, much in the same way as she had "felt" him looking at her during their first encounter. Looking around, Emily saw Blain standing back against the wall hidden by the foliage from the ten captives. Her eyes locked onto his and he smiled.

"Hello Emily. If you have some time I would like to visit with you for a few minutes". Of course the greeting and request was not verbal. Neither was Emily's response. "I will meet you outside." Blain turned and quietly left the room unnoticed by the group. Emily got up and excused herself saying she would be right back. She too exited the room. The ten Humans continued telling their abduction tales.

Emily had not seen or spoken to Blain since he brought her on board the intergalactic craft. She had wondered where he was and what he was up too, and, what was his status within the milieu of the intergalactic space travelers?

Out in the passageway, Blain was standing by one of the two person transport lifts. Emily approached Blain and extended her hand for a handshake human fashion. "Hello Blain. I thought that perhaps we left you on Earth, we have not seen you anywhere around here." Emily gave him one of her crooked grins.

Blain smiled back and taking her hand in his, he returned her human handshake. I have been kind of busy trying to locate Klaxo and his group. They are hiding somewhere in your solar system. It is really quiet large when one is looking for such a few individuals and they do not want to be found."

As of yet Emily was unaware of Klaxo's plan to destroy the Human species from the earth. She believed they were just responsible for kidnapping the ten humans on the ship and holding them captive before delivering them to the intergalactic space ship. She did not know about the other eight Human-Andrian Hybrids. She was unaware her parents were murdered by them nor did she fully understand her role in the drama being played out or what stakes were involved. As of yet, she believed she was just an above average gifted Human that could do unexplainable things. She was unaware that fate of the Human species hung in the balance and would not bode well for them should Klaxo not be caught to stand before the "Council of Yield" and be judged for his crime of treason.

"That and a couple of other reasons is why I wanted to see you. Actually I wanted to invite you into our "home", as you would say. I have a son and a daughter who think you have horns and fangs and walk around saying, "Duh", all the time. I guess on earth this would be construed as an invitation to dinner."

Emily was taken aback, totally by surprise! Since her arrival, and the other captive's arrival before her, they

SEED OF HOPE

have been kept totally separate except in a classroom setting. For the most part, the experience from the Andrians point of view was one pretty much similar to humans being on exhibit in a zoo. Emily did not care much for their attitude, but then whose space ship was it anyway?

"And what would your wife have to say about that? After all, I am one hot earth girl!" Emily smiled up at Blain with the joke. "I imagine she would have a say in an invitation to another women to have dinner in your home."

Blains response surprised her. "I have had several consorts. Right now I have only two. They are not "wives'" in your sense of relationships. Because we are such a rather small isolated group, our DNA and genome pool must be managed to a greater degree than what would be required on earth". Looking down smiling at her, Blain said, "You do not need to worry about any jealous wife trying to space you! Besides I think you would make a nice addition to our family."

Emily smiled up at Blain pleased with the invitation. She did not know if Blain was serious or not but she was not too sure if she would enjoy being part of that kind of family relationship. As of yet she had not had the opportunity to make any kind of assessment of her own regarding the Andrian culture. So far, other than Blain, she had personally met the geneticist, Flata, and Breveka, the specie group dynamics intercessor, a long title for group sociologist. "I would love to visit your quarters and meet your family."

CHAPTER 43
SELF DELUSION

Klaxo was becoming impatient with Zelegark and the group he had sent to retrieve the prisoners. Ever the self-delusional, with a superiority complex times "infinite space", Klaxo was beginning to disdain the stupid Humans even more. He was becoming obsessed; which, if the truth be known, he was well past the point of no return. He had become so blinded by his greed for earth and power that to view himself and his followers as being on anything other than a holiday, never entered his mind. And, his mind was substantial. He was indeed, even superior to his birth mate younglings by the Andrians standard. Unfortunately the pathology of an extraordinary mind was equally and diametrically opposite to a well-ordered mind. Thus, his self-delusional fantasies totally eclipsed his judgment, once again, most fortunate for the Earth Alliance. He simply did not even consider any additional protective options.

Thinking to himself, Klaxo believed there was no way for the "Council of Yield", to find him and his cohorts on Jupiter's moon, Europa. He had prepared well, carefully. He had sought out those likeminded as he and proposed his plan to thwart the, "Council of Yield's", plan to enhance humans. He believed that they, the Andrians, needed the planet to survive.

SEED OF HOPE

The decision to set up their base on Jupiter's moon Europa was a masterful stroke. The moon was a dirty ice ball. The eccentric orbit caused great magnetic field induced tidal forces on the ice covered moon, thus the frozen surface cracked continually. The top surface was eternally frozen but the inside remained liquefied. The tidal effect generated intense heat and steam which forced its way to the surface causing long rifts across the moon's ice frozen surface.

But fortunately for Klaxo, Andrian science had located a large geological formation of a rock shelf just below the surface ice and thus they built their base on that foundation. They then covered the entrance with clear nano graphite constructs with light bending technology. This technology rendered the entrance invisible from space.

Their science enabled them to break the water molecules down to generate breathable oxygen. The domes contained the oxygen and the steam provided plenty of heat and drinking water. Their machines also controlled the strong and flexible gravity field so that the field on their base was consistent and walking was not a problem. It was not exactly a home away from home, but, it was a good beginning. Soon they would call the planet Earth home.

Klaxo was very pleased with himself, if only Zelegark would hurry up and return! Then he could develop the biologicals to cleanse the stupid humans from face of his new earth! Klaxo unconsciously wrung his hands in anticipation.

CHAPTER 44
MORE ENEMIES

Captain Swenson was wearing an alien heavy armor suit retrieved from one of the three saucers. He had enough heavy armor for three men, himself included. The other nine commandoes were wearing the alien light armor coveralls. It was much better stopping ballistic projectiles than the current military armor. The earth's military armor was superior in camouflage, not so good at stopping projectiles.

The research and development departments was working twenty-four hours, seven days a week, in an effort at back engineering the nano polymers woven into the fabric of the coveralls. They have had some success at this endeavor. However, so far, the pliable ceramic heavy armor was beyond earth science abilities to unravel, even with the help of two of the hybrid young people assisting in the research. The research and development people working on this wanted Dr. Abbott's expertise on the project but his services with the saucers received a higher priority.

Captain Swenson watched two saucers land; the third saucer hovered off to the side at a high altitude. From his camouflaged ceramic command post, he watched as six aliens exited their saucer. This time they were somewhat more cautious. One alien from each saucer was outfitted

SEED OF HOPE

in heavy body armor. The other four aliens were wearing the light armor coveralls.

Captain Swenson thought, "This was not going to be any picnic!"

The six aliens reached the rear door of the facility. As before, they used an electronic device to open the repaired door.

After the last alien had entered the building and closed the door behind them, Captain Swenson pushed a button on his control. The floor of the room divided in the middle quickly swinging downward with the sides hitting the lower level walls with a resounding crash. At the same time huge ceiling fans blew downward. There were large fans at the lower level sucking air out of the upper room and blowing down a long passageway tunnel creating a suction that literally whisked the aliens downward. The lower level had a divider forming an upside down "V", or an apex designed to divide the aliens into two groups.

The aliens, again caught by surprise, fell into the lower room onto the curved surface of the outer walls. These walls were treated with nano oil which made them super slick allowing no purchase and hastened their fall into the divided room separating the aliens into two groups As the aliens landed near the bottom into their respective cells, they found themselves adhering to the floor and walls with a new crowd control sticky glue. They were stuck in whatever position they landed down the twenty foot slide, on their back or on their side. Either way, not one of them could lift a weapon.

After about fifteen minutes, four commandos and two young hybrids exited the building. Four were wearing armored coveralls and two was wearing the battle armor. They split into two groups of three, each group entering a saucer. The hovering saucer had been distracted at that moment by several jets which were headed directly for their position. As soon as the two groups on the ground were safely in the saucers, the jets were ordered to veer away and leave the area. Both saucers lifted from the ground and joined the third. All three saucers left for the vicinity of the moon after the building was blasted.

Captain Swenson breathed a sigh of relief as the saucers lifted from the ground and joined the other saucer. "So far everything was working perfectly", he thought. Then, using his newly constructed tunnel, he exited his camouflaged bunker and quickly jogged a downward slope until he entered the chamber containing the trapped aliens.

One wall of the chamber was nano plastic, one-way mirror, manufactured in such a way that those entombed within saw only a black wall, thus providing little information as possible to the enemy. All six of the aliens were stuck in various positions on the forty-five degree slopes. One was head down with legs splayed, head turned toward the one-way mirror. He was glaring at the nano mirror with hate and malice in his eyes. The two aliens in body armor had super strength, thus, nozzles were turned upon them that sprayed thick foam like glue that completely entombed them in place. They still had their

SEED OF HOPE

blasters therefore it was important that they were totally immobilized.

Captain Swenson then pushed another button on his control panel. A knock out gas filled the enclosure and four of the six aliens were fast asleep. The two aliens in the body armor were not affected by the gas; they remained conscious and cognizant of their surroundings. Because of this, Captain Swenson knew they were extremely dangerous. He would have to be careful with them and come up with a way to extricate them without having to kill them, or, they, killing any more commandos. Captain Swenson then activated the evacuation switch. Both containers detached from their magnetic holding positions and were forced smoothly along a long tunnel by hydraulic pressure, pretty much like the money tubes of old in the earlier banking transport system.

The aliens, in addition to being glued to the walls of their container cells, were incommunicado because their communications were jammed. Having had the good fortune of obtaining other full battle armor suits from the earlier captured saucers, the Research and Development group learned how to immobilize the armor and jam their communications, thus even though the two aliens in the armor suits were conscious and aware, they were blind, deaf, and, inoperative. Captain Swenson smiled at how easily they had entombed the aliens into their "Burr Rabbit" trap. They had captured and whisked the aliens away within eight minutes of them entering the prison hospital. In fact, they were evacuated before the other teams entered their saucers and lifted from the ground.

Earlier they had all agreed that in order to put on a good show, the team leader would blast the building to atomized particles from her newly acquired saucer. This was done with such efficiency and effectiveness that there was nothing left of the two story structure except a large black smoking hole about seventy five feet deep. After all, even though the aliens exhibited a higher intelligence, surly even they would not be so stupid as to return to the same fly trap three times. Thus, the decision to destroy the building appeared to be a judicious one.

CHAPTER 45
INTERGALACTIC HOMES

Blain escorted Emily thru the intergalactic carrier on a maglift transport vehicle with standing room only, for two. Seats were considered undesirable in inter-ship travel as exercise was paramount in maintaining strength conditioning. The carrier had many areas with its own gravitational field which could be adjusted according to need. However, exercise was still a necessity.

The maglift transport traveled about fifteen minutes before stopping perpendicular before a long passageway. Upon exiting the maglift, Emily walked with Blain for about fifty yards, passing hatchway entrances on both sides.

Stopping in front of one of the hatchways Blain looked at Emily and said, "Welcome to our home Emily." Opening the hatchway door he escorted Emily inside carefully closing the hatch behind him.

Emily did not know what to expect but she did not expect to see what she saw. She found herself in a long clear ceramic glass tube open on both sides with a ceiling about twelve feet above her head. There were several winding staircases placed intermittently along the passageway ascending into what Emily believed to be private sleeping quarters. At the end of the passageway, there was a large bulbous room completely of ceramic glass.

Walking toward the clear ceramic glass she was mesmerized with a view of uncountable stars strewn like diamonds across a black velvet scroll. There appeared to be a galaxy cluster in the distance. She reached up and placed her hand on the ceramic glass, the glass felt cold and shimmered beneath her touch.

From behind her Emily heard a new voice. "You must not touch the force field! Everyone knows that."

Removing her hand from the force field Emily turned around. She was facing a young female child who appeared to be at least ten to eleven earth years of age. The child wore a frown on her face. Emily bowed her head and said, "I apologize. I have never seen anything so beautiful in my life." She then greeted the child in Andrian fashion, the child being the greater, she the lesser. The child like children everywhere, accepted acknowledgement that she, the child, was right, and Emily was wrong, and seemed to be mollified. Emily followed the child around the circular pattern of the large bulbous living area. Looking thru the ceramic glass again Emily saw hundreds of spires extending from the outer skin of the intergalactic carrier disappearing around the curvature of the outer structure. At the end of each spire there was a bulbous tip which evidently served as the inhabitants living quarters.

There were several chair loungers spaced throughout the living area. Each lounger had a small table with some kind of fruit in a decorative diamond bowl. Standing in the middle of the room was two Andrian women and a young male child that appeared to be about eleven or twelve earth years of age. The young girl stood off to the side. Blain was behind the women.

Blain verbalized, "Emily, these two ladies are my consorts, Sharla and Chandra. To his two consorts he said, "This is the Human female I have told you about. Her name is Emily. Emily, you have already met my daughter, Hanlee. And, this is my son Jawane". Neither the women nor the children said a word. They were all very quiet, each making an assessment of the first Human they have ever met in person.

Emily quietly bowed her head and greeted them in Andrian fashion, the lessor to the greater. Telepathically Emily said, "Thank you for inviting me into your home, it is very gracious of you." Both women quickly glanced at one another then the one who appeared to be the oldest said, "I am Sharla. It is unprecedented to have anyone in our living quarters. Our living quarters are sacred to us. Personal space is highly coveted."

Emily again bowed her head in acknowledgement and said, "I do understand. I am humbled by your acceptance of me in your personal space."

Sharla pointed to a lounge recliner and said, "Come. Sit!" Each of them sat in a recliner positioned in a circular fashion, each able to enjoy a view of the cosmos above and to the side and also each other. They all stared at Emily. Emily felt like she was definitely a bug specimen under a microscope, or perhaps the fly in the ointment, depending on one's point of view.

Chandra then said, "Blain has told us a lot about you. It seems you and the male Human is the exceptions for your specie. You are the only ones that can speak telepathically and you seem to have intelligence above average for your specie."

Emily chose her words carefully. "We are able to determine ones worth differently from you. I have never thought much about what kind of mores, rules, and regulations would be required in a star faring society such as yours. The sacrifices you make must be many."

Blain smiled. The women and children stared. The women were thinking, "This Human women must be mentally deficient in some way even though her telepathic skills seem almost equal to our own. How could one possibly think any different than they? And any form of self-importance exhibited by Humans stem from their inability to acquiesce to the greater good."

Jawane, the young boy said, "We have had the other ten humans in our class. They are blind, lame and stupid. They can only speak with verbal words and they cannot even comprehend spherical math."

Emily responded, "It is true that the ten humans you speak of are not telepaths, very few of us are. And, as far as the math is concerned, the Humans on the earth are not yet ready for space time travel; we have no need for spherical math."

Hanlee the young girl said, "They even refuse to eliminate the blind and the lame ones. They are using up precious resources. Even when the controls were going to do it for them, they all became very rebellious and dangerous. Then a couple of, I guess, "Normals", even volunteered to be eliminated instead of the blind and the lame ones. What good would that do? The useless blind and lame ones would still be using up precious resources!"

Emily looked at Hanlee and smiled. "What you have observed is absolutely the very best in Human behavior that we could possibly show you. I am very proud of them. You must try and think what your lives would be like if you were not limited in space and resources. Try to understand why you think the way you do. You travel among the stars! You see different worlds! You discover new life forms! But, for this privilege, you pay a very high price in personal sacrifice! I do not think I could do it for a very long time. I love seeing the things I have been privileged to see. I feel blessed to sit here with you in your home and I feel comfortable doing so."

Each of the Andrians could feel and see the fervor with which Emily shared her convictions. They were all moved and truly liked the young Human women. However, they were all shocked by what she blurted out next.

"I think it would be fun to have you come and visit me on earth! You could all stay in my home. My parents left me a lake house that I have never used. It is sort of isolated so you could get accustomed to being on earth before you run into any more people! Wow, we could really have a good time!"

Sharla got her voice and composure first and responded, The "Council of Yield", would never allow that. I am the ships chief fusion physicist! And, I am primarily responsible for the younglings!"

Emily enthusiastic response of, "Bring them with you!" elicited looks of terror on the two women's faces. Blain's face even blanched white. The children smiled big smiles thinking of the possible adventures as all children do. It was truly a thought that had never entered their mind or psychic.

Blain watched the exchanges between his consorts, children, and Emily. They were becoming more animated. He was caught off guard with Emily obviously sincere invitation to be her guest in her home. As of yet Emily did not know the gravity of her species situation. It was becoming apparent that soon she must be informed; the sooner the better. He would talk to the "Council of Yield", tomorrow.

The rest of the evening passed with pleasantries and small talk, Emily loved giving the children a challenge and said, "Duh", several times, and placed her hands next to her ears with one finger extended in the caricature of horns, each time eliciting a giggle from the children. The women were amazed with how easily she disarmed the children, and, if the truth be known, they themselves. All the family liked Emily. Blain knew he had made the right decision in bringing her here to his home. Initially he was not so sure and had avoided contact with her by design.

CHAPTER 46
SAHARA

As preplanned, Lt. Sasha Palangin had her genius young assistant laser a short micro burst message report telling the alien occupied saucer that all the hybrids had been destroyed along with the twelve hospital assistants. The captured aliens advised, during the interrogation process by Space Intelligence that the Andrian aliens always referred to humans as "The Humans", or, mostly, "The Stupid Humans". The "Human-Andrians", were always referred to as, "The Hybrids". Naming the groups this way allowed the aliens to depersonalize the human species thus easier to destroy. That is assuming of course, that they had the same values for life as humans.

Lt. Palangin sent a laser message to the aliens stating that they learned where Zelegark was being held captive by "The Stupid Humans". She further advised she did not know for sure how he was captured but one of the" Stupid Humans", at the hospital had told them, upon the pain of death, that Zelegark and the other two soldiers were asleep when they were attacked at the hospital; thus having been taken by surprise by the "Stupid Human's", military, the two soldiers were killed while defending Zelegark and Zelegark was taken prisoner. Oh yes, all the prisoners and humans were eliminated before we left. We just blew the building as a nice finishing touch!"

Having given the coordinates of Zelegark's supposed whereabouts, Sasha took the lead to fly to the pre-arranged coordinates in the middle of the Sahara desert. Upon arriving at the coordinates, Sasha sent a laser message to the saucer with the aliens telling them to dress in full battle armor and search what appeared what to be an old aircraft hangar assuring them that it was a secret base. She further stated they would stand guard above the area to take out any "Stupid Humans", that might be in the area. As after all, this was one of their secret bases.

As directed, the aliens landed their Saucer in the exact coordinates provided. Donning their battle armor they exited the saucer, walked to the building and entered thru a partially opened door. As soon as the aliens had gone from view, two commandoes and a young woman crawled from a camouflaged ceramic bunker and ran ten feet to the saucer, lowered the lift and were soon aboard the craft. Once they assumed their respective positions, the young Human-Andrian female took control of the saucer craft and smoothly lifted about fifty feet into the air, then shot skyward out of view. When the saucer had reached the designated altitude the other two saucers, also piloted by young Human-Andrians, approached their coordinates and maintained watch over the area.

The three aliens carefully searched the building but they were unable to locate or detect any signs of Zelegark. The building was obviously abandoned. They exited the building thru the door they had entered but they did not see their saucer. The three aliens at not seeing their saucer believed they must have somehow become confused and exited the wrong door. They reinterred the hanger and crossed the wide hanger area to the opposite door. Again they could not see their saucer. They were beginning to get a stomach churning inclination that somehow, something must be wrong. But of course, that could not be possible. They then walked around the entire structure. It appeared they had lost their saucer. "Our fellows must be playing some kind of joke on us by taking our saucer", stated team leader three.

The alien designated as team leader three-pointed his laser communicator skyward and said, "Team leader three to team leader one." There was no response. Again, the alien tried to make contact; "Team leader three to team leader one ". Team leader three was now becoming uneasy. The alien tried to contact them again; "Team leader three to… team leader two, come in team leader two."

On board the three saucer crafts the commandoes laughed quietly. Sasha was smiling brightly as she heard the tension begin to stress the alien's voice. Finally, keying her mike Sasha said, "Team leader one to team leader three, go ahead." It seemed to her that military protocol must be universal, so to speak.

Sasha keyed the mike again as there was silence on the other end. "This is tem leader one to team leader three. Go ahead team leader three".

"Team leader three stammered to his two companions, "That is a women's voice! We did not did not have any women in our group. How can she read what we say to the three saucers?

The other two aliens looked at one another and had a look of disbelief on their faces. "It appears, Team Leader Three, that we have somehow, some way, been duped by the Stupid Humans."

Team leader three felt bile come up into his throat. He thought he was going to throw up. This, in and of itself, was a brand new experience. Team Leader three, talking more to himself then to his two fellow assassins, said, "What happened to Team Leader One, and what about Team Leader Two? What happened to Zelegark? He was invincible! Surely they were not all taken prisoner!"

Team Leader Three looked around. The hot earth sunburned down on their armor suits. He could see nothing but sand dunes as far as his eyes could see, even more never ending sand with the enhanced vision of the combat armor. They heard and felt an explosion behind them. The hanger structure had been blown up and now there was not an opportunity to use it for whatever meager shelter it would provide. They did not bring any rations of food and water, after all, to what purpose? Team Leader Three then remembered his training. It was standard procedure to have food and water available upon leaving the saucers. It was elementary teaching; even younglings knew it was required. Team Leader Three was brought up abruptly from his musings with the receipt of more communications from the Stupid Humans, again, that stupid female no less!

"Andrian personnel, be advised you are prisoners of war. If you give up peacefully you will receive all the rights and privileges of prisoners of war as accorded by the Old Earth Geneva convention. If you choose not to submit to our demands you will be obliterated!" The women's tone had become menacing.

Lt. Sasha Palagin continued, "I like our new toys. I wonder what this laser gun will do to your body armor. We do need to test it on the armor to evaluate its effectiveness. So, do not think you are going to escape." In a chilling cold voice she further said, "Exit your suited armor or I will push the button..., Now!"

The three aliens looked at each other. Leader Three stated, "This is only temporary. When Klaxo hears of this he will come for us. Do as the Stupid Human female commands." The three aliens exited their body armor. It was scorching hot. The air burned in their lungs. Their eyes were almost completely closed to protect them from the glare. Their feet quickly became burning hot as the heated sand encased their lightly shoed feet. In effect, it was nothing like any of them had ever experienced before.

"Team Leader One! That would be me!" Sasha exuded flush excitement on the communicator. "Team Leader One to Base!"

"Base to Team Leader One, go ahead", responded Lt. Swenson, smiling into the communicator.

"Team Leader One, to Base, The packages are waiting for pickup!

"Well done Lieutenant. That was a job well done. Transport team should be arriving within ten minutes."

Approximately fifteen minutes later the Andrians heard a droning noise in the distance. Off to the horizon they saw a spec. The spec turned in to an antiquated airplane with two large propellers pulling the plane thru the air. As the plane came nearer into view, five specs emerged from the back of the plane. Each spec bloomed into a large white upside down bowl that collected the air and slowed the specs down. Soon the aliens understood that the specs were men dangling on strings suspended beneath the large white upside down bowl. The men landed close enough to see that they were wearing Andrian combat support coveralls. The Andrians also noticed the military precision as the group of five men spread out into a defensive line. As they got closer one of the Stupid Humans said, "Welcome to Earth".

Each Andrian was handed a pair of heavy baggy coveralls which they put on. Then, they were fitted with a wide webbed harness that crisscrossed at the chest and formed a seat around the legs at the crotch. A long rope with a snap hook was then attached to the back ring of one alien and to the chest ring of the other. They were then seated in a row with Leader Three in the front with a spacing of about twenty feet apart.

The aliens heard a loud hissing noise behind them and upon turning around to look they saw a large red balloon object rising into the sky. The balloon object had a long webbed rope attached to the bottom of it, and then it extended to the back of the webbing of the last alien crewman in the row.

Leader three turned and looked at the last crewman and smirked. "Those Humans are so stupid, they are truly aptly named. They actually think that balloon is going

SEED OF HOPE

to float us out of here!" All three aliens had a long belly laugh.

Pretty soon they again heard a drone in the distance. The drone was accompanied by a spec. The drone grew louder, the spec turned into another old airplane. Leader Three looked on with interest. The Stupid Humans were grinning at him, having overheard his comment. The commando in charge leaned down to the alien known as Leader Three, and smiled at him.

Leader Three looked at the Stupid Human mystified as to his meaning. Looking back at the plane he noticed it had lost altitude and was flying very low, close to the ground, and, it was headed straight toward them! Leader Three and the other two aliens looked on. They began to get somewhat nervous as the plane did not deviate from its flight path. Then Leader Three, looked up at the balloon floating about one hundred feet up in the air then looked back at the airplane. He then observed a large "Y" shaped appendage attached to the nose of the aircraft. Enlightenment flashed thru his brain as his astonished horror emulsified into comprehension!

"No! Surely not!" screamed Team Leader Three.

The lead commando saw the aliens astonished face and leaned down to Team Leader Three and said. "This is what we Stupid Humans call, "Beam me up Scotty!"

The plane flew swiftly overhead with a loud roar, collecting the webbing held aloft by the oversized balloon. The three aliens were jerked aloft as the plane passed overhead; their screaming drowned out the roar of the aircraft engines! Soon they were three specs swinging wildly behind the swiftly departing aircraft, yet their screams could still be heard diminishing like the sound of a train whistle as it left the vicinity.

All five commandoes had tears streaming from their eyes covering their faces as they laughed so hard that none of them could stand. They fell to the ground howling beating the sand with their fist and rolling in the sand! Earlier they had set up a satellite cam to record the extraction. The same response was achieved whenever and wherever the video was shown to the rest of the commando units worldwide.

Lt. Sasha Palangin ordered the saucer to land and pick up the five commandoes who were still on the ground laughing and crying. Another saucer landed and retrieved the three armored suits. Lt. Palangin had planned and executed the extraction. She had designed the operation to terrify, breakdown, and demoralize the alien commandoes. Sasha grinned to herself patting herself on her back thinking, "Well done!"

CHAPTER 47
TEDDY BEAR

Emily had basically become part of Blaine's family and spent a lot of time with his two consorts and two children. When Emily was not busy seeing to the needs of the ten captives or conducting her own research and study, she could most often be found in his quarters. She loved the children and they loved her. However, instead of her teaching the children, the role was reversed. The children taught her. Emily was an eager and astute student.

Emily soaked up as much knowledge as she possibly could; the children, being eager teachers, having never been in such a role before, never tired of showing Emily new things, especially regarding astronomy.

Sharla and Chandra enjoyed Emily's presence, it freed up their time to participate in other projects. Emily had suggested, and Sharla had accepted, though be it somewhat reluctantly, Emily's suggestion that she allow Robert Aaron to observe her as she made her rounds inspecting the fusion drives on the intergalactic carrier. Robert had expressed an interest in the drives and wanted to learn how they worked. He proved to be an apt student and soon Sharla looked forward to his presence as he accompanied her on her inspection rounds. He also intrigued her as she looked more closely at his physic. He was not built any different than Andrian men but strange thoughts were beginning to form in her mind. They were thoughts that she had never had with any Andrian male. That part of her mind she kept absolutely and carefully shielded. Unknown to her, Andrian male pheromones were diluted to enable a more efficient specie population control. With Robert being in his prime and never having had sexual relations, his testosterone levels were off the charts thus his pheromones were strong and potent. It appeared that there were soon to be interesting developments.

Emily had made two small stuffy teddy bears and had given them to Hanlee and Jawayne as gifts. Giving gifts of material things was not a practice of the Andrians. Again, it was a matter of material requirements verses utility. The children were totally mystified.

Hanlee intoned, "What is a teddy bear and what utility does it serve?" a totally mature response from a ten year old.

Emily responded carefully and took the teddy bear and held it to her bosom rocking it back and forth and said to the bear, "I love you". "Sometimes earth children become scared. Maybe they lost their mother; maybe they fell down and skinned their knee. It may be that you are just afraid of the dark. It just makes them feel better to imagine someone or something is with them. Then the earth child will hold the teddy bear close and say, "I love you"."

Both Hanlee and Jawayne listened to Emily very carefully. They did not understand the utility or use of the teddy bear but they considered the practice and explanation a firsthand lesson on human behavior from a real Human; thus a very beneficial learning tool. Because they loved Emily, they both dutifully clutched their respective teddy bears to their bosoms' and intoned, "I love you'.

Since Andrian family structures were different from Humans, they did not understand how important it was for an earth child to lose a parent. Their family units were organized for the greater good of their specie. Sexual mores were braided around concepts of need with the least expenditure of sexual desires. The desires were intentionally muted. Population control was extant upon expendable resources. These resources were fiercely guarded. Fortunately for Hanlee and Jawayne, neither of them had to experience any degree of separation from a parental figure. However, in the Andrian culture, should that had been the case, so be it. There were to be no tears.

Emily was glad she had made the teddy bears for Jawayne and Hanlee. It gave her a feeling of belonging in that she could give the children something so… "Human". They could not relate to what she had told them and she hoped they would never experience loss. However, from personal experience she knew loss was inevitable and always seemingly just around the corner. Again she thought how much fun it would be to take Blain and his family home with her to visit the Earth.

CHAPTER 48
RELIEF

Once again Admiral Cleary stood before the assembled group. However, this time there was a large presence of Space Defense Commandoes assembled along one wall and also in the back. Seated on the dais behind Admiral Cleary, were Commander Johnson, Captain Swenson, and a young women that most of them had never seen before. However, Agents Jessop and Reese immediately recognized her as the women in the Blaizon University sweat shirt that gave Commander Johnson a package the day they had gone to Defense Intelligence to deliver their evidence of Emily Smith's abduction. She too was wearing the uniform of The Space Defense Commandos. The ten young Human-Andrian Hybrids sat on the front row either side of, The President. Special Agents, Jessop and Reese were sitting more to the front as their normal seats in the rear was taken up with other government, industry, and military officials, thus their easy recognition of the young women. She again caught Agent Jessop looking at her and again she winked at him. And as before, Jessop turned red in the face. And also again as before, Reese gave Jessop a light elbow jab to his ribs.

Admiral Cleary cleared his throat in an effort to stop the chatter and focus attention to the front. When all was quiet he began. "We now have in our possession six alien

SEED OF HOPE

saucers and seventeen alien captives. The captures came at a high price. We are going to honor the five Space Commandoes who died in the initial capture of Zelegark at a future date. Their sacrifice will not go unnoted."

This statement came as a stone cold shock to everyone in the room except the commandoes as no one was told about the specifics of how Zelegark had been captured. Jessop and Reese looked at one another with a pain of loss in their eyes as they have been one with Commandoes since their induction into the intelligence group.

Admiral Cleary continued. "What we have learned is that the group that governs the community of space travelers is called the "Council of Yield". They have developed a council of twelve members, four each from their respective intergalactic ships. There are about five thousand occupants per each ship, or a total of about fifteen thousand individuals. The adults are engaged in scientific research and they travel the galaxies looking for habitable planets. They, meaning their species, have been intergalactic travelers since before man was on the face of the earth. Because resources in space are limited, stringent controls have been necessary to keep their population stable. All of their individuals have been born on the ships. Very few of the occupants have ever set foot on a planet. Most of those who have been off the ships have been their military groups. Their personal accommodations are limited to about nine square feet per traveler. They can adjust their gravity fields so their common areas are not restricted to a flat surface. Families have about one thousand square feet of space; the personal space is included within this area."

"The most prestigious and influential individual on the craft is the geneticist. This individual basically decides who lives and who dies. There is absolutely no room for the weak and the infirm; resources are reserved for those who are healthy and can produce to the benefit of the group as a whole. Personally, to me, it does not sound like Shangri-La and it seems like a high price to pay for flittering around the universe. Our scientific community needs to study their model and see if it is applicable to human space travel."

"The source of our problem is that there are those within their group that covet our world. Many of their home worlds are overcrowded as is their ships, thus, the eternal quest for new worlds to inhabit. I think I can understand why this character Klaxo, a former member of the "Council of Yield", and the leader of the defectors from the ships, wants to possess the earth. However, the age old problem of ethics looms its head and some individuals choose to go outside of the mores and constraints of society to get what is coveted; in this case, what is coveted, is the planet, our planet."

"We, as specie, are seen as inferior, and not deemed worthy to occupy this good earth. I guess in some ways, they are pretty much like us. We most always seem to want what someone else has and we will do whatever it takes, and justify whatever it takes, to obtain that which is coveted. However, in this case, billions of souls are at stake."

"Now, that was the bad side. Let us discuss the good

SEED OF HOPE

side. We have within this group of alien space travelers, individuals that have gone to great lengths to help improve our human condition. Instead of blasting us from the face of the earth, the "Council of Yield", decided to make an upgrade, so to speak; or, if you will, a human 2.0 ". There was laughter around the room; it helped to ease the tension that had come with the knowledge that there was a group of humanoid extraterrestrials that wanted to eliminate the human species. "The results of this experiment are the fine ten young people sitting with The President, on the front row. Ladies and gentlemen, meet our new and improved, Human 2.0!" There was laughter and cheering accompanied with a standing ovation as the ten young people stood up facing the audience taking a bow!

"It appears that our ten fine young men and women are above average in intelligence and abilities in solving difficult problems. All of our alien captives, every single one, say that… and I quote, "Ten younglings were inserted into our population". What that means is, if your care to really think about it, is that …this intergalactic, star fairing humanoid specie, truly believed, that these ten, fine young people, can be a viable solution to the saving of our specie instead of the extermination of our specie. That in and of itself is a very sobering thought."

Admiral Cleary looked around the room. It was very quiet. "The "Andrians", that is what they call themselves, cared enough about us as a specie, to try and create an advancement in our evolutionary development. They wanted to do this to help us avoid our own self destruction, and the destruction to the planet."

"But, Ladies and Gentleman, there is a paradox. All the Andrian captives insist that ten and only ten younglings were inserted into the womb of their human earth mothers. If that is true, where did the other two genius children come from? I am speaking of Emily Smith and Robert Aaron. There is no doubt they exhibit the same, off the charts, mental characteristics of our fine ten young people here in this room.

Agents Jessop and Reese looked at one another surprise on their faces, Jessop mouthed silently to Reese, "How did we miss that!" Reese mouthed back, "Beats me!"

Captain Swenson was watching the byplay of his two detectives smiling to himself, even his intrepid two detectives missed that amazing salient fact, and they all had until one of the young people had brought it to the attention of Captain Swenson who had presented the information to a small group of people earlier.

Admiral Cleary continued, "Emily and Robert were definitely singled out and abducted by the Andrians. Emily's parents were murdered. Robert's parents and sisters are fine. They are in protective custody and have been apprised of the situation and receive daily reports detailing any new information. Our ten young people were definitely singled out by Klaxo. Their parents were murdered and they were incarcerated by Zelegark and his assassins. And, in addition to Emily and Robert we have learned of ten additional captives taken by Zelegark and delivered to the intergalactic carrier spacecraft in lieu of

SEED OF HOPE

the younglings. We have no idea who they are or where they are from. They were delivered to the spacecraft with the intention of destroying the efforts of the "Council of Yield". Oh, and if you have not figured it out yet, Klaxo is a renegade member of The Council of Yield."

"I imagine in the social structure of the Andrians, Klaxo and his one hundred and fifty followers are considered traitors; therefore, he has nowhere to go but here. He has nothing to lose. He and his followers are very dangerous. Right now, the only thing standing in their way is us."

"We have been so fortunate with the past three operations, notwithstanding the loss of five of our own. We have seventeen prisoners, six saucers, nine battle armor suits, and twenty pair of armored coveralls. In the way of armaments, we have twenty-four heavy blasters and forty laser handguns. We have numerous scanners and other small devices that we have turned over to research and development labs to determine their function. And of course, our greatest of all assets is our fine ten young people on the front row." There was a round of applause with that statement. "So far, our primary weapon has been the alien's blinded self-delusion of superiority. Fortunately for us, on every encounter they under estimated our resourcefulness and, I guess, our intelligence. Because of their errors in judgment, we now have the capability to go to Jupiter's moon, Europa. That is where the alien's base is located. The base is on the surface with lower levels being constructed daily. It is camouflaged and nearly impossible to see. However, we have the exact coordinates."

Admiral Cleary became very grave. "In our planning we have decided the first thing we need to do is go to Jupiter's moon Europa, and capture or destroy every single one of their saucer craft. We cannot leave them with any means of escape. Second, we must capture or kill the one hundred and fifty or so aliens on the moon. Third, we must board and retrieve our twelve citizens being held captive on one of three of the intergalactic cruisers." At that point, Admiral Cleary made a military about face and returned to his seat. There was absolute silence in the room. The despair was palatable.

Commander Bob Johnson then took the floor. "Thank you Admiral Cleary. In light of the gravity of this situation, it is imperative that we plan our next move very carefully. It could well be our last. Therefore, I am going to call upon Captain Swenson, who is in charge of mission planning, to further advise us of our course of action." Commander Johnson made an about face and returned to his seat.

Captain Swenson came to the podium. "Thank you Admiral Cleary. Thank you Commander Johnson. It is important that we review some of the operations on the ground at boot level. It is imperative to keep the enemy guessing what we are doing. For this I call upon Lieutenant Sasha Palangin." Captain Swenson made an about face and returned to his seat.

Lt. Palangin stood, squared her corner and marched to the podium. She squared her corner again and faced the audience. Because of her short stature, the podium was electrically lowered to allow her to see and be seen. She was not smiling. Even so, she was absolutely beautiful. She was petite in stature and her blue eyes stared into the crowed without blinking.

Agent Reese looked at Agent Jessop. Leaning over, she whispered, "These military brass types are really anal. Why don't they get to the point? What is coming next, the cook? It really sounds like were screwed."

Agent Jessop, always the stoic, replied, "Yep, you got that right."

Lieutenant Palangin turned and faced the seated officers and stated, "Thank you Admiral Cleary. Thank you Commander Johnson. Thank you Captain Swenson. Then once again she turned and faced the audience who by now looked somewhat bored with the military protocol.

The commandoes along the wall knew what was coming next. They enjoyed watching the civilians looking confused and apprehensive.

Lieutenant Palangin continued, also looking very serious and concerned with her brow furrowed. A picture came up on the large screen behind the podium. There were three aliens sitting in a row facing the same direction. They were in a desert. They appeared to be attached to one another with some sort of web tether. The three aliens, although in captivity, looked directly into the camera with a haughty look of disdain and hatred.

Lieutenant Palangin said in a loud plain voice, "Okay Ensign! Run the training film!"

The film unfroze as the aliens looked away in unison. You could hear the increasing drone of an airplane as a plane approached out of view of the camera. The look on their faces turned from haughty to speculative as they continued to stare away toward the droning.

A commando leaned down toward the first alien in line and said, "This is what we humans call, "Beam me up Scotty!" The loud droning became more pronounced. Immediately the three aliens looked absolutely terrified. A plane flew overhead and collected a tether being held aloft by a balloon that was previously unnoticed by the audience. All three aliens were snatched from the ground screaming in terror! The evacuation of the aliens was a classic, "behind the lines", extraction method, used by the military in the by gone days of the last century. The extraction method had never been viewed by any of the civilians in the audience. The drone of the plane was drowned out by the screaming aliens as they became diminishing specs following the plane in the cloudless sky.

There was complete stunned silence in the room. Then Lieutenant Palangin, grinning her lopsided smile, said, "And that ladies and gentlemen, is how you would extract an alien from the middle of the desert!"

Everyone stood simultaneously cheering and laughing, some with tears streaking down there cheeks. The heavy somber spell that possessed the audience earlier was completely broken. Even hardnosed Agents, Jessop and Reese, had tears streaking down their face. Oh! What they would give to whisk away a suspect or two like that!

Now Lieutenant Palangin's lop-sided grin was changed to a grin from ear to ear and transformed her face with a beautiful glow. She saw, The President, give her a thumbs up, for a job well done. She was the one responsible for the extraction planning. She was pleased with its outcome. Admiral Cleary was proud of his staff. The whole operation was executed with the utmost professionalism and planning. But, he knew, that the next operation would be in the aliens court. They could not, under any circumstances allow them to escape. Thinking to himself, he said aloud, "How in heavens name do you fight an enemy on Jupiter's moon of Europa?"

CHAPTER 49
EXCURSIONS

As Blain expected, he found Emily in his quarters with his children. He said, "Emily, would you like to take a short tour of your solar system? Robert can come along if he would like to do so."

Emily jumped up off the couch shouting, "I would love to Blain". She was fully energized by the prospect of having the opportunity of flying the saucer. She had already done so on several occasions and was becoming quiet proficient. The planets in the solar system would be an exciting excursion; for Emily, it was a dream come true. Since she had traveled so far away, the solar system had become her home, not just her planet.

Emily contacted Robert using the ships communication system and asked him if he wanted to go. He turned her down saying he and Shayar were going to enter the fusion room to adjust some of the ion resonators; he was really excited about the prospect of seeing the quark analyzers up close. The pixilation of quarks and the tuning of the resonators was the essence of spherical mathematics in relation to space-time travel. He was also beginning to fall in love with Sharla, which was as alien to her as the Andrians method of procreation was to him; but since he had never had a relationship with a women before, he believed he could accept whatever form of relationship she was able to abide, they would have to meet in the middle if there was such a thing. However, Sharla was beginning to feel the pressure of attraction toward Aaron greater than any other male in her lifetime.

Blain and Emily left the intergalactic carrier which was positioned in the area designated by earth scientist as the "Oort Cloud", the Oort Cloud being beyond the Kuiper belt with the Kuiper belt extending beyond the orbit of Neptune at about approximately thirty five to fifty five astronomical units from the sun. The Kuiper belt is twenty to two hundred times as massive as the Asteroid belt which is located between Mars and Jupiter. The Asteroid belt consists of an untold number of rocky body asteroids, large rocky body planetoids such as Ceres, Vesta, Gaspera, and Pallas among numerous others surrounded by an untold number of ice chunks; whereas the Kuiper belt is composed of primarily frozen volatiles such as methane and ammonia with numerous ice chunks. There is also numerous dwarf planets with Pluto being the most well-known. They were staying hidden among the asteroids to avoid detection by Klaxo and Zelegark. Several drones and satellites had been left behind to monitor the solar system in the hopes that Klaxo would reveal his position. Once the Andrians had returned to the solar system, additional drones and satellites were launched and those left behind were retrieved and analyzed.

Emily piloted the saucer through the heavily populated asteroid, and planetoid infested Kuiper Belt trying to conceal their return to the solar system. Using her growing telepathic skills and knowledge of spherical mathematics, the double helix formulas began to make more definitive sense. Even more exciting to Emily was the ghost like tendril of thought that began to define a third strand in the helix.

There was a slight vibration, the wall of the craft turned from opaque to clear. As the vibration ceased, the holographic vision presented the planet Uranus before them. The planet was rotating on a ninety-seven degree inclination of equator to orbit, thus it rotated on its side in relation to the sun. However, from Emily's point of view it was upright. Uranus was blue in color, the methane atmosphere, though small in comparison to the hydrogen-helium content, adsorbed the red spectrum of light frequencies thus giving the planet its pale blue hue.

The closest moon to the planet and to Emily and Blain was Miranda. Miranda was one of the smallest of the five major satellite orbiting Uranus and just one of its twenty-seven known moons. As Emily hovered over the surface of Miranda, she was fascinated with the large, long furrows and right angle grooves carved into the moon's surface. To her the furrows appeared to be a large plowed field. (1986 Voyager 2) 1. PIA01490.tif.jpg; 2.PIA00043.tif.jpg; 3. PIA00038.tif.jpg

Blain advised, "In the most ancient past, even before our specie entered this quadrant of the galaxy, the surface was mined by a star faring specie that was obviously very advanced and had mining technology that could cut the grooves into different elevations. We do not know what mineral they were interested in, but, whatever it was, there had to be extensive deposits on the surface.

SEED OF HOPE

Emily remembered seeing the photos taken by voyager two, which was a space probe, launched by Earths old National Aeronautics and Space Administration back in 1977. After the successful attack on Washington D.C., the old NASA was replaced by the SDIA, Space Defense Intelligence Agency.

After circling Miranda, Emily entered another coordinate for a new destination. After the vibration ceased, Saturn and its rings hung in the black void. Several of its fifty-three moons were visible. The closest moon to Emily's position was Hyperion. 2. PAI07740.tif, jpg. The oddly cratered moon was matched by its just as odd tumbling, rotating orbit. Emily, in her research of Earths early space program remembered seeing a picture provided by NASA'S/JPL, Cassini, Sept. 2005 mission, of a clear, large, view of the moon. Upon closer inspection Emily had found a bright neon green looking light in one of the craters. The light was a small pinpoint but stood out in the otherwise dull grey surroundings after magnification. The light was located in the upper right hand quadrant of the picture of the moon's surface in the large, multi- cratered depression.

Upon mentioning the anomaly to Blain, he advised that the Andrians had a robotic mining facility on Hyperion and they have been mining for a scarce trace chemical. The use of the robotic mining facility allowed them to collect the trace chemical in usable quantities when they periodically returned to the solar system. Blain had Emily fly the saucer over the facility where she observed extensive structures with small tractor like robots moving about the surface. The small green light seen from the old photo became an intensive spray of light beams that were reflected from the subsurface laser mining apparatus below the ground.

Emily then moved the saucer to the vicinity of Saturn's Iapetus This moon was Emily's primary interest. For generations there have been rumors that the moon was an artifact/construct. This was Emily's first visit to the moon. Emily placed the saucer level with the twelve-mile high wall. The wall ran half way around the moons equator in a straight line and disappeared over the curvature of the horizon. The wall also had a twelve-mile wide surface area that was very intriguing. Hovering over the surface of the wall she observed that it was honeycombed with multiple cones whose depths could not be measured with any know instrument. The interior of the cones was a maze of crisscrossed girders which originally had been supports for the interior walls.

Emily carefully and slowly explored several of the cones looking for some kind of entrance. Upon descending a particularly deep cone that allowed access to a great depth, they observed an access tunnels that ran parallel to the surface. Again there were no wall but the remaining girders were a maze of densely packed forest of girders which had a tunnel clearly accessible. Emily proceeded thru the tunnel for about twenty minutes carefully navigating thru pitch darkness.

Blain was amazed that Emily had found an entrance so easily. The entrance was in a cone among the rocks and deep craters and crevices. The Andrians have been

SEED OF HOPE

looking and exploring the artifacts on Iapetus for a thousand years. They have never found a way in. And, they have been using sophisticated scanner equipment which has as of yet, not even been imagined by earthlings.

Blaine continued to be amazed with her achievements. "How did she do that? She was over the moon less than twenty minutes and she found an entrance."

The depths of some of the crevices and cones were not discernible with or without sophisticated sensors. The opening cones were gray which faded into the blackness even darker than space.

Emily moved the saucer carefully into the darkened round corroder, which was an abyss of crisscrossing structural beams. The beams disappeared into the gloom in all directions. Except for Emily's superior navigation skills and the saucer's wizardry, it would have been impossible to move about the interior of the structure, much less finding their way out. Emily continued floating thru the corroder of girders that at one time, eons earlier, had made up an access tunnel to the interior of the construct/artifact/moon. After about thirty minutes they came to an area of the tunnel that had material walls as they had not, as of yet, caved in.

Blain carefully analyzed the incoming sensor data to avoid a catastrophic collision with any objects. Then to his surprise, he noted a slight elevation of the ion matrix indicator. That meant that there was a power source nearby other than their own, and that should be impossible! Adjusting the levels of the delicate instruments, Blain confirmed the ion source was exactly thirty degrees to starboard. Emily maneuvered the saucer to the direction of the ion source.

The infrared scanners indicated what appeared to be a large round solid portal with small access ports on four sides. Blain had spent an enormous amount of time exploring the giant artifact as had many other Andrians over the times past. He was again stupefied as to how Emily could not only find an entrance but then enter the interior and navigate unerringly to a power source and an inner access point! Blain very deftly operated the controls within his ceramic sphere. Several robotic instruments exited the base of the craft and approached the access portal. Another robotic instrument returned unerringly the way they had come and exited the artifact. That particular instrument divided itself into two halves. One half took up surveillance above the entrance, the other half returned to the intergalactic carrier with the information gathered about the artifact.

Two of the robotic craft approached the sealed portal and examined the exterior for access controls. Upon finding a panel on the bulkhead next to the large access point, Blain x-rayed the control panel to examine the interior circuits. To his and Emilie's surprise, the large entrance slowly opened in an aperture fashion, the center rotating and collapsing into the next outer ring.

Emily said excitedly, "Let's go in Blain! Let's go now!"

Blains response was one of a seasoned explorer, which he was. "Not yet! Let's see if we can operate the access point several times to make sure it will continue to work." Blain then directed the robots to x-ray the panel

SEED OF HOPE

again. The access slowly closed. After repeating the process four more times successfully, Blain then sent in a robot to find a similar panel on the inside of the large room. There was an access panel centered on the four sides of the access port which indicated that at times this area did not have a gravity field. Each and every panel operated the access port.

Blain then sent another robot into the large room to view the room and other areas. The robot found a six-foot portal on the opposite wall of the entrance portal. Blain x-rayed the controls on this portal and again was surprised when the outer portal closed. The robot on the inside then sent pictures and data indicating the inside six-foot portal had opened after the larger entrance access port had closed. The robot then entered the smaller access point and x-rayed the panel next to the door. The smaller door closed.

Then to their utter surprise, the surveillance instruments indicated that the second room, sealed off from the outer portal, was filling with breathable, one hundred percent pure oxygen! Blain and Emily looked at one another surprise registering on both of their faces.

Again, Emily excitedly said, I want to go in Blain! We can go in can't we?" I want to see for myself!

Again Blain's extensive exploration of artifacts subdued his own excitement and he heard himself say, "No". He really wanted to say, "Yes". He was just as excited as Emily, and he wanted to see firsthand what beautiful treasures awaited the intrepid explorers! The more experienced explorer side of Blain cautioned him and brought to mind about how impossible and out of any normal parameters of expectations, that anyone could devise, that would explain a working oxygen system within the ancient construct/artifact that had actual working parts.

Blain's hands were shaking when he sent another robot to retrace their steps and exit the portal. The robot would then communicate the impossible finding to the intergalactic carrier. If this area had a working oxygen system then it could well have a functioning automatic defense system. Therefore, they had to proceed with the utmost caution.

Blain and Emily watched the 3D images as the now oxygenated interior was being explored by the robot. Everything was gray and featureless; there were not any tables, chairs, or other items that could be construed as furniture. The walls and ceiling were perpendicular and square. The bland features were suddenly interrupted when the robot rounded a corner and came within inches of an alien face!

Emily screamed! Blain was shocked enough to have the color drain from his face. To Emily, the alien was grotesque. It was..."Alien", in every sense of the word. Emily had long since quit believing that the Andrians were "Aliens"; they were not. They were just a different type of human; they were just short one finger, nothing more, and nothing less. They were fellow travelers.

This grotesque being floating, suspended in the zero gravity, was different. It was alien by any definition of term which one may choose to use. The being was wearing a space suit. That was indicative that the being was of higher intelligence. The clear plastic type substance shaped in a bubble completely encased its head. The eyes were a series of lateral visual ports that encircled its head. The mouth was a vertical orifice with two sets of lateral tusk which was sprouting fine saw like teeth. There were no holes, or ears, where one would expect them to be. But then what would one expect with a being that had eyes placed laterally around the circumference of its head? The skin was a mottled gray with small green spots that had what appeared to be suckers centered in the middle.

Blain observed panels along the new corridor in which the alien floated. He aimed the robots infrared detector at the panels and emitted an x-ray beam toward them. The panels in the corridor and room began to glow with a soft red tinted light which glowed with increased incandescence. Soon there was enough light to see the entire physic of the alien. There were four long apertures that were its "arms". They were of equal length, two angled from the top and two angled from the bottom. It did not appear to have legs. It was completely encased within a hard suit. There was a small tank on its back and the tank had four hoses that entered the sides of the helmet. Evidently, whatever the alien used as a respiratory aid was in the tank, and it was long gone.

Blain again released another robot and coded it with a priority key that allowed the robot to defend itself from any unforeseen enemies. This robot must reach the intergalactic carrier. Once outside the artifact, it immediately began transmitting video streams on the ion molecules that were in abundance throughout the galaxy. The defensive mechanism was initiated to provide an assurance that the encoded information would be received by the intended recipients.

Blain moved the robot behind the floating alien and extended two pincer devices. The pincers took two alien arms and moved forward bringing the alien out of the room into the exterior hanger. After the robot closed the inside hatch, the large outer aperture sensor was activated which opened the larger outer aperture. The robot brought the alien specimen directly to the saucer where it could be easily observed. There was some kind of script engraved on the side of the tank attached to the aliens back. It was not like anything Emily had ever seen before. After bringing the alien to the saucer the robot closed the larger aperture access. Blain had the robot move the alien to the side for later retrieval.

The second robot continued into the oxygenated interior of the artifact. All the rooms were now bathed in a red glow and were fully oxygenated. They did not locate any more aliens. On one of the bulkheads Blain observed a rack which contained spheres with protrusions. The spheres were about twelve inches in diameter. They were secured with some type of band which extended from one end to the other. Blain did not know what they were but he believed that it would be to their advantage to retrieve the alien with the robots and exit the artifact before anything untoward happened. So far, they have had an amazing productive and safe exploration.

Emily was excited. She did not want to leave. "I want to go inside Blain! I want to see more! We cannot possibly

SEED OF HOPE

leave now! We just got started!" Emily's eyes were big and actually shined with excitement. There was a slight quiver to her voice. They had been in the artifact for over four hours yet it seemed like only minutes.

Blain could not physically touch Emily but he could fill her mind with his presence. "Emily, you can never explore an artifact alone or without special defense detectors. There is also an array of robot assist units that we use. We must check for dormant biological contaminants, chemical trace contaminants, and for possible weapons. Nor can we bring the dead alien or the robots that handled the body back onto this saucer. The carrier will send a special biological receiving unit for that purpose. The exploration team will send nano bots into the interior to check for known explosives. The exploration of this artifact has gone on for a thousand of your earth years. You are the first person to ever find an entrance, a power source, and, against all known logical parameters, oxygen!"

Emily smiled her crooked grin. "Am I? Well I went the way I did because it just seemed to be the way to go. Oh! Have you ever seen an alien like this one? Boy he was frozen solid. I wonder how old he is. Do you think he is the specie that built the rooms in this artifact? I wonder if there are any more of them in there. I guess he was in one piece because he was sealed in the airless chamber for who knows how long. Do you think the oxygen that filled the chamber would be okay for us to breathe? When are we going to go back in? I am going to get to go aren't I?" Emily had to pause for breath.

Blain looked at Emily. He did not think she was ever going to stop asking questions. She was so excited she had verbalized the entire conversation without ever realizing it was not necessary as, telepathic communication would have sufficed just fine. This was the second time this evening that she became excited like that. She must be a natural born explorer. She was looking at him expectantly like a child breathlessly waiting to ride a carnival ride. Her face was again flush with excitement. And, she was so beautiful! That thought caused Blain to pause and examine his growing attraction to Emily.

"No. you may not go back in until the area has been cleared and has been deemed safe. We finally have found an intact access point to conduct an intensive research and exploration of the interior of the facility. But most importantly, we cannot afford to lose you."

Emily was surprised she would not be allowed to go back into the artifact; after all, it was her find. Surly that must be worth something. The fact that Blain had said, "Most importantly we cannot afford to lose you," did not enter her mind.

Blain, having read her mind said, "Exploration teams are specially trained. There have been several fatalities. These places are never as safe as they seem. Unfortunately we know of this type of alien. The most surprising thing is to find it here. It is a mystery that must be solved. We are at war with this specie in another galaxy. They are a ferocious, cold-blooded killer. They never take prisoners. They will destroy an entire world down to the last living thing regardless of specie. Yes Emily, this is absolutely the most important find in the last thousand years in this galaxy. It may well mean our time is short. Your importance to your world has just been magnified by a hundred fold."

Emily was mystified by Blains speech. As of yet, she had not been told why she was abducted. And besides, why was she so important?

Soon approximately twenty saucers arrived from the intergalactic carriers hiding in the Oort Cloud. One of the saucers was at least ten times larger than she had seen before. Blain said, "Emily, the large craft will take the alien and the robots that handled the alien. Our work is done here. It is time for us to leave."

Emily was dejected. Earlier she had been so excited, she had never felt such a rush before in her entire life! Not to be able to continue was disappointing to say the least. Emily piloted the craft back to the galactic carrier in silence. She did not think that she personally, was any big deal.

CHAPTER 50
BRAINSTORM

Admiral Cleary, Commander Johnson, and their combined staff, debated ways to destroy Klaxo before he destroyed the human race from the earth; there was no longer any doubt that Klaxo was planning to do just that.

Addressing the group, Admiral Cleary advised, "We need some fresh ideas. The standard approaches to warfare on a distant moon are not the same as warfare on the earth. I suggest that we broaden our input. We need new and fresh ideas. We have the best military minds in the world, the best scientific minds with the most enlightened approaches to a new kind of problem, and yet, none of them will come close to working an assured success. We need something else. I believe we need to think outside the box. If the ten young people are as astute and intelligent as we all believe, then we should include our ten young people. They may offer some unique or novel way to approach our problem which we have not thought of before."

The ten young people eagerly and excitedly accepted the challenge. They had all the information that military intelligence possessed, Including, the possible scenario plans of attack. They quickly threw the Military plans away. They believed them to be too cumbersome.

Setting around a table they rapidly, with

unprecedented speed, did what they did best, they provided solutions to a very difficult problem. They began by stating the objective. They asked for and received a list of resources required to achieve the objective. And, they quantified the duties of each individual within the group and developed clear chain of commands. And most important, they came up with not one plan but two.

One plan was to have commandoes to go to Europa like it was a normal every day excursion. After all, Klaxo had been expecting the return of Zelegark and his minions at any time. They were already long overdue. They would catch them by surprise, engage them and defeat them. This operation did not necessarily require a stealthy approach. Why not arrive as expected? And plan two; send one saucer craft as ambassadors to the intergalactic ship to intercede on behalf of earth's citizens, if they could find it. Both groups, without exception, would include all of the gifted Human-Andrian young people. All the young people had discussed and agreed that it was necessary for them to go to the intergalactic carrier for evaluation by the Andrians. After all, they were their creation.

CHAPTER 51
REALIZATIONS

After the think tank session involving the planning of the attack on Klaxo's base on Jupiter's moon, Europa, and the role they would be assigned, the mood of the young people became muted and quiet. Jake and Ashley returned to the dorm strolling hand in hand. They had been excited to actually use their talents and their abilities to help make a difference and to save lives. The plans for the attack on Klaxo and his group had seemed so logical; they just did not understand why the military planners did not think of it first.

Even though they had constantly been together since they had been freed from their imprisonment, they never considered themselves more than friends. Part of that line of thinking was the result of being isolated during their most formative social developmental years. The other part of it was that they did not yet have a concept of what love was. They just knew they liked being together and did not want to be separated. They believed they were just comforting one another. They both lost their parents when they were thirteen. Then, they were drugged into oblivion for four more years until they were seventeen. The drugs, having been finally been purged from their bodies and mind now for about six months, represented a new awakening for them.

SEED OF HOPE

As they walked into the common living area of the dorm, Jake started to sit down where they usually spent their time together. Ashley took his hand and pulled him with her toward her living area and said, "Not this time, Jake. You are coming with me." Jake grinned and sheepishly followed; always having been a shy boy he allowed Ashley to tug him down the hall to her room.

Once in the room Ashley shoved Jake against the door. "Jake, I do not know or understand the feelings I have for you. But since we have been rescued, we have been constant companions. I think I love you. I know that I do not want to be with anyone else. There is a possibility that either one of us, or perhaps both of us, may be killed when we participate in the next military operation. I want you to hold me and make love to me. You do love me don't you Jake?"

Jake, being shy looked down and replied, "With all my heart and soul. There will never be another".

They took their time undressing one another, crawled into bed and consummated their union. Afterward they went to sleep in each other's arms, legs tangled, breathing on one another's cheek.

They knew that the plans they had made in the think tank was daring, dangerous, and had only a fifteen percent chance of succeeding. To them it seemed right to share their last days before the operation began, together. They hoped they would succeed. They wanted to spend a lifetime together; preferable a very long life.

The surveillance officer in charge of their safety observed the two young people enter the young women's room. They had never done that before. After hearing the audio of their fears and declaration of love and the visual of them beginning to undress one another, he turned the surveillance system off. That was against protocol but after hearing their words he believed they deserved their privacy. They also represented the most likely, best chance, of survival, for the people of earth. The surveillance officer left his desk and went to get a cup of coffee.

CHAPTER 52
MOONBASE

The Andrian watch officer contacted Klaxo's personal communicator and advised, "Sir, Zelegark and the others are returning. They are maintaining communication silence as advised. Earth's forces are in the area and may possibly detect the communication signals. There are at least four earth vessels strung out on the other side of the planet. They do not want to possibly alert them of their and our presence."

"Very well, when they arrive quickly open the outer access to allow them entry. Do not delay, and make sure Zelegark comes straight to me."

"Yes Commander".

As the fleet of six saucer craft neared Europa, and the access dome came into view, Sasha said, "The Andrian technology for camouflage is absolutely amazing. Camouflaging a suit of armor is simple compared to the magnitude of hiding a complete base!" Had the coordinates not been provided by the alien prisoners, the commandoes, in all probability, would never have located the base.

The Andrian sentinels, having been watching for the return of Zelegark and observing the four earth ships strung out on the other side of the planet, paid little attention to the saucers as they approached the base. They were more concerned with the earth ships; no one knew the exact coordinates of the base except Zelegark. After all, who else could it be? All six saucer craft bear unerringly directly for the base. They were obviously theirs. The sentinels opened the outer access. All six saucers hovered before the entrance maintaining perfect formation, then, they glided slowly inside.

Ashley was excited, apprehensive, and focused, on controlling her craft. The flight to Jupiter had been flawless. Jake was operating the saucer to her right, or starboard. She smiled when she thought of Jake. The night they had spent together was the first of eighteen. Time had flown by. If they were not training in the saucers and going over attack plans, they were together in Ashley's room. She just could not get enough of him, and him, her. She had never known such a deep and abiding love. Then she thought of her mom and dad. They loved one another too. They must have felt the same way. It must have been like her and Jake. Then she became pained thinking of the premature death of her parents. She had believed they had died in a car accident but then Agents Jessop and Reese advised her that her parents, along with all the other young people's parents, had been murdered by Klaxo and his henchmen. Ashley steeled herself for what was to come. It was payback time for her loved ones. She put all else aside and put all her concentration into controlling the craft. And, Ashley's concentration was formidable

Lt. Palangin looked to her left and observed Ashley. She, as with all the personnel engaged in destroying

SEED OF HOPE

Klaxo, loved the ten young people. She felt like she was herself a better person just in knowing them. Ashley was young and driven, as they all were. Sasha, thinking to herself, wondered if, "Had the Andrians ever considered what a formidable foe the Human-Andrian Hybrid children would be after murdering their parents and holding them prisoners all thru their adolescent period of their life, depriving them of their freedom? Well they should have! This operation was designed by them." Sasha smiled at the thought."

Sasha said, "Okay folks, time to implement "Operation Dummy"! The outer gates closed, enclosing them within the hanger. The hanger pressurized and the inner gates opened. The six saucers glided to their designated positions.

"All right Ashley, keep the engine hot, watch your behind and keep your finger on the trigger!" Sasha flashed Ashley a beautiful smile and touched her arm reassuringly. "These jerks are going to be sorry that they ever messed with ya'll!" Then Sasha quickly exited the saucer wearing the battle coveralls. Her commando team was right behind her.

There were sixteen commandoes per each saucer in battle coveralls. There were four additional commandoes wearing the full battle armor. Thus, there were a total of one hundred commandoes and their commander that swarmed from the saucers into the hanger area. The aliens had their twenty saucers parked in their designated spaces. Two commandoes were dispatched to each saucer; one commando secured the inside of the saucer and one stood guard outside the saucer. Fortunately for them, they knew the layout of the saucers and knew somewhat what to expect. There was also one commando in full battle armor that was assigned to assist on the hanger deck should it become necessary.

The Andrian sentinels were exactly where the captives said they would be, in the adjoining break room playing three-dimensional chess. The six Andrians were caught completely by surprise when the three-man assault team entered the recreational area. The assault team was armed with one blast rifle, one laser and two Tasers

Even though the Andrians were caught completely by surprise, they recovered and acted quickly. Too bad for them! The commando with the blast rifle blasted two Andrians in half and another one's head vaporized. Of the remaining three, two were tasered into unconsciousness, the third raised his arms. That particular move appeared to also be universal. The team did not have time for prisoners before achieving their objective. The commando with the laser fired a red beam in a circular pattern around the heart. The smell of burning flesh accompanied the circle of smoke that emanated from the cauterized wound. The laser had effectively cut the heart and arteries from the body. The Andrian dropped to his knees with his arms still raised. The words on his dying lips were, "You Stupid Humans."

Klaxo was sitting at his desk eagerly awaiting the arrival of Zelegark, impatiently tapping his pen light on his desk. His aides sat on either side; they too were eagerly waiting to hear of the disposition of the ten hybrids. They really wanted to hear that they had been destroyed. Thus when the door opened he was expecting to see Zelegark. Instead, five humans in armor coveralls and one in battle armor entered the room. He could not believe his eyes! The human that appeared to be in charge was a diminutive, Stupid Human, female, and she had a blaster pointed at him! Klaxo could not say a word; he was so confounded at the turn of events that his tongue would not move and his eyes bulged! It was impossible yet there the Stupid Humans were standing right in front of him.

The ugly little diminutive female said, "I am Lieutenant Sasha Palangin, of the Space Intelligence Commandoes. Are you Klaxo the Andrian, traitor to the "Council of Yield"?"

Klaxo could still only stare. Utter surprise and disbelief that this could possibly be happening again tied his tongue. When he did try to talk he could only stutter and spittle flew from his lips. His face was contorted. His surprise slowly turned from anger to hatred. He turned his formidable mind to direct its energy toward the hated Humans in an effort to generate massive hemorrhaging in their brains.

Smiling sweetly, which only infuriated Klaxo more, Sasha responded, "Your mind energy will not work Klaxo. We are all wearing protective neural mesh to protect us against your directed mental energies. They were supplied, by the way, by the young Human-Andrian Hybrids you wanted to murder. I was going to take you prisoner to stand trial for murder and kidnapping. However, since you just tried to murder me and my team,

I will with great pleasure, send you off to whatever eternal damnations are reserved for beings like yourselves!" Sasha had the blaster pointed at his head and having said what his judgment was going to be, pulled the trigger. Klaxo's head vaporized in a clouded mist of red DNA. His neck, being cauterized did not spurt blood, but the neck ring to which the head was attached, sent curls of smoke upward toward the ceiling. Then, the body simply dropped straight downward to the floor.

Klaxo's two aides looked in horror at his body as it fell headless to the floor. A fine, red mist settled over their faces and heads. They then looked at the small diminutive women who had just killed Klaxo. She was just standing there smiling at them! Her blaster was in her hand but her arms were down at her side.

"Stupid, stupid woman; did she not expect they would react to Klaxo's murder!" thought Klaxo's first counselor? "Stupid Humans, did they not ever learn!"

Unknown to the Andrians, this scenario was very carefully rehearsed time and again. Thus Sasha, appearing defenseless, was giving them a chance to surrender. Or not! Of course, blinded by their hatred, their surrender in all probability was not ever in their minds. And since their focus was on Sasha, they never again noticed the other commandoes wearing familiar body armor standing motionless in the background. Both Andrians jumped up at the same time armed with laser weapons. And, before they could raise their weapons, both Andrians were sliced with lasers multiple times by the four commandoes who had gone unnoticed in the background. Their arms fell off. Their heads rolled to the side still having murderess anger permanently plastered on their facial features. Then the top half of their bodies tipped sideways as their legs buckled to the floor in the opposite direction carrying the waist with them.

Sasha let her breath out unaware she was holding it in. She was pleased with a job well done. Her team's primary mission was to capture, if possible, the traitorous leadership. But they knew that in all probability, they would not surrender. If that was the case, then they were to be eliminated. With the decapitation of the leadership they hoped the rank and file would surrender. That remained yet to be seen.

After two hours of light resistance they had one hundred and seven of the one hundred and twenty three aliens rounded up in the large dining area. The sixteen remaining aliens had fled into the deeper recesses of the construction area of the base.

The four ships the team had stationed on the other side of Jupiter and used as decoys to keep the aliens attention focused away from the approaching saucers were now in orbit around Europa. The saucer craft was loaded one by one into the carriers. They would be ferried to earth orbit where they were to be divided into groups on different bases.

Lt. Palangin looked over the one hundred and seven prisoners. They returned her observation of them with looks of pure hatred and directed energy. Their combined effort to destroy the human's brains was almost more than the neural net protective caps could withstand.

In a loud voice Lt. Palangin declared, "Andrians! You are under arrest for the murder and kidnapping of Earth's citizens! Your sentence has been decided by a military tribunal on the Earth. You will remain imprisoned on this moon until you are dead. If any one of you attempt to escape, that individual will be sentenced to death and be spaced. If any one of you successfully escapes, this whole colony will be spaced!"

With that declaration, Lt. Palangin turned on her heal and left the room. Her back was guarded by the four commandoes in complete battle armor with blasters. One by one they left the room, boarded the saucer and were the last to leave the moon base of Europa. The success of this mission was due largely to the assistance and inclusion of the young Human-Andrian Hybrids. What a marvelous asset they were becoming to the citizens of earth.

As Lt. Palangin's back disappeared thru the door the remaining Andrians looked at one another. Each had the same thoughts, "Did that ugly little diminutive, Stupid Human really kill Klaxo as the video showed?" And. "How did those stupid humans capture them and their base anyway?" Without Klaxo to encourage them on, they drifted to their berthing areas and went to sleep.

CHAPTER 53
OBSERVATIONS

As the small flotilla of six saucers and four cargo carriers left the vicinity of Europa, they were observed by an advanced robotic satellite. The robotic surveillance satellite had the capability of both seeing thru the camouflaged cover, building, and ice. Everything that was said and done within the premises was recorded. The satellite was sent by the intergalactic ship that had just arrived and was now waiting among the many objects of the Kuiper Belt. Initially the Andrians believed that the six saucer craft that approached Europa was Zelegark and his crews. Subsequent surveillance revealed it for what it was.

"Council of Yield", member, Shayar spoke. "It appears the humans have mastered the art of deception and eliminated a major problem for us. Klaxo and his two counselors have been eliminated by the same diminutive Human female soldier that used the unorthodox extraction method in the desert. Sasha had informed the Andrians on the Moon base that Zelegark and his followers are imprisoned upon the earth and one of Zelegark's followers had been killed."

"It is a mystery to me how the humans could have accomplished so much with so little. They are extremely resourceful and imaginative in their planning.

Human-Andrian Hybrids were piloting the crafts from Earth to Jupiter, and then back again, upon their return; obviously they have mastered the science of Three Dimensional Mathematics. It may very well be that they were the source for the masterful attack on the moon base. The twenty saucers that Klaxo had in his possession are now in the possession of the humans and are being ferried to Earth in their cargo vessels. I do fear that they are completely unaware of the destructiveness of the weapon technologies incorporated in every saucer."

"The remaining one-hundred and twenty three traitors have been marooned on the moon, Europa. They have brought shame upon our specie. I recommend that they be destroyed. The human standard of compassion and justice is perhaps, "alien" too us, but, the Humans do not understand the threat the marooned Andrian traitors can be to their survival. When I recommended that the traitors be destroyed, I meant that they should be eliminated immediately!"

The "Council of Yield", agreed unanimously to eliminate the traitors on the moon Europa.

CHAPTER 54
DEMONSTRATION

Admiral Cleary was in his office when summoned by Commander Johnson. When the Admiral walked into the Command Intelligence Control Center he saw about twenty service personnel watching a large center screen. The view was of the Andrian prison base on Jupiter's moon of Europa. The signal was relayed to earth via three communication satellites that were placed there specifically for surveillance support of the moon base prison. The scene was not viewed in real time but transmission was only about a fifteen minutes lag, not bad for such a long distance.

Three saucers had taken up positions over the base. Admiral Cleary was advised the saucers had entered Jupiter's orbit from the outer solar system, the Kuiper belt. The intelligence officers watched as the three saucers used their laser weapons too methodically and systematically destroy the canopy over the base. Debris started floating quietly away from the base in slow motion from the destroyed canopy. Some of the debris was bodies. After about ten minutes of systematic destruction two of the saucers moved away from their position. The remaining saucer then emitted a large directed beam into the center of the exposed base. However, this beam was green and so bright that the surveillance satellites had to dim the lenses for protection. There was a huge explosion of light as enormous amounts of debris erupted from the base's central location. Then in the blink of the eye, the center of the explosion became a black point and all the debris around the moon reversed course and shot back into the hole. Immediately the moon material near the black hole folded into itself and about one third of the moon disintegrated in a blue and green light before disappearing into the black hole. Jupiter's large ice moon had just been reduced by one third. The green laser was turned off. The saucer joined the other two saucers and they returned slowly the way they had come.

The room was quiet. They were all stunned into silence. The amount of energy generated by that one beam was more powerful than all the nuclear weapons on the earth. The green beam had somehow generated a small black hole that vaporized one third of the moon. They observed quietly as other large chunks of Europa floated slowly, tumbling toward Jupiter.

Admiral Cleary said, "Bob get on the horn right now and ground all saucer craft. No one is to touch them until we know more about how to control the weapon systems. We cannot afford accidents like that! Gather all our staff, scientist, and think tank; and include the young people. We are going to need all the help we can get."

Commander Johnson replied, "Yes Sir!"

CHAPTER 55
ACKNOWLEDGEMENTS

The usual crowd was in the room. This time there was chairs only in the front as there was standing room only in the back half of the room. The ten young people had become celebrities for their contribution to the planning and execution of the assault on the Alien base on Jupiter's moon, Europa. It was there idea to place decoy ships on the far side of Jupiter but still detectable by their systems. The six saucer craft approached the base directly and slowly so as not to arouse suspicion. The commandoes, once they were inside, did what commandoes do best, they moved quickly, quietly, and lethally; they achieved their objective, and then they left. Then three other saucers approached Jupiter's moon Europa and took up positions above the traitor's base.

The video was replayed in silence. You could hear the intake of breath, even from the young people, when they observed the black hole devour almost a third of the moon Europa. No one was aware of the saucers potential for destruction. All the men and women in the room were fearful. It was palatable; it hung in the air with every breath exhaled. What kind of defense could they possibly design against that degree of advanced technology? Up until that very moment all the prior events, even though serious, seemed more like a game of Human vs. Alien.

They never realized how much the cards were stacked against them. Not anyone spoke, not anyone moved.

Finally, Jake got up and walked to the podium. Admiral Cleary looked at Commander Johnson in askance. Commander Johnson subtly shook his head no, indicating that Jake should be allowed to speak. Heaven knew that he did not have anything constructive to say.

As Jake stood at the podium he could barely see over the top. One of the Admiral's aids retrieved a tall wooden decorative speaker from the side of the stage and laid it lengthwise on the floor at the base of the podium.

Jake stepped up on the speaker and looked around and exclaimed, "Oh, there you are!" His words generated a soft laughter around the room. "We must needs be remembering why we are all here. We have shown ourselves, and any others who may care to watch," gesturing with his eyes in the upward position indicating the aliens, again getting around of laughter, "that, when we are in control we can do okay. Now, it should not come as a surprise to any of us that the Andrians obviously have some incredibly powerful weapons. We just saw an example of one of their laser weapons. And you know what? I bet what we saw was one of their baby weapons!"

"Ok, if they did not really want us here, we would not be here; and certainly my new found friends and I would not be here either. Remember, we were specifically genetically engineered to help save our specie from self-destruction. I mean really, their specie have been knocking around the universe before we ever got out of

SEED OF HOPE

the trees! I can imagine that there must be some pretty tough customers out there in the universe somewhere. Perhaps they are the equivalent of an inter-galactic sheriff. Klaxo, Zelegark and his followers have obviously broken some kind of law; they have shamed their specie before us, "Humans". They paid the price. I bet agents Jessop and Reese could relate to their kind of thinking better than anyone of us."

And, that was exactly what they were thinking. Jessop and Reese sat stone faced, as several pair of eyes turned and eyed them.

Once again, Commander Johnson thought, "They look like deer caught in headlights. Gosh I love those two!"

Jake continued," There is no doubt they were aware of our surveillance satellites. They knew we would be watching. I think that allowing us to see that demonstration of their power was there way of telling us not to do anything stupid."

Ashley then got up and walked up to the podium and stepped up on the other end of the speaker and stood by Jake. Fortunately, the speaker was the right dimension to allow her to easily take her position next to Jake.

"Jake is right! There is no way we could ever sneak upon an inter-galactic carrier. The first saucer we sent to the Kuiper belt area was unable to make contact with them. Apparently they did not wish to make contact with us at that time. And, we were able to fool the other Andrians because they must obviously, have been the "stupid's", of the bunch. We must not make the same mistake they did. It is really simple. I mean, my mom would say, "They just got too big for their britches!"

There was genuine stress relieving laughter all around the room, and a smattering of applause. Jessop and Reese marveled at the logic of what both young people were saying; they, as well as the rest of the room, including the military types, received peace and comfort at the "rightness" of her words. When they had finished going thru their logic-decision tree, it left only one course of action.

Ashley said in a loud voice, "Let's go out there and say hi to our cousins!"

CHAPTER 56
NEW ADVENTURE

Admiral Cleary was in an intense conference with, The President, and his advisors. They had decided that they would send three saucers carrying emissaries to the intergalactic carrier. They were going to take the prisoners being held in their custody in the hope that they would exchange them for earth citizens kidnapped by Zelegark and Klaxo and being held on the intergalactic carrier. They had agreed with the young people that the most correct and beneficial way to start a new relationship with an obviously, much more advanced humanoid specie was with a show of humility rather than an arrogant, defiant, display of pride.

There was much discussion as to who the right emissaries should be. It was apparent that the ten young people would be included; they all but demanded space on the saucers. Of course their logic was flawless when they pointed out that, "they", were what all the fuss was about. The young people also "suggested" that Agents Jessop and Reese be included. They reasoned that it was their initial investigative work that identified Emily Smith as an abductee, found them incarcerated in the hospital, and then set the facts straight about their parent's untimely death. Therefore, it just seemed like a natural evolution of events that they should be the ones to go and bring

Emily Smith, Robert Aaron, and the others home. Agents Jessop and Reese looked somewhat horrified when told they were going, but being the intrepid investigators they were, they reluctantly agreed, especially when they were told the young people wanted them to be included. The young people were the only ones that looked upon the excursion as nothing more than a holiday event. Indeed, to them it was sort of like a homecoming!

Earl Abbott earned a position on the saucer because of his extensive scientific knowledge and his contribution to awakening the young people's mind and enabling Spherical Mathematics to be deciphered. Without his assistance the same objectives could no doubt be achieved by the young people on their own but at a much slower pace. Therefore, it was deemed he should go as, "The President's Scientific Representative"; also included as "The President's" representatives were a medical researcher and one very senior diplomat who had the power to initiate whatever treaties and agreements that was deemed necessary to assure the survival of the citizens of earth.

The military was to keep a low profile. Admiral Cleary would lead the contingent and Lieutenant Palangin would act as his attaché. There were several marines to guard the seventeen prisoners. All the prisoners and the marines were on the same craft; the Andrians had been sedated into unconsciousness and a neural mesh net was placed over their heads as advised by the young people. They wanted to prevent any catastrophe enroot to the intergalactic cruiser. The latest intelligence indicated that the intergalactic cruiser was hiding somewhere in the Kuiper belt beyond Neptune, among the numerous asteroids and planetoids. It was time to go.

CHAPTER 57
THE COUNCIL

Shayar and the "Council of Yield" were in deep discussion regarding the Human-Alien Hybrids mathematical achievements of totally mastering spherical mathematical equations to the point of flying a saucer thru space without help. Shayar advised, "We know the Hybrids are extremely intelligent as is the Hybrids, Emily and Robert, were also exceptionally intelligent when they arrived when they arrived. With tutoring they became even more so. The Hybrids Emily and Robert have even expounded additional probabilities in spherical mathematics that we have not here to fore observed. It is truly astounding what they have accomplished in such a small amount of time. But that is with tutoring. It stands to reason therefore, that the Human-Andrian Hybrids on the planet was also, in all probability, tutored. And coupled with their success in finding and defeating Klaxo and his minions, we should from here to ever after, as a specie, quit referring to them as the, "Stupid Humans".

Flata listened closely to what Shayar had said. "Yes, it will be very interesting to evaluate all the humans we come in contact with from here on out. I would like to meet their tutor."

Blain requested entrance into the conference with a message. "My eminence, it appears that a human contingency is approaching the vicinity of our ship. I do not believe they offer us any harm as they are broadcasting on all radio and light frequencies. There are three saucers in the contingency. Our onboard sensors indicate that they have a full contingency of passengers; the traitor Zelegark, along with sixteen of his followers is also on board. They are alive but unconscious. The compliment also includes the ten Human-Andrian hybrids and they are controlling the craft. It is not known at this time how the humans captured Zelegark and his men and took them prisoner; nor do we know how they found the Human-Andrian Hybrids. Flata, would you assist in setting up a quarantine area where a cursory, level three, decontamination can be effected? Then should any of them wish to stay, they will be submitted to a molecular cleansing at that time to eliminate all parasite genera life forms?"

"The Council of Yield", voted unanimously to allow the humans to enter their intergalactic carrier. This appears to be a season of first for the Andrians. No one other than Andrians had ever entered their intergalactic carrier unless they were captured and retrieved for a specific scientific purpose. Now it appeared the Humans would be "knocking at their door", so to speak! Blain was also thinking that, "No Andrian had ever been taken prisoner by a Human."

Shayar advised, "Send out a craft and escort the Humans inside. We do not want any accidents. Oh, and by the way, did you say ten Human-Andrians? Exactly how is that possible when we have two of them on board?"

Blain responded, "Perhaps I was in error on the count." Blain thought privately, "Now how did I miscount?" Then responding to Shayar he advised, "I will take a craft out to escort them to the ship; it is highly unlikely that any untoward thing could occur with the Human-Andrian hybrids operating the craft. I would also like to take Human-Adrian Emily with me to meet the three saucers."

Shayar advised, "As you wish. You seem to make a good pair," Shayar said with a slight smile.

Blain looked up at Shayar with a strange, mystified look on his face. Thinking, "What ever could she mean by that?" He then turned and left the room.

Shayar watched Blain leave. "It is interesting how Human-Andrian, Emily Smith, has captured Blain's heart in the Human way. He is blind to the way he looks at her and even when he says her name it is with tenderness. His attachment to her is not the Andrian way but there does not seem to be any harm in his strange affection. Perhaps we should keep an open mind to the Human way of developing relationships."

CHAPTER 58
THE SEARCH

The small flotilla of three saucers had long since passed the dwarf planets Pluto and Sedna, and, had come to the edge of the Kuiper belt upon passing Neptune. The Kuiper belt was extended from Neptune with Neptune being thirty astronomical units from the sun and then extending up to another fifty astronomical unites and is twenty to two hundred times as massive as the Asteroid Belt which is composed mostly of rocky bodies. The Kuiper belt primarily consists of frozen volatiles such as methane and ammonia and water ice. There are also several dwarf planets with Pluto being the most well-known. The number of asteroids in the Kuiper belt was astronomical and was present in all sizes and shapes. The Oort cloud being located farther out still, is located approximately one third distnce to the next star Proxima Centauri was almost a light year distance from the sun.

Fortunately for the Humans, the Andrians had moved their intergalactic carrier fleet among the planetoids of the Kuiper Belt. They were unable to locate any signs of any other craft in the vicinity. Admiral Cleary speaking to his new attaché, Lieutenant Palangin, said, "Sasha, have the other two saucers search on a one-hundred degree ark, one to port, one to starboard. We will continue dead ahead until one of us contacts the intergalactic carrier. Have each saucer also broadcast radio frequency signals on a sliding scale; then emit a kaleidoscope of light frequencies to insure we make a lot of noise. We do not want them to misconstrue our intentions and think we are trying to sneak upon them.

Sasha provided the instructions to the astrogators and the saucers obeyed the command. They were already becoming a fairly unified fighting force. Soon after the order was given by Sasha to make a lot of noise, the astrogator advised, "Admiral! The saucer on our starboard side reported contact of a small craft bearing zero niner zero on the starboard quadrant sir, she is not moving, Sir!" The young female astrogator looked at Admiral Cleary smiling. By calling the other contact a "she", meant that the pilot was obviously a women. The Admiral then advised, "Sasha, have all ships turn to starboard and approach contact. But do not call it a "she"; after all, there are some pretty good male pilots too! Discontinue the broadcast to assure them that we are aware of their presence and do not have hostile intentions. All ahead slow and steady."

"Yes Sir, Admiral. Sasha relayed the message to the astrogators.

CHAPTER 59
RENDEZVOUS

Astrogator Ashley called out, "Captain Jake!" She looked at Jake and smiled. Jake returned her smile blowing her a kiss. One of the marines assigned to their group rolled her eyes in mock admiration batting her eyelids. "You two love birds are just getting me all excited!" There was laughter throughout the saucer.

"It appears, Captain Jake, there is a saucer on our starboard side at zero niner zero degrees. Jake sent a laser message to Admiral Cleary's saucer advising him of the contact. Upon receiving their orders all three craft made a smart sharp ninety-degree turn and headed toward the saucer contact and followed it thru an asteroid field

Blain watched the maneuvers on his holographic vision and smiled thinking to himself, "Those young Human-Andrian Hybrids were as bright, but not quiet bright as Emily, yet!"

Emily, standing beside him observing the craft said, "Blain, who is that? You never said why we are here."

Blain responded, "It is a surprise for you Emily. I think you will be very pleased. You know, you have become proficient enough that you can control this craft by yourself. Why don't you give those guys a run for their money and see if you can lose them on the way back to the ship. I bet you cannot navigate this craft half as well as you think." He grinned at Emily knowing full well that she would not pass up a challenge.

Emily looked at Blain and smiled. She then focused her newly awakened formidable mind on the controls and linked telepathically to the fusion drive. She maneuvered the craft relatively fast to see if the other three saucers could follow. They did not seem to have any trouble. Emily then immersed herself into the magnificent mind of the machine and melded as one. The only thing she saw was the tracer which led her to the intergalactic carrier. She increased her speed and received an all-encompassing feeling of wellbeing with a kind of fellowship with the saucer. It had to be alive! The saucer missed asteroids and space debris avoiding collisions that were measured in nanoseconds. She could also sense the other saucers following behind with maneuvers not quite as efficient as hers but they kept up nonetheless. The intergalactic carrier seemed to be before her all too soon as the saucer came to rest in its proper position. Moments later the other three saucers followed suit stopping in their designated positions.

Blain let out a sigh of relief as did the occupants of the other saucers did the same. Blain looked at Emily with adoration and awe. He could not believe she handled the craft in such a manner. He himself was good but was he really as good as Emily? He did not think so. The saucers were designed with a biological electrical matrix that was able to sense ones thoughts, receive and execute telepathic commands; but, the connection that Emily had achieved with the machine had seemed almost magical.

It could easily be compared on the same scale as an ordinary human coming into contact with and Andrian, and then some! Now, he, an Andrian, had come into contact with a being that far excelled him doing the one thing in which he was most proficient; And not only that, he was absolutely the most gifted saucer pilot in the three intergalactic fleet.

Emily safely led the other three saucer craft into the docking area and attached her saucer to the extended umbilical. The other three saucers did likewise. Emily then prepared to unlink her mind from the machine. For some inexplicable reason she felt a warm caress meld thru her mind, she had the impression it was like a good by kiss from a loved one. When the connection was completely broken it took a moment for Emily to regain her focus to her surroundings. She became conscious of Blain standing in front of her holding on to both of her arms. He had a sheepish look on his face.

"Emily! You have out flown me and all the other pilots in the fleet! You were marvelous!"

Emily looked around the saucer seeing it thru new eyes. It was aware, she did not know how. She felt it in her mind. It was like an awakening. She felt tears run down her cheeks. How could an inanimate object be alive? She ignored Blain, still being engrossed in her thoughts. She walked to the bulkhead with myriad panels of kaleidoscope colors and touched the panels softly and gently stroked them. "I love you," she intoned; she may have imagined it but it appeared the panels flickered momentarily brighter.

Emily and Blain exited the saucer craft. Emily placed her arm in the crook of Blains arm and said, "Thank you Blain for allowing me to fly the saucer. It is not like anything else I have ever done in my life! Of course there are so many things I have done lately that I have never dreamed they would be possible for me to ever experience!" She looked up at Blain and gave him an endearing smile and to Blain's surprise, Emily reached up, placed her arms around his neck and gave him a tender kiss on his lips and said, "Thank you Blain."

Blain was able to read her mind and also heard the non-verbal, "I love you". The kiss shook Blain to his very soul. The revelation of her Human love was in itself staggering. It was so different from Andrian, cerebral sensuality.

Emily released her embrace and changed her demeanor realizing her feelings for Blain. Thinking to herself, "It must have been the saucer experience that made me think and say that." To Blain she said, "I need to go see Flata immediately."

After entering the Intergalactic craft Blain and Emily parted ways, she never even had a second thought of who was on the other saucers, and, she was able to tuck away her new found revelation of her feelings for Blain into the recesses of her mind…somewhat.

CHAPTER 60
NEW ENTITY

Emily parted from Blain after leaving the saucer in the hanger bay. She was in somewhat of a stupor. Thinking to herself, she wondered what happened. "It is a machine! How could I connect with an inanimate object? The impression was as if "It" was alive! I was immersed in "It" and "It" in me. I felt so free, so powerful! I could see forever!" Then more subdued she thought, "I loved every minute of it! Yes, "it", was alive!"

Emily could still feel the neurological impressions and insights as she maneuvered the saucer thru the asteroid field. But then again she really did not "maneuver or steer", the saucer. She just told the saucer where she wanted to go and how fast, and "It", did her bidding. Every fiber of her being was engaged. She could feel the neurons coursing thru the veins in her arms and legs. She had even connected with the other saucer craft and guided them along! It was real power! It was…godlike!

Blain watched Emily as she and he separated at the entrance to the hanger. Her eyes were glazed over, nostrils flared and her walk was without deviation. She was going to see Flata and nothing was going to stand in her way. Something had happened to her when she was piloting the saucer. He was the best pilot in the fleet in this galaxy and he could not even come close to her skill.

Blain was aware that the saucer had an organic biomass processor and he had superficially connected with it but evidently, not in the manner as had Emily. To Blaine, that made her more of an enigma than ever.

Emily proceeded directly to Flata's quarters breaking all Andrian protocols for personal space. She did not even knock or announce herself. Upon entering the bulbous living room Emily saw Flata and three Andrians. They were all female.

Flata looked up startled by the unprecedented intrusion into her personal living quarters. Seeing the look on Emily's face and feeling the turmoil of her mind she became very apprehensive and somewhat fearful. "What could possibly have happened to Emily to have her act in this manner?"

The other Andrians were even more startled than Flata. They had never before seen or met the Human-Andrian, called Emily. The only thing they knew about her was what they heard. Evidently she was unique and different from all other Humans ever encountered, even the male Human-Andrian, called Robert, and was considered different, just not as evolved as Emily.

Before Flata could speak Emily said, "It is alive!" It was a precise statement of truth, no equivocation.

The three other Andrian women thought the woman was mad. She had burst into Flata's private quarters, an unprecedented flagrant violation of one's personal space, claiming "It", was alive! What was "It"?"

Flata stood and approached Emily, hands outstretched taking Emily's hands in her own. Flata looked her in the eyes and searched her mind. "Yes, it was true. Emily had made a connection with the bio mass in the saucer's mechanical-neurological bio matrix!"

Somehow she, Flata, had made a cognizant being of a mechanical device! Quietly, barely audible, Flata said, "What did it say?" Flata keeping her thoughts in line trying not to show emotion was articulating telepathically to the Human-Andrian, Emily, as clear and concise as possible.

"Tell Me!" Commanded Flata.

Emily responded, "I do not understand. My mind, being, and very soul were immersed with the mind of the machine. I could see, feel, and know everything all at once! It was like flying down different dimensions of being yet being a singular whole! I could feel the heat of ions as they coursed thru me; the power of the gamma rays was gulps of fresh air. And most importantly, dark matter pulled me into a different dimension where I saw more of those ugly creatures. I was there just momentarily but I saw thousands of them! They were in rows moving away from me in a uniform manner and at the front of the group they disappeared into a black void. They were all wearing the same style of space suit as the alien we found in the artifact, moon, Iapetus."

Flata stood there stunned listening to Emily's revelation. It was all her mind could do to take in the possibility that she, Flata, had created a living mechanical entity, and, that Emily could mind meld with "It". But most importantly, that Emily was somehow transported to an alternant reality and observed their most dangerous and deadly enemy they have ever encountered! How was that possible? Furthermore, what were the implications of what she had "seen"?

Again Flata asked, "What did "It" say?"

Emily, looking peaceful and tranquil, replied, "It" said, "I love you, Emily."

The other three Andrian women had looks of fear on their faces as they looked in awe at the Human-Andrian Hybrid. They wondered if what she had said about their enemy was true. They were at war with this strange biological form and the struggle in a distant galaxy had become desperate. And, the information that she had found one on Saturn's moon, Iapetus was not known to them. Evidently the "Council of Yield", wanted to keep the information from the general population. And, how in the stars could a machine love anyone, and not only that, but what was love? It was obviously some kind of Human emotion that is important to Humans.

Emily's next statement was just as startling and perhaps more revealing as to the magnitude of Flata's creation. "The saucer is mine and no one else's. I love the entity within and "It" loves me. There is four more like "It". "She says they are one cohesive unit."

Again Flata looked surprised. You said "She"?

Emily thought for a moment and then said, "I guess so. It just came to me and it seems so right. "She" also said that we will never again be separated and if we are it will not be for long, "She" will find me."

Emily looked pensive and thoughtful, then she slowly said, "She also said more entities just like "her", must be built quickly or she, the Andrians, and all the living species under Andrian control will be destroyed by the "Beings", from the eighth dimension."

Flata jumped back startled into saying a verbal, "What!" The three Andrian females also jumped at Flata's vocalization.

Emily turned from the room saying verbally over her shoulder, "You better listen to "Her"; she has more knowledge of the cosmos in her brain than you Andrians have collected in the last thousand years.

Flata turned to her three friends and excused herself. She said, "Emily, you must relate your impressions and experiences to the "Council of Yield", and, you must not tell anyone else what you told us. She then relayed the same information to her three friends who were still standing and staring in awe of the young Human-Andrian, Emily Smith.

As Emily and Flata left the room, Flata's eyes shined bright. The implication of Emily's short statement about connecting with a mechanical device was equivalent to controlling a star burst! She had done it! She had taken biological mass and fused the neurons into a cohesive whole with a dynamic mechanical property; and somehow, the resultant, "entity"?... had made contact with Human-Andrian Hybrid, Emily Smith! And not only that but somehow the "Entity", could immerse itself into the cosmic spirit using the saucers sensors. "Yes! This was an unprecedented achievement."

CHAPTER 61
ARRIVALS

The three saucers came to rest at the appropriate docking port. Everyone was preparing to exit the craft except the seventeen aliens who were sedated and still unconscious. Sasha's heart beat rapidly as was everyone else's. No one knew what to expect. She checked on the prisoners one last time. Turning to one of her fellow marines she intoned, "Are they going to be surprised when they wake up!" As they were walking down the passageway away from their saucer, six Andrians in the same style of uniform and clear Plexiglas helmets passed them and entered the umbilical access to the saucer. They did not acknowledge them as they passed, looking neither to the right or too the left.

"They certainly looked serious! They did not even stop to say hello", laughed Sasha.

Flata watched the group enter into the assembly area. She immediately recognized the short diminutive female who orchestrated the extraction of the three Andrian assassins. She would certainly make a point to visit with her later. She rather liked her style, even if she was only human, and of course, "Only Human", was not the same thing as "Stupid Human".

There were approximately thirty-five human visitors, including the ten Human-Andrian hybrids. " Now, there was a real mystery! How did that happen? She knew beyond a doubt that Emily and Robert were hybrids, and even perhaps, something more! She would look at these ten more closely."

The visitors observed a woman and a man standing before them on a raised dais. The female was wearing purple coveralls, gloves and a clear plastic, bubble helmet. The male was dressed in similar fashion except his coveralls were blue. The woman cleared her throat, more to quiet the assembly than to accommodate a bodily function. Everyone quieted down, the room became totally silent.

"Welcome Humans. My name is Flata. I am the ships chief geneticist, or, medical doctor, if you will. For any of you to proceed any farther into "our", home, it will be necessary to cleanse you of contaminants such as parasites, bacteria, and viruses. This cleansing will be a superficial cleansing and will take about seven of your earth days. This superficial cleansing is all that is required for you to come aboard our vessel for a short visit; a short visit being up to two earth months. Should any one of you wish to stay longer with us, you will be decontaminated down to the molecular level. This process would take three of your earth months, if not more."

"We are aware of your mores and proclivities regarding nudity. We do not have similar mores here. However, in deference to your customs, we have set up two separate decontamination areas. When you leave the room, males will exit to the right, females to the left. Once you are in the next room you will disrobe completely. Place you clothing in the designated receptacle. They will be destroyed. This includes your wallets, ID's, belts and shoes. All rings, watches, and jewelry will go thru a different class of decontamination. You will get these items back at a later date. Place them in the proper designated container. Please assist us in this endeavor. It is not an option. If you do not comply you will not be allowed aboard our craft. If you do not have the maturity to follow these simple requirements we do not want you aboard our craft. Now, we know you may be uncomfortable being nude, we apologize; there is absolutely no room for modesty. We are making a great concession in dividing you up by sex."

With the end of her speech, Flata pointed toward the two doors. A female Andrian was standing by one door and a male Andrian was standing by another. They too wore the same style of clothing with the bubblehead cover. Both made motions with their hands indicating they were to enter.

Jake squeezed Ashley's hand and kissed her on the lips. "I will see you later love!" The male and female Andrians blanched and looked away. As Jake was walking by the Andrian male he said, "You ought to try that sometime, you would love it.

Once thru the door, there was a long passageway with a large round receptacle at the end of the hall. Jake quickly stripped naked and threw his clothes into the receptacle. He was startled when his clothes, almost out of view down the dark receptacle, burst into flame. The ashes were quickly sucked into the void.

Jake placed his feet in the designated position on the deck, legs spread wide apart. Agent Jessop took the next designated position beside him and stood in similar fashion. Jake was startled to see the scars on his body, several looked like gunshot wounds. If Agent Jessop knew he was staring he did not acknowledge it.

Soon there were twelve naked men standing in a row in the designated positions. The lights in the room dimmed. They then began to change color in a kaleidoscope of rapidly changing colors. The light resonated at different light frequencies that killed different strains of bacteria, viruses, and insects of various varieties. After the lights ceased there was a warm, damp breeze that caused tingling sensations on the skin. A clear tube came from the ceiling and completely encased them in a vacuum tight seal. A light spray spewed from the top of the containment capsule. All the lights in the room went out leaving them standing in pitch darkness. A longitudinal blue light wave followed by other longitudinal waves of different frequencies swiftly went over their bodies. The light was definitive and did not mix. Again there was another strong flowing of air from top to bottom. When the air ceased, the Plexiglas case lifted. A voice in their head told them to go thru the door at the end of the hall. Once all the men exited the room, another group of men entered and underwent the same cleansing process.

As Jessop entered the second room he observed what appeared to be a shimmering glass wall. A voice in his head said, "Walk slowly thru the shimmering wall." As he walked thru the shimmer, he felt a mild burning sensation, even between his legs. They were then all directed into a third room. Again they were instructed to stand erect, legs apart, within the designated circle.

This time a tube came up from the floor sealing them into the place with a definitive click and change in air pressure. Again Jessop, as all the rest of them, heard a voice in their heads say, "The glass tube will begin filling with a gelatinous substance beginning at your feet; the substance will fill to your neck line. Keep your hands to your side. Stand very still. A small circular tube will descend from overhead. The tube will insert itself into your mouth. It will not be uncomfortable. Do not fight the tube insertion. Just relax".

The gelatinous substance quickly filled from Jessop's waist to his neck. He could feel a strong tingling sensation all over his body. As for moving, once he was encased in the jell, he could not even move his fingers. He heard the voice in his head again. "Nano bots will be collecting and cleansing debris from your body. Just relax." A tube came down from the top of his body and inserted itself into Jessop's mouth. One breath and all sensations ceased. Jessop, like the rest of his companions, were fast asleep.

CHAPTER 62
THE REUNION

Sasha slowly regained consciousness. She felt languid and totally rested. She allowed herself a long satisfying yawn and stretched her arms above her head. She then observed the billowing sleeves the color of a soft hued, pink rose, as they slid down her arms to her elbows. Raising her head from a soft satin pillow she looked down and observed she was clothed in an extremely thin, one piece, lightweight, garment. There was a sash fastened around her waist. The sash was darker in color and added an accent to the garment. Sitting up in the lounger and swinging her legs to the floor, she saw her slippered covered feet. They too were colored a darker pink. It was then she noticed the deep cut of the upper garment exposing the cleavage of her ample bosom. This exposure caused her cheeks to burn; she always had her breast tightly bound so as not to accent her female assets. It was a necessary thing working in the capacity of a commando. Men will always be men, even in the most difficult and strangest environments; distractions could get one killed.

Across from her she saw young Ashley waking up. Ashley sat up observing her garment and noticed the deep cut exposing Sasha's ample breast. Then she looked down and observed she was equally exposed, even though her breast was not bountiful like Sasha's, they were well formed and quite desirable. Ashley looked up and observed Sasha observing her. Their eyes caught on one another and each smiled a strangely sensuous smile. Then Sasha remembered her strange dream. She blushed, looking away, as did Ashley. It was like they had the same dream or, could they read one another's mind?

Sasha, thinking to herself mused, "What in the hell was that all about? I know I am still a virgin but surely I am not attracted to women! What was that dream? I cannot quite recall it."

There were only fifteen women in their group. Five of them were military; five of them were the young Human-Andrian Hybrids. The other five women were civilian scientist and one police officer. Sasha observed Agent Reese. She had seen the bullet wounds and knife wounds when they undressed. She was in excellent shape. Now it was apparent that she felt as awkward as Sasha, both being extremely conservative in dress and mannerisms, mostly because of choice of careers. She felt a kindred spirit for the female detective so she approached her and gave her a hug and a greeting. Reese had the same kindred spirit for Sasha. After all, they were a minority in a very violent, primarily, men's domain. Reese returned her embrace with a greeting and a smile. Both women had utmost respect for the others skill. Reese had seen the extraction of the three aliens from the Sahara on the holographic and upon learning it was orchestrated by Sasha she knew they could be friends. And, Sasha had researched Reese's career and upon learning of her many encounters knew that in any violent encounter she could

SEED OF HOPE

trust Reese to watch her back. As the rest of the group woke up they murmured greetings to one another and examined their clothes. All were dressed in the same billowing one piece, super thin, breast revealing, with a wraparound belt accenting the waistline. It appeared the Andrians did not offer much in the way of color selection. They were all the same color. And, because all the women were conservative, they all felt equally exposed.

Flata entered the room standing silently to one side observing the group. Looking approvingly around the room, her gaze landed on Sasha. Flata sent her a telepathic message, looking directly into her eyes, gauging her perception. Sasha returned her gaze to Flata and knew she was being asked a question. She was not sure but she thought the women asked how she was doing. Sasha smiled at her and verbally responded, "I am fine, thank you", then she telepathed ,"I think". Flata's smile broadens. She was pleased with her enhancement of the Human female's telepathic abilities. Flata nodded her head in acknowledgement, and then she turned around and left the room. Flata was pleased with the results. She had enhanced Sasha's ability to communicate telepathically when she was being decontaminated. She had also removed all cell destroying pathogens and healed several serious life threatening contagions from all the human population.

The five Human-Andrians and Sasha followed upon hearing the telepathic command to do so. The remaining humans followed the young people because they did not want to be left behind.

In the men's section of the decontamination lab, the men began to wake up. All of them were dressed in the same fabric except for color, it was pale blue. They too had a belt like sash around the waist and sported a plunging neckline. All of the military men and Agent Jessop were broad at the shoulder and narrow at the hip. That is of course, except the scientist and the politician. They were plumper around the waist. None of them felt comfortable.

Blain entered the room. He was dressed in the same fashion. With a practiced eye of a combat warrior, he observed the military men and Agent Jessop. He mused that in hand-to-hand combat they would be formidable opponents. Well, bigger men than they had fallen before his fighting skills. Still, it was nice that they were not enemies, at least not yet. All the men had noticed his scrutiny and they eyed him in return, suspiciously.

"Hello. My name is Blain. Welcome to our home. If you will follow me, we will meet with the others in the conference center."

Agent Jessop eyed the man named Blain. He did not see the abductors face in the surveillance video but this individual's height and weight matched the man in the video. He could very well be the same individual that abducted Emily.

Blain stopped and turned around facing the group but addressing Agent Jessop, "Detective Jessop, you are a fine investigator. Yes, I am the man that abducted Emily. I did so to save her life. As you well know, we believed that Klaxo had his assassins were out to murder or kidnap her. You know her parents were murdered by them. We do not understand how they missed her. As you will soon see, she is in good health and has greatly expanded her intellectual abilities beyond our comprehension. And, we are all…grateful, for your superb investigative skills that were instrumental in finding and freeing the ten young people." Blain turned and left the room. Jessop was flabbergasted that Blain was so knowledgeable about his role in recovering the young people and his investigation into discovering Emily's fate.

The group entered a large area which could easily hold up to one hundred people. The fifteen women of their group were already in the room. Jessop heard a sharp intake of breath from one of the marines standing beside him. He observed that the marine had just seen Sasha in a very un-military like fashion garment. She was stunningly beautiful. Sasha caught his admiring gaping stare and gave him a full smile. The marine smiled back sheepishly and looked away with a blood rushed face.

Jessop said, "She is indeed a beautiful woman. What a strange profession she has chosen".

The view of the cosmos and the planet had its intended effect. Neptune had a twenty-nine degree inclination to its orbit thus it had seasons like the earth. The view showed the humans where they were, who they were, and most importantly, who was in charge.

There was certainly no argument there. The men moved to the women's side of the observation room. Jessop saw Reese give him a "thumbs up" and pointedly stared at his groin. The thin material was very revealing.

Jessop smiled at her and shrugged his shoulders and held his hands out in an upward position. As for Reese, he had never seen her look so good. How could he but help to admire her toned athletic body? They stood side by side holding hands, enjoying the closeness, and admiring the view.

Blain entered thru a side access and stepped up on a dais. He was accompanied by Flata and Breveka. They were waiting a moment to allow the Humans to enjoy the view and evidently for another group.

Agents Jessop and Reese were on the outside of the group admiring the panoramic view of the cosmos when another door opened. A group of approximately twelve people entered the room. They instantly recognized Emily Smith and Robert Aaron. They did not know any of the other people. Both investigators approached Emily and Robert. "Ms. Smith, Mr. Aaron, we are detectives Jessop and Reese," extending their hands for a handshake. Both Emily and Robert were caught completely by surprise. They were almost speechless.

Emily responded, "You know who I am? How do you know that?" Even though Emily could read their thoughts, she was so caught off guard that she was unable to do so.

Reese replied, "We have been looking for you since you disappeared from the University campus. It is a long story. We will fill you in later."

Then Emily could hardly believe her eyes. She felt like Alice, again falling down the rabbit hole, for a second time. She saw Earl Abbott walking toward her, arms extended. She ran falling into his arms burying her head into his chest, just like she did with Warren! Small tears began rolling down her cheeks, soon becoming a sobbing flow.

Earl said, "Everything is going to be alright Emily. You are coming home. These two fine detectives tracked you down." Jessop and Reese each placed reassuring arms around Emily's heaving shoulders. They too had tears running down their cheeks.

The two groups looked at one another appraisingly. They both wondered how each other fit into the strange milieu of circumstances and how each came to this utterly, out of the world, strange place.

Emily could feel the ten young people probing her mind. They were inquisitive and somewhat distrustful. They were wondering why they had been taken captive and imprisoned and she was not. Emily responded, "I do not know. But the one thing we have in common is all our parents were murdered by Klaxo's henchmen. And thank you, James Carroll, for trying to save my parents. I will be forever grateful". James nodded his head acknowledging her heartfelt thanks. Emily had somehow been able to discern his actions from all the other mental communications among the group. And, she was grateful and truly moved. They sensed her emotions and sincerity and believed her honesty, and as one, moved to Emily and Robert and placed their arms around them. They were truly part of their group. Then all the group intermingled with the original ten captives sent to the Andrian intergalactic ship, everyone talking excitedly at once. The Andrians watched and listened to the group. They were pleased. In their minds eye they knew they had made the correct choice.

CHAPTER 63
NEW GIFT

Shayar allowed the groups to mingle and visit for about twenty minutes. Then, she called to them to get their attention. "May I have your attention please?" Shayar waited until all the whispering ceased. Everyone turned toward Shayar who was standing on the dais next another female and male Andrian. Behind them was the panoramic view of a blue Neptune, the color derived by the methane in the atmosphere, and the last of the giant gas planets in the solar system. The rings were easily discernible due to the closeness of the planet as was several of its moons, Triton being the largest. The cold ball of ice was easily visible and was smooth on one side and rough on the other.

Shayar continued, "I am Shayar, president of the "Council of Yield". We, those of us on the three intergalactic carriers, would like to apologize to you ten Humans who were captured and delivered to us by the traitor Zelegark. Our accommodations and treatment of you here has not been as hospitable as it should have been. Our failure in this area was brought to our attention by Human-Andrian Hybrid, Emily, at which time, we did our utmost to correct.

Emily's eyes popped open wider! Her heart skipped several beats. She never ever thought of herself as a

Hybrid. She knew she was different from her fellows having some amazing intellectual gift, not to mention that she could also connect with a mechanical biological entity. But that was all. They were just gifts. She remembered Blain having told her she was different, she was like them, but she had never before put a name to the difference. She really did not realize and or believe, she was a hybrid. Actually, she never thought of it. Deep down, she now realized she was afraid to know the truth. She could feel the other ten Human-Andrians stroking her mentally to help eliminate her fear and distress. Emily, for the first time, looked around with new eyes. She finally understood how she could understand Spherical Math, converse telepathically and l link with a biological machine.

She heard Shayar continuing and had to concentrate to understand what she was saying. The knowledge she just received had been a tremendous shock. Before the meeting this morning she had no knowledge of the other ten Human-Andrians..."Our treatment of you should have been more hospitable but when we learned you were not the ten Human-Andrians which we were to retrieve, and became knowledgeable of the traitorous duplicity of Klaxo and his followers, we chose to keep you on sustainable rations until we could reach a decision as to your fate. Fortunately, Emily and Robert arrived and Emily interceded on your behalf before we spaced you..." said in a nonchalant, rather dismissive manner, disregard for Human life.

At first the ten captives looked horrified, then, with

SEED OF HOPE

open hostility, and some looked around with resigned indifference; all of them now understood why Emily could order the Andrians around. Even if she did not know she was one of them, she was obviously much smarter than the everyday, run of the mill humans.

Emily looked at them smiling and said quietly, "I love you".

Shayar continued, "At that time, we chose to follow Emily's, uh, request." She looked at Blain who was smiling at her obvious misspoken truth. She then looked at Emily and smiled. "Because of Emily's intercession on your behalf, we expended more sustainable rations on you. Emily also "requested", that we use our science to heal your lame and you're blind. The two of you humans that had been blind and lame from birth have been made whole." They both shouted simultaneously, "Thank God!"

Shayar looked at them somewhat annoyed.

Emily smiled at her and telepathically said, "Yes, we thank our God. And, we thank you, for your generosity in expending your precious resources and knowledge to help us."

Shayar looked pacified and continued, "Now, to the Human-Andrians". Shayar turned and faced the group. "We are truly sorry for the pain and suffering caused by Klaxo and Zelegark when they murdered your parents and put you in prison. Our intention was to keep you together as family units. There is nothing we can do to bring your parents back or to return the time you spent in prison. You are now on your own. You will have to form other alliances for family support. I suppose it is time to enlighten you as to your purpose. You have learned only half of the truth. The truth you have learned is that the earth is in dire straits and is about to become uninhabitable if measures are not taken to control existing debilitating circumstances resultant from your many manufacturing process. I am speaking of the many manufacturing processes which no control is exerted to make certain industries stop polluting the atmosphere and poisoning the water. They are putting profits and personal gain above the greater good. I suppose in your culture, it would be called flag waving and free agency to make profit however one chooses to do so. To us, it is total insanity.

How can your governments not see that the many cancers and other deadly illnesses are caused by this pollution? The truth is, they do see and they choose to turn a blind eye; again, for personal profit and gain. How can they believe that their children and grandchildren are immune to such practices? They just look the other way and go sailing off in their fine yachts in your polluted oceans. If that is not proof of a demented species then we do not know what is. Should intervention not occur, then the Earth will be uninhabitable within eight hundred years. The Earth will become just like the planet you call Mars."

Everyone looked at one another. That was a heavy revelation; could the ten Human-Andrians actually stop the destructive processes; and, if the Andrians keep talking about only ten Human-Andrians, what of the extra two? Where did they come from? It was confusing to everyone, Humans and Andrians.

"Now, it will not be necessary for you to find consorts within your group. You may procreate with any other human. Your Human-Andrian DNA will be passed to your offspring. What we have tried to do was to make an assessment as to the viability of allowing earthlings, humans if you will, to continue to occupy the planet. We believe you can make the difference between annihilation and life."

Now that statement angered every one of the humans, even the Human-Andrian Hybrids. How could they come to their world and make a decision that they were unworthy to live on their planet!

The Andrians could read their thoughts and feel their emotions. Shayar continued, "It may seem cold to you. From your point of view, it is. But, your lack of self-control is destroying the planet. You seem to have no concern for the very habitat which gives sustenance to your lives. The truth is there are many intelligences clamoring for a chance to occupy and colonize the earth before it is totally destroyed. We are but one of those intelligences. You think there is an infinite number of worlds in habitable zones though out the galaxy; there are, in this galaxy and many more galaxies. However, the intelligences within our sphere of contact, which is very substantial, are on worlds which are overcrowded. Your world is crowded, but not like other worlds. And, what few of you there are is destroying what you have."

"It seems your planet is well hidden and known only to a few other space faring intelligences. You are not in a highly dense convergence zone; the flux in this arm of the galaxy is minimal. Thus, you are relatively safe from outside incursions. But even so, if you continue on the path you are pursuing, you will make your planet uninhabitable like the planet you call Mars, within a few short generations."

"Instead of removing your species from the planet, we chose to insert genetically altered younglings into your population. We believe they are capable of exerting influence enough to remedy the most immediate critical problems your species face. Then, they and their offspring could preserve your species and the Earth."

"However, we have just recently discovered an interesting development for which we have not planned for nor expected. We know we inserted ten and only ten younglings into the population. We have before us twelve. Our "doctors", geneticist, and their entire staffs, have exhaustively studied your DNA on the molecular level. Each of you are Human-Andrian Hybrids. Therefore, where did the other two Human-Andrian Hybrids come from, and which ones are they? What is their source?"

"Our most eminent scientist-geneticist, Flata, has come to the conclusion that what has resulted is not a hybrid of Human-Andrian, but a totally new humanoid species. She believes this to be true because of the exponential increase in mental powers that far exceeds even our own."

"Our greatest advantage as Andrians over Humans is our keenly developed mental skills. We do not have more sophisticated brains or larger brains. Our brain size is almost exactly the same. But, one of the parameters we used to determine your fate is the existence of a small pinpoint growth next to your hypothalamus. A genetic nano scan has determined that this growth, in the Human-Andrian Hybrids, or possibly the new specie is rapidly developing. This development is creating a new chemical enzyme which we cannot yet identify"

"We have gone back over our previous records of earlier Human contacts and looked for this small growth. It was present but was passed over due to its tremendously small chemical trace identifier. It appears all humans have this small chemical trace. What this means is that there is a potential for a DNA renaissance into a better and improved Humanoid already in place upon your earth. This can be the only possible explanation for the two extra young people. This renaissance of human neurological development is already in process and the two extra young people are at the very cusp of this development."

Turning and speaking to the ten initial captives, Shayar advised, "Unfortunately for you, we believe it will be in your best interest that we remove any and all memories of us and your experiences here. You will wake up in the cities in which you were taken. You will have memories implanted that you have been part of a government work program and have contributed to integral research pertaining to inventory management of machine parts. Sounds dull? It is but you will love it!"

The ten captive had a real laugh for the first time since they had been abducted.

"You will be provided with expertise in this area. You will never meet each other again. All of you will work at businesses that are fronts for the intelligence service; you just will not know it. This is necessary to help the new coalition maintain security for our programs and to give you some semblance of your former freedoms and rights. And of course, your expertise will be utilized to advance our collaborative scientific programs."

"Now, for the two of you who were recipients of our superior medical knowledge, you will wake up in different cities from which you were taken and will remember that you were recent participants in medical experiments for which you volunteered. You too will have jobs working for business that have been established for the intelligence community. Also, you will submit yourselves for medical study at least three times a year so earth science can be advanced. You will all be amply rewarded for your time away from home and the trauma which you all endured."

"We all thank you for your time and patience."

Several of the former captives laughed. One said, "Our pleasure".

"It is necessary that we meet with your military and the Human-Andrians in private after this meeting. We have serious issues to discuss. But for now, Please, watch the holograph…".

CHAPTER 64
AND, JUDGEMENT

The **holograph covered** one bulkhead toward the end of the room. The visual showed the planet Jupiter, and the moon identified on the holographic, as Europa. The moon was an icy ball a little smaller than Earth's moon. The surface was covered with ridges, smooth icy plains, and dark colorations. The dark colorations were a result of tidal friction from the gravitational forces encountered as Europa circled Jupiter in its eccentric orbit. The audience watched captivated as they observed four saucers approach Europa. They entered a large cavity that opened as they neared the surface. It was the traitor's hidden base. Soon a group of freighters neared the base. Other saucers were flown from the base into the freighters. Four saucers exited the base, the large cavity closed for the last time and the freighters and saucers left the area, leaving Jupiter and Europa behind. The visual was time lapsed so the time frame for viewing was shortened.

Soon, three other saucers approached Europa from a different direction. They were near enough so that the saucers and the moon were clearly visible. Three beams of red light extended from the saucers to the canopy that covered the hidden entrance to the base. The beams systematically cut into the canopy. Material and some bodies floated out into space thru the openings. Then two of the three saucers moved farther away from the moon. The one remaining saucer then emitted a large green beam into the cavity exposed by the destroyed canopy. A black hole appeared on the surface of the moon. There was a flash of brilliant light as the area exploded in a large cloud of ice, rock and metal. Debris was ejected with rocket like force from the surface of the moon. Then, just as quickly, all the material was sucked into the small black hole that was in the center of the former base. And then the group watched in horror as a large chunk of Europa detached itself from the rest of the moon and drifted toward Jupiter, pulled by the planets immense gravity field.

Shayar then said, "Look out the viewing window. What you are now seeing and everyone on the three intergalactic carriers are seeing, is the ejection or spacing, of the remaining traitors returned by Earths Space Defense Commandoes. We commend you for a job well done." And looking directly at Sasha, she continued, "And we applaud you for your ingenuity and intelligence."

All in the room watched as the bodies sailed swiftly to ward the blue planet Neptune. The wind of Neptune at times has been recorded as much as one thousand miles an hour. Some of Neptune's thirteen known moons were visible, the most prominent being Triton, which orbits Neptune in a retrograde orbit. The surface of Triton is frozen nitrogen and is a minus three hundred and ninety one degrees Fahrenheit and yet, spews geysers of material up to five miles above the surface of the moon; again, the ejection of material being the result of tidal friction generated by Neptune's magnetic field.

The traitors, in their suits, would eventually freeze solid but live long enough to regret their traitorous activities. Over time they would collide with other frozen debris and ice objects and be broken into numerous pieces, their DNA would become part of the frozen rings forever circling the planet, Neptune. It would be an ignoble death. Their bodies tumbled and rolled toward the planet. They would be conscious for several hours, time enough to contemplate their actions.

CHAPTER 65
ALLIANCE

The "Council of Yield", was all present on the raised dais. That was unprecedented for them to physically be in the same place at the same time. They were always, without exception, viewed on holographic. However, their efforts to save the specie on the Earth, and the discovery of the corpse of one of their deadliest enemy, on Saturn's moon Iapetus, caused them to change their protocol this one time. The dictum about using holographic vision came about when the entire council was murdered by one malefactor over a thousand years ago; also included as Andrian representatives were Flata, Breveka, Blain, Sharla, and military representatives.

The earth's delegation consisted of the government representative, the military officers and enlisted men, scientist, including Earl Abbott, the twelve young Human-Andrian hybrids, and of course, Agents Reese and Jessop.

Shayar commenced the meeting with a welcome and greeting, and then skipping the preliminaries, she got straight to the issues at hand. "We would like to extend an invitation to your government to send envoys of various scientific disciplines to participate in educational programs aboard our ships. We in turn would like to insert medical and scientific representatives among your populations, primarily to attempt to solve the mystery of the extra two Human-Andrians, for which whom, we cannot account. We also would like to observe your development up close to see how you handle your environmental issues. It is your lives and your futures that are at stake. And of course, we will add more fingers to make us appear physically normal and we will do our best to act Human". That statement elicited some laughter. And unknown to the conferees and to the great embarrassment to Blain, and Sharla, their two children, Jawane and Hanlee, having been thoroughly infected with Emily's sense of humor, ran to the front of the conference room from their hiding place and gleefully danced around the room saying, "Duh, Duh, Duh" and placed their hands beside their ears with one finger sticking up in a parody of horns. Emily quickly got up and said and did the same and she was soon followed by the other ten Human-Andrians. That did elicit quiet an uproarious laughter from the Human side of the contingent. The Andrians were not known for their sense of humor stared in complete shock. After the laughter died down, Emily took the children by the hands and walked them from the room. On the way out she looked at Blain and Sharla and telepathed, "It is my fault; please do not chastise them overly much. We humans need laughter to help us assimilate painful and difficult information."

Shayar, having regained her composure, stiffly said, "Well I guess we all now know how we are going to fit into the Human population." That too elicited a good round of laughter. She did not intend to be comical. "Now onto the serious side of this meeting, it is imperative that representatives of your military train with our units. I cannot stress enough the realities of the danger we both face by the life form that Emily and Blain discovered on Saturn's moon, Iapetus. We believe that it may possibly have come from another dimension, Emily will discuss that later. We have our most imminent scientist working on this theory. Its' DNA, and chemical structure is not like anything in any of the galaxies we have visited. We do not normally invite any other specie to join with us in any endeavor. However, we believe the Human potential to evolve exceeds even our own evolutionary processes. We do not want to be left behind." That too received a room full of laughter. Again, Shayar was not being comical. "But we believe that this new enemy could possibly mean the extinction of all our species. I would like Emily to revisit her experience when she was flying the saucer and leading your delegation back to our intergalactic carrier. Emily, if you please?"

Emily stood at the dais and looked toward the other Human-Andrians. "Those of you who were the pilots and astrogators of the saucers that was following me back to the intergalactic carrier are still wondering what happened. What I mean is, is that there was no way for you to navigate thru the asteroid fields and keep up with me on your own. What you experienced was the assimilation of your mind with the living entity created by the chief geneticist, Flata. This living entity is a combination of neuro bio mass and machine. And whether you like it or not, you are now melded with that particular machine's entity."

There was complete silence in the room. Very few people were aware of Emily's experience. The military presence in the room leaned forward on their seats as one. They definitely wanted to know more. The young Human-Andrian astrogators and pilots sat opened mouth in awe. They knew that something amazing had happened, they just did not know what it was and they were afraid to talk about it.

Emily continued, "Because of my numerous flying experiences, courtesy of Blain, my continued presence allowed the entity to be assimilated into my neurological-structure to the point where I was able to become completely cognizant of its presence. I, in effect, became part of the machine. I could feel the spirit of the cosmos flow thru my being. I could see vast distances. My being could immerse itself into the numerous subatomic particles that sing the songs of the universe. And in some way, somehow I was transported into the eighth dimension. I cannot verbalize to you the truth of this statement. I do not know how I know it was the eighth dimension. What I saw there was thousands of the ugly beings that Blain and I found on the moon Iapetus. After you see one of them you know what an "Alien", truly is. I saw them from the back, looking down upon them. They were all wearing space suits. They were all facing forward and moving rapidly until they disappeared into a black void." Emily ended her experience and sat down. The mood in the room was pensive.

The meeting continued for several hours with work groups being formed to address the issues incident to both Human and Andrian. Also, there was much discussion about Human behavior aboard the intergalactic carriers and Andrian behavior on the Earth. Breveka was the designated point and it fell to her the responsibility to liaison between the two groups. She would be on the Earth at one of the military bases but would have complete freedom to come and go as she pleased.

It was further decided that Robert Aaron would assist Sharla in developing fusion drives to be used to enhance Earth's military and civilian space infrastructures. They both would be commuting between the earth and intergalactic carriers when required. Dr. Abbott would spend most of his time on an intergalactic carrier as per his personal request.

Sharla's "marriage" to Robert was a great festive occasion for the Humans and it was performed in the large viewing room with the planet Saturn in the back ground as the intergalactic carriers had moved further into the solar system. However, they decided to save their physical union until they were on earth, much to the relief of Sharla.

While the meeting with the "Council of Yield" was still on going, Blain went to the dais and asked everyone for their attention. "Some of you have been wondering how I fit into the "milieu" of this merry band of intergalactic travelers." The statement elicited laughter all around. "Emily, if you must know, I am the Military Commander for all the Andrian forces in your galaxy. " Emily's jaw dropped as she stared wide eyed, up at Blain. She had no idea that he was … military? "And as such I would like for everyone to know what a special young women you are. You have exhibited courage, calm before the enemy, and maintained an acute presence of mind when faced with new and mind blowing revelations." Everyone was quiet as "Commander" Blain, publically extolled Emily's virtues. "Also, you can ask more darn questions in one minute than any other female life form in the entire galaxy!" Everyone stood and cheered with the last declaration.

 Emily looked up at Blain and said, "Thank you Blain."

CHAPTER 66
HOME COMMING

Dr. Earl Abbott and Emily walked up the driveway to Dr. Earl Abbotts home. They entered the house thru a side door and walked into the kitchen. It smelled so good to Emily, she loved roast pork. How long had it been; almost a year? It seemed like forever. Karen, Skip, Billy, and Warren were sitting around the kitchen table preparing to eat. Warren looked up and saw his father; at his side stood Emily. He could hardly believe his eyes. He blinked them once, then twice. She was still standing there!

Karen, having seated herself with her back to the door, saw the opened mouthed startled stare of her eldest son, turned in her chair, and observed Earl and Emily standing just inside the doorway. Karen literally flew out of her seat and rushed into her husband's arms. He embraced her gently murmuring all the things that lovers say to one another.

Warren just sat in his chair disbelieving that Emily was standing in the room in which he was seated. Emily walked slowly to Warren not taking her eyes off his. As she reached his side she embraced him to her breast and hugged him close. She telepathically sent him words of love and endearment. He returned the hug, snuggling close, still in utter shock at her sudden appearance.

SEED OF HOPE

Warren was still not sure if Emily was real. He dreamed of holding her close for so long that often time's what was fantasy and what was reality, was indiscernible, and had blurred his judgment. Was she really here? Was her arms wrapped around him? Did she really pull his head to her breast and hold him there? Maybe she isn't really there. Maybe he was just going completely crazy.

Billy and Skip, mesmerized by the sudden appearance of their Dad and Emily, watched the tender embracing reunions. They knew the moment was sacred and that they should be quiet, it was a very personal moment for all of them. Tears rolled down their cheeks. They loved Emily, they believed, as much as they loved their mother.

Later that evening, Emily explained that a band of Gypsies had accosted her by the park, chloroformed her, and carried her away. She said when she awakened, she was somewhere in the middle of Europe, tethered with a rope. She had been captured and used as a cooking slave. Emily said, "Those poor people, they must have really been hard up for a cook! And then those two fine detectives Reese and Jessop, who was working with Interpol, tracked me down! Earl had become involved because of his association with Admiral Cleary, who was some high up muckety muck in the navy."

Warren did not know what to believe. He knew he loved Emily. And, if Emily said it was so, then that was the way it was.

Billy and Skip listened carefully to the story not wanting to disbelieve a single word Emily said. They gave each other a knowing look and politely excused themselves from the room stating it was late and they needed to go to bed. They both embraced Emily tightly and gave her a kiss on the cheek before leaving the room.

As they were leaving the room, Emily gave them an approving look. They knew she was not telling the truth. They did not know why, they just loved her too much to pry. She was pleased she could not suffuse, redirect, or diminish their skepticism. She knew they would use the internet computer to Google the clue she gave them. She did not think they had ever heard of Admiral Cleary and knew he was not a muckety muck. He might be high up, but it was an important position, of that they were sure. Good! She wanted them to think for themselves. She knew they had not been idle while she was gone. They listened and researched daily any news that seemed strange. The most obvious clue to them that something was up was the detectives Jessop and Reese. It appeared that they had dropped off the face of the earth. As for Warren, her sudden disappearance had deeply injured him. Emily knew she would have to nurse him back to health.

Looking outside in the darkness, Emily could hear raindrops on the roof, smell the rain with her nose, and hear the wind move the limbs of the nearby tree. It was so good to be home. There was so much work to do. But for tonight, she would just hold Warren.

Then, without thinking, she turned to Karen and Earl, and said, "Warren and I are getting married tonight, right now. We can get a priest, a pastor, or a rabbi, I do not care which. We will keep our marriage secret. No one needs to know but us and God. We can have a public wedding with a Justice of the Peace, later."

Karen and Earl looked at one another then back at Emily. They both saw the resolve in her eyes. And, they knew she was right. Warren was looking up at her still enraptured by her return, from the dead, if you will. He could not believe his ears. He was getting married! Tonight!

Earl kissed his wife on the cheek and said, "I will be back shortly". He left the house and drove off in the rain. Even though it was one in the morning he had no doubt that he would find a clergy member to perform the ceremony. Minutes later he was knocking on his pastor's door.

Emily took Warren by the hand and said, "Come on Husband to be! We both need to shower and dress for our wedding. And I for one intend to take a long, hot, shower!" Warren did not need any encouragement. He jumped up and allowed Emily to lead him upstairs to his bedroom to prepare for their wedding.

Within the hour, Earl had returned with their Pastor and his wife. They were very excited to be asked to perform the wedding. They knew the story of Emily's disappearance and was aware of Warren's anguish. This was to be a very auspicious occasion, even if it was one in the morning.

Warren was wearing a dark suit and tie. Emily was wearing a grey skirt and white blouse, which belonged to Karen. She was also wearing Karen's white veil. Her wedding dress was just too small. Skip and Billy were wearing dark trousers and white shirts, their hair neatly combed. They were excited for the turn of events with Warren and Emily getting married. When they were suddenly rousted from their sleep they had no idea what was going on.

Karen had gone outside in the early morning darkness and drizzling rain and had cut a bouquet of roses from her rose bushes. Karen glowed with satisfaction thinking, "It would not do for Emily to get married without a bouquet." She was beside herself with joy at the momentous turn of events!

Karen herself was dressed in a pale blue suit with a rose colored blouse. And as usual, she was as beautiful as ever. Adding to her surprise was that Earl was wearing the same suit that he and Karen had gotten married. It floored her to think that he remembered and not only that but he had carefully preserved it in a clothing preservative unit. The fabric was as fresh and laundered as the day he had put it in storage so many years ago.

She saw Earl grinning at her surprise and he said, "You did not think I remembered, did you?" She reached up and placing her arms around her husband's neck, she kissed him lightly on the lips and said, "I love you so much. You always surprise me." Fortunately for Earl, these last few months had caused him to slim down to his younger year's weight so he was able to fit nicely into the suit.

The wedding was performed quietly. The Pastor and his wife sensed the profound sacredness with which Warren and Emily said their vows as they looked into one another's eyes. They congratulated the young couple which they knew had endured so much adversity; if they only knew the truth. They left thru the side door which they entered. There was no fanfare. Emily kissed them all good night and then taking Warren by the hand led him upstairs to his, and now her, bedroom.

    The consummation of their marriage was everything Emily had expected it to be. She now lay in the crook of his arm and listened to Warrens even breathing. He was sound asleep clutching her lightly in his arms. Emily put away the heavy weight of knowledge of things to come and peacefully went to sleep in her husband's arms.

CHAPTER 67
INTERLUDE

As the rain beat softly on the outside window pane, Karen and Earl were embraced in a tangle of arms and legs, Earl said, "Honey, how would you like to go on a study sabbatical, enjoy different cultures. You know, just to get away from it all?"

Karen, thinking, "Goodness Earl, you just got home." Instead she said, "Well Honey, how long would we be gone dear? You know you just got home?"

"We should not be gone…, not less than one year nor more than two. The extended length would be up to you," replied Earl.

Wow, that was a lot more than she anticipated! "Where are we going, Dear?"

Earl smiled in the dark, his mind racing, "It will be someplace new, an out of this world experience; we will be having opportunities beyond your wildest imagination."

Karen looked up into her husband's face. In the dim light she could see he was smiling at her. His words might momentarily be verbalizing on his "sabbatical", but his eyes were soaking her up and she knew the look on his face. She knew the power she had over her husband. His love for her was like a child discovering the wonder of his mother's breast for the first time. She loved Earl deeply. He was so "Holly Wood" handsome and wonderfully made and…so socially awkward.

His marvelous brain did not leave much room for social interaction. She fell in love with him the moment she laid eyes on him. He never saw her for a long time. She had cornered him and carefully courted him. Of course he did not know it. He just suddenly found himself married and honestly, he did not know how it had come about.

"Who would care for the boys," Replied Karen? "I mean you just got home!"

"I think Warren and Emily is up to that task, Dear. The boys love Emily as much as we do and they always pay attention to what she says. That is more than we can say for ourselves." Earl chuckled at the thought.

"I know they could do it Earl, but gracious, they may be out of high school by the time we get back. They might even be in their first year of college if it is a two year sabbatical! Surly we could come home for the summer."

Earl responded, "I do not think so, Dear. Nor will there be any short weekend trips home."

Karen looked at her husband as she leaned back on her elbow. "Where on earth can we not go that we cannot come home for Christmas, for goodness sakes?"

Earl's smile grew even larger. "It isn't on Earth, Karen; it is not even in our solar system. I am sure we will be knocking around our solar system for a while but eventually we will be traveling to another star and maybe, perhaps, even to another galaxy."

Karen looked at Earl in shock, then laughing heartily and hitting his shoulder with her little fist she said, "Oh Earl! You are such a kidder! That is why I love you so much! You really had me going there for a minute! I am going to get ourselves a nice cup of warm tea; we might as well have one, were both awake. Then we can discuss your sabbatical some more."

Karen got up and after throwing on a robe, left the room. Earl could hear her humming as she went about the business of fixing their tea. She returned to the bedroom carrying a tray bearing two warm cups of tea and a pile of Earl's favorite homemade cookies. Setting the tray on the night stand, Karen tossed her robe aside and sat on the bed as she stirred cream and sugar into their steaming cups. They drank and ate in silence.

Setting her tea on the night stand, she turned and faced her husband who was nibbling on the last cookie. "Earl, you were not kidding were you? We are going to go where Emily was."

The statement was a resigned acquiesces of acceptance. Karen knew her husband would not have asked her to come along if he did not really want to go himself. He really wanted her to come with him. She truly believed, that in this one instance, he would leave her behind.

"Yes I will go with you Earl, only because I do not trust those hot alien women! I bet they do not have anything I don't have! " Or, maybe…not."

CHAPTER 68
NEW OPPORTUNITIES

Upon Emily's and Earl's return it was decided that she and Warren would be married again by a Justice of the Peace at Emily's lake house in upstate New York. The gathering would be attended by her "cousin", Blain and his three children, Jawane, Hanlee, and Persha. Persha was a young Andrian female about eighteen earth years of age. She was included in the group because Blain had assumed custodial management when her Father and Mother were both killed by the new alien intruder in a far distant galaxy. They were both officers in the Andrian defense force. Blain believed that the earth assignment as a molecular chemist would be a good diversion for her. He and Emily and thus Warren, had decided that when Blain was away, the children would be staying with them. Of course Warren knew nothing of the Andrians. All of them would have genetically altered fingers to more easily fit into earth society.

There were no other family members on Emily's side of the family as her Mother and Father was all she had and they had been murdered. Warren's side of the family was almost as sparse, with six surviving cousins.

Also to be attending was Detectives Jessop and Reese. They too were planning on getting married at later date. And of course it would not be a wedding if the ten

Human-Andrian hybrids were not present. Ashley and Jake married on the intergalactic cruiser with the cosmos for a fantastic setting and would enjoy being one of the "older" married couples there.

Breveka would be attending as a friend and Social Scientist. She was very interested in the ceremony, even though she had seen it before. The binding of relationships for life was a mystery to her and she wanted to analyze the unknown practice in a more detailed study. Breveka would be staying with the ten young Human-Hybrids at the secret military installation until other accommodations could be made.

Emily had talked at length with Billy and Skip and told them that they were all going to go to her lake house to live for a short period of time. When they heard the first mention of her, "Uncle Blain, and his three children", whom, before this very moment, have never been mentioned, they knew something was up and they were all ears. Emily had said on several occasions that she was the only child and had no other living relatives.

Sharla and Robert would be working with the military on the ion drives that moved the intergalactic carriers thru the cosmos using space time Spherical Mathematical concepts. Emily had suggested and Warren had accepted, Robert Aaron as his best man. Sharla would be her bridesmaid. Sharla, as was the children, were totally terrified of the assignment on the earth. Sharla and Robert would be going to the ship from time to time, therefore she reluctantly agreed with the assignment. Of course Blain had assisted with her choice. After all, she did marry a Human.

Lt. Sasha Palangin was promoted to commander and would accompany one hundred and fifty space commandoes to the intergalactic carrier for extended duty. All personnel involved were volunteers and there was no dearth of men and women who considered the assignment a most exciting opportunity. The group was mixed one third female and two third male, as upper level commanders considered this to be the most opportune mix for a fighting unit. Sasha was personally requested by Blain at the insistence of Shayar, the senior member of the "Council of Yield", to be the commander of the unit. Shayar was impressed with Sasha's improvisation and "out of the box", thinking that enabled her to defeat Klaxo and his mutinous companions.

The "Council of Yield" was unanimous in extending treaties that were mutually beneficial to each other's advancement. It appeared from early research assessments that Human "Two Point O", was well under way. The earth inhabitants just did not know about it yet.

The ten abducted humans who were taken by Zelegark and sent to the space craft were enhanced neurologically and had their dormant telepathic abilities enhanced. These things were procedures that were done as a sort of payback for being subject to Zelegark's duplicity. However, it was decided that it was in everyone's best interest to remove any memory of the Andrians and the previous events. Thus when they went to sleep on their last night on the intergalactic craft, Flata put them into a deep sleep and altered their memories so that they would remember nothing of the Andrians, and memories was implanted that led them to believe they had been involved in some sort of secret military project, they would remain asleep until they woke up on the earth. They would then be reinserted into society and given jobs with the government which would explain their absence from their family and friends. The lame and the blind were led to believe that they were made whole due to some military experiment for which they both applied.

The new evolution of humankind has been enhanced and accelerated by design to help save the planet and their very lives. An intergalactic council was established to oversee the administration of the new environmental programs. "The Council of Yield" believed this level of cooperation was necessary, and, as the Humans would say, "The right thing to do"; especially since the Andrians had come so close to annihilating the Human Species. All groups worked together to clean up the environment. The militaries worked in conjunction with one another to locate the home of the new invaders and enemies encroaching on humanoid space.

Emily and Dr. Abbott deeply researched the helix formation of spherical math. It was their discovery that if one more strand was added to the helix, that not only space time travel could be achieved but inter-dimensional travel appeared to be possible. It was a beginning to help them discover where the inter-dimensional destroyer specie came from. To travel to a different dimension was definitely a bold new adventure for the humanoid spirit. And, the journey has just begun.

CHARACTERS IN ORDER OF APPEARANCE

KLAXO	YIELD COUNCIL MEMBER
SHAYER	YIELD COUNCIL MEMBER
ROBERT AARON	ENSIGN, LAGRANGE POINT FOUR STATION
AVERY CLEARY	ADMIRAL, SPACE DEFENSE COMMANDER
BOB JOHNSON	COMMADER, SPACE DEFENCE INTELLIGENCE
FLATA	CHIEF GENETICIST
EMILY SMITH	PHYSICS STUDENT
DR. CALENDER	DOCTOR EMERITOUS PHYSICS
WARREN ABBOTT	EMILY'S FIANCEE
BLAIN	ALIEN ABDUCTOR, MILITARY COMMANDER
EARL ABBOTT	FATHER, SCIENTIST, INVENTOR
GARY JESSOP	HOMOCIDE DETECTIVE BLAIZONHILLS PD
CAROL REESE	HOMOCIDE DETECTIVE BLAIZONHILLS PD
SGT. WILLIAMS	ANALYST, SPACEDEFENSE INTELIGENCE
The PRESIDENT	THE PRESIDENT OF EARTH ALLIANCE

ANDRIAN	ALIEN HUMANOID SPECIE CLASSIFICATION
BREVEKA	FEMALE ALIEN, SPECIE ANALYST
JOHN SMITH	EMILY'S FATHER, DECEASED
MARTHA SMITH	EMILY'S MOTHER DECEASED
JAMES CARROLL	ACCIDENT WITNESS, HUMAN-ANDRIAN
MR. JONES	ESTABLISHED PRISON HOSPITAL
ZELEGARK	ANDRIAN ASSASSIN
MARLA RAINES	HYBRID IN GOVERNMENT PROTECTION
ALLEN PAISLEY	HYBRID IN GOVERNMENT PROTECTION
CAPTAIN SWENSEN	SPACE DEFENSE COMMANDO
DAVID LONGORIA	HUMAN ABDUCTEE ON SPACE SHIP
KAREN ABBOTT	WIFE OF EARL ABBOTT
SKIP ABBOTT	SON
BILLY ABBOTT	SON
ASHLEY	HYBRID IN GOVERNMENT PROTECTION
JAKE	HYBRID IN GOVERNMENT PROTECTION

TOMMY	HYBRID IN GOVERNMENT PROTECTION
SASHA PALANGIN	LT., SPACE DEFENSE COMMANDOE
SHARLA	CONSORT OF BLAIN, MOTHER OF CHILD
CHANDRA	CONSORT OF BLAIN, MOTHER OF CHILD
JAWANE	CHILD OF SHARLA AND BLAIN
HANLEE	CHILD OF CHANDRA AND BLAIN
PERSHA	ORPHANED ANDRIAN CHILD
THREE DIMENTIONAL MATH	ALIEN MATH FOR SPACE TIME TRAVEL

EMILY SMITH TRILOGY
BOOK 2
ASSIMILATION
CHAPTER ONE
ANTICIPATION

Blain gathered the three children into the control room before entering the saucer to help encourage them in their new assignment. Jawane and Hanlee were excited and wanted to go even though they were afraid; the only reason they were willing to go was because they knew Emily and trusted her with their lives. And, truth be known, they had developed a new kind of love for her that was foreign to their Andrian species.

Persha was of a different mindset altogether. She did not want to go. She wanted to join the Andrian military forces and fight the "things", or life form, or whatever they were that had destroyed her parents. So many Andrians have been destroyed, including three fully populated solar systems. Not one life form had been spared on the planets and the six intergalactic carriers that were defending them. All personnel on board had been vaporized with a new kind of weapon. The last place she wanted to be was on the earth. The Humans were so, so..., stupid! Blain said, "Remember to do what Emily says. She loves you in the earthly way Humans love and she will not allow anything to happen to you. And Persha, I believe that at this time, this assignment will be in your best interest and to the best interest for the "Council of Yield". They are depending on you to help channel and direct other young Andrians that will be following soon.

Persha acknowledged Blains word of admonition by indicating she was the lessor and he the greater, but he knew she was not pleased. Blain also knew that with the devastating loss of her parents, as she was one of the few, who had known no other, being with Emily was the best thing for her. Emily would help her heal.

All four boarded the saucer and left the intergalactic ship. Since the enemy had been discovered on Saturn's moon, Iapetus, all craft leaving the carrier had a small contingent of military. The saucer quickly located the proper coordinates, and hovered in the landing position.

Blain and Persha exited the craft first. Persha stayed close to Blain as they moved to the side. Jawane and Hanlee huddled close as they stepped off the lift next. All three children were terrified and had second thoughts about the great adventures they might have on a planet.

Everything was green. There were things called birds flying everywhere, some of them making a grating noise. A wind was blowing softly, and the smell, it was unlike anything they had ever sensed before. It was very pleasant. And the sun, it was so bright and hot but for some reason, the air was somewhat cool. It was also disconcerting not to have a ceramic glass or cover protecting them from the cosmos. Looking around they did not see any barriers whatsoever separating them from their surroundings. It looked like they could walk forever! Then they saw Emily standing near the trees with her hand vigorously waving.

CPSIA information can be obtained
at www.ICGtesting.com
Printed in the USA
LVHW032256130222
710624LV00001B/15